Harry Ritchie

The Third Party

HODDER

First published in Great Britain in 2006 by Hodder & Stoughton
A division of Hodder Headline

This paperback edition published in 2007

A Hodder paperback

1

A CIP catalogue record for this title is available from the British Library

ISBN 978-0-340-82714-7

Typeset in Sabon by Hewer Text UK Ltd, Edinburgh
Printed and bound by Mackays of Chatham Ltd, Chatham, Kent

Hodder Headline's policy is to use papers that are natural, renewable
and recyclable products and made from wood grown in sustainable
forests. The logging and manufacturing processes are expected to
conform to the environmental regulations of the country of origin.

Hodder & Stoughton Ltd
A division of Hodder Headline
338 Euston Road
London NW1 3BH

Part One

I

10.07 a.m., Monday 8 April

RICHARD
Oh, I don't know. Who, in fact, could know which would have been the best route in, supposing such a thing even exists, because who's to say that the whole of London isn't as chocka as this? Though surely that can't really be the case, I mean, there must be some traffic moving somewhere. Although having said that there was that time a year ago, maybe two years, when everywhere seemed to be completely clogged up in one enormous jam that stretched, in my experience of it, all the way down to Marylebone, then all the way from Marylebone to Uxbridge or wherever it is that London can finally be said to have petered out into what might just conceivably pass for countryside, and then, because I was heading for Stow and los parentes, all the way along the M40 to the Oxford turn-off – six hours (I mean, seriously, *six hours*) of heel-toeing clutchwork that had my ankles aching – but this can't be as bad as that and, come to think of it, even if it is, it won't be for me because I'm only trying to get to the office in Clerkenwell, not Gloucestershire.

Actually, the truth is that it doesn't seem to matter which route in I take these days. Even if all the omens are good – in

3

an ideal world: I feel like I've had some sleep, there's no atmoss, breakfast goes without a hitch, the car starts first time, I get to the end of the street while whatever song on the radio is still going, I manage at some point to get into second or even third and career along at, oh, twenty, fifteen miles an hour, thinking, this is what it's supposed to be like – then there's always something, somewhere: roadworks, a diversion, a wonky traffic light, or, as now, a rubbish-lorry backing into non-existent space, because that's the best time for rubbish-lorries to be out and about and reversing into traffic, rush hour . . . But perhaps the rubbish-lorry will sort itself out in a moment and the next green will release lots and lots of cars and we'll all be rattling along, two lanes of happy motorists zooming into the heart of the city . . .

No.

Still here.

. . . If this goes on for much longer I'm going to start fretting. But then I remind myself to not let, not to let the little things get to me. And I do. Not let them get to me. Because the fact of the matter is that even a Monday-morning snarl-up can't compete with what was a picture-book weekend, including as it did a trip en famille to the zoo, the big zoo in Regent's Park, on Saturday, Bongle held in mid-dangle by the pouch thing in front of me, a nostalgic wander round Clissold Park yesterday, self pushing Bongle in his buggy, followed by a successful roast-lamb dinner, cooked by, although it doesn't behove me to say so, me, the three of us sitting at the kitchen table, one of us, admittedly, less keen on the solids and slightly smearier around the fizzog than the others. There was a moment, on Saturday, at the zoo, near the entrance, when

4

I bought, on impulse, a balloon, and Ali laughed and her face lit up with one of her best-ever smiles, a smile that shone in her eyes, a smile that was full of wonder at our extraordinary good luck at having this Bongle bundle dangling in a pouch and not noticing the monkeys, and I remember thinking: who could have hoped that it would have turned out not only all right in the end but as miraculously all right as this?

As I gaze out of the passenger window, my glance falls, for a moment only but nonetheless, on the briefly revealed legs of a girl, a very tall black girl, twenty or thereabouts, overtaking me on the pavement, her long coat having flown open at the back at the very split-second that she turned, probably to avoid an oncoming person, to display a skirt that's not going to keep her warm in this weather and an astonishingly long stretch of unhosieried jet-black limb, with a correspondingly elongated   part-of-the-body-I-don't-know-the-word-for   or possibly part-of-the-body-there-is-no-word-for, the back of the knee, which I've always found such an endearing bit of the female form, as well as strangely erotic, the ligaments or whatever they are, those taut cords, if they're firm and have exactly the right prominence, as Ali's, for example, most certainly do, which makes it a bit surprising that this could be a part of the anatomy that has no name, not even a proper medical one, though surely doctors don't talk about the back of the knee, they'd have some technical term, one would have thought. Ah, Carruthers, take a look at this X-ray of the kneecapula reversum, would you? Good Lord. A growth in the ligamentuloid canal. Let's hope it's not malignant. Malignant? I'm afraid so. How long have I got, doctor? I'm sorry. You mean . . . The zoo. The zoo. Ali and Bongle at the zoo. Buying the balloon. Ali's smile. I have so many lucky stars to thank. I really do.

Far, far up ahead the lights change to green, but whatever good fortune the cars at the front have had has run out long before it could reach up here, what with the ongoing gridlock and the still-reversing rubbish-lorry. I'd turn off the engine if I had any confidence that the damned thing would start again . . . That Ealing comedy we watched on Saturday, after the zoo, self retaining only the vaguest notion that Alastair Whatshisname wasn't a real professor but actually a criminal of some sort, because I'd been too busy staring at the backdrops – acres of road empty save for an occasional squat, round, black Austin trundling sedately by, or a solitary bus, of the kind that used to be everywhere but that you hardly see at all these days, the buses with a snouty radiator, an open platform at the back and a pole up the middle of the open platform to hang on to. London in the days of black and white and London as I can – just, in tiny snippets – remember it, from family treat trips, usually at Christmas but not always, and I don't think it's my memory playing tricks on me when I can't relate any of that childhood London to London now, so that I can't set up a pair of spot-the-difference images, there being as much point in that as trying to spot the difference between a . . . crocodile and a . . . teddy bear. BBC 2, I think, or at any rate the only channel within our terrestrial grasp that wasn't devoted to horse racing or somehow spivvy-looking men in suits being excited about the half-time result at Bolton United, and, making this a bit of a date for the diary, we settled down to watch it, taking advantage of the long, post-zoo afternoon nap, the two of us on the sofa together, quite snuggly really, shoulder to shoulder, and who would hope for more?

The lights up ahead have gone green again, but again there's not even the slightest hint of a shunt forward. I could be here for hours, getting in just before, or during, or blimming hell, after lunch at this rate, to find all the phones going nuts, Bob in a mutinous sulk, Shirley trying to hold the fort against impossible odds . . .

The pang of guilt carries with it the threat that this post-weekend lightness of heart might disappear, to be replaced by the usual fretful boredom of office exile. So it's high time, I'd say, for the song test. I fiddle about with the radio to find a song, any song, but there's only wittering. 'Slow moving on the South Circular . . .,' 'next up is Alan from Ching . . .,' 'coming up for thir-teen minutes past ten . . .,' 'here on one oh two point . . .,' 'here on Magic F . . .,' 'you're listening to . . .' Finally, I hit 'The Power of Love' by Jennifer Doodad on Melody. Okay. If I get to the McDonald's sign by the time Doodad's finished, I'll make it into the office before ten-thirty.

. . . Ah. Not even close. Still four cars to the McDonald's sign. And a motorbike.

Right, then, Fossett Major, let's get started. A list . . . Maybe I should do it properly, write it all down, reach over to the back seat, fetch my notebook out of my briefcase . . . Yes, but wouldn't that be a sure-fire way of inviting a surge from the four cars and the motorbike in front, a sudden yawning space in front of me, the engine stalling on me and everyone behind me leaning on their horns. On the other hand, going by the take-your-umbrella-and-it'll-never-rain principle, perhaps

I should do exactly that, to guarantee a miraculous unblocking of traffic. Not take my umbrella, of course, but fetch the notebook . . . No. So. In my head, then. Get to work, find parking space, in the side streets if the spaces at work are all taken, in the multi-storey if the side streets are full, and the multi-storey's menacing ammoniac stink, not to mention the multi-storey's astronomical charge, then quick-march to the office, airy wave hello to Callum in reception, eyes down in lift and corridor if lift and corridor occupied by younger, female colleagues from, for example, *Life & Style* or *Mode*, another airy wave hello to all staff, by way of a collective apology, swerve past Bob, get to cubicle before Shirley starts up with an account of her weekend, get coffee, check emails, reply to emails, then swot up for meeting at 12, then go to meeting at 12, be bored by meeting at 12, and, whenever it's eventually over but surely by lunchtime, out for a quick shop. Snappy Snaps for the photos, Boots for Sudocreme, Huggies, formula and some of those Hippo jars if they have any. Bisley and Ainscombe's Ludicrously Overpriced Dry-Cleaning Emporium to pick up Ali's floral dress. Toni's for one avocado, cheese and tomato sandwich and one bottle of still Malvern water. A desk lunch then talk to Bob about . . .

The most extraordinary thing. A young black man just whooshed by the passenger-side window. And he was – presumably still is – wearing a pair of purple pants. Only. I can still make him out, gliding it seems, and at a fair old speed, presumably on roller skates, between the lanes, past the lights . . . and now out of sight. But he really was completely naked, save for that pair of pants . . . And therefore, it occurs to me, living out one of my old nightmares, one of those which

8

plunged me down into the middle of school assembly, wearing only a blazer. Anyway . . .

Got it. Talk to Bob about this month's production schedule, if there's any chance of talking to Bob about anything rather than listening to Bob bang on about the football, the Pyramids, last night's TV or any of the many other topics Bob likes to bang on about. And then devote the rest of the day – i.e. five or ten minutes – to actual work with Shirley on the next issue, if we get the flatplan, because where would the domestic-construction industry be if its premier trade organ failed to appear?

First things first, though, and that's to get beyond these blimming traffic lights.

10.07 a.m., Monday 8 April

EWAN

'Something something busy today. But the property itself is in quite a quiet location. Though handily located as well for the something something.'

I nod as though in agreement with the twelve-year-old estate agent at my side. He has a suit on, dressed as a grown-up. He also has no idea that he might have to speak up now that we're out of his office. He has to stop chatting away to himself though, while he negotiates his way through the first two lanes of motionless cars. He stands there in the middle of the becalmed traffic, waiting for me to catch up.

The moment I've done so, he's off wittering again. 'And a key factor is that something something very up and coming. I really think we'll be something a boom round here very soon. Something something something to Islington and the City just down the . . .'

I shuffle sideways to let a harassed-looking woman past but she stops and lowers her two crammed bags of shopping like a weightlifter who's done with the dumb-bells. So now the three of us are standing there in a row in the middle of the road. All of us in prime position to observe a bin-lorry backing out towards the cars. 'This vehicle is re*vah*sing,' announces the bin-lorry as though this is a grand event.

Now Mrs Harassed makes her move – picks up her dumb-bells and off she goes, between the bumpers. Head down, shoulders hunched. Probably quite a few years younger than me but she moves like a crone.

Suitboy, by contrast, is too busy mumbling drivel to do anything but continue standing in the middle of the road. '. . . the up,' I think I hear as a few fluted words drift by on the gritty breeze. '. . . investing . . . twenty per cent an annum . . .'

I do more nodding and shiver. It's a cold grey January morning in April and I'm dressed for July. T-shirt, linen jacket, very thin cotton breeks. And it's getting difficult to remember a time in my life before I was standing here in the middle of the road, vibrating with cold, not listening to Suitboy.

Suddenly, through the chilly gloom, a vision from Miami flashes by. A young guy on rollerblades, whooshing between the queuing cars. Swooping past the NatWest and the AfroEuro Cosmetic Hair Centre Wholesale & Retail. Zooming down beyond the halal butcher's, the bogus shopping centre, and the McDonald's. Singing along, presumably to whatever he's hearing through a pair of fluffy pink earmuff-sized headphones. More to the point, here's what else he's wearing – (a) two rollerblades (b) a pair of burgundy hot pants which sparkle with sequins and (c) there is no (c). Fair play to the boy, especially in this weather.

Because the spectacle didn't involve real estate or a sale at

Next, Suitboy remains completely oblivious. 'This way,' he says, in case I've forgotten that we are halfway through crossing a road. I follow him across then down towards the shopping centre then left. Halal butcher. Fishmonger. A presumably well-used police station. Another halal butcher. Bagel place. And now a street market. Stalls selling pirated leisurewear, household cleansers and improbably cheap fruit. A tiny Cantonese woman bawling shrilly at her stall of T-shirts: 'One poun. One poun. Comeanavealook. Chip chip cheap.'

Twenty yards in and Suitboy and I are in the middle of a jostling, shouting mêlée of shoppers and folk just milling about, putting in some valuable jostling and shouting practice. Eventually, Suitboy veers left, past a forbidding pub and up a street that I suspect is the one where the flat will be. A street of three-storey, beige-bricked Victorian houses. All but a few looking down on their luck.

And here, indeed, the flat is. Suitboy having darted left and jogged up a short flight of stone steps, smartly, like they were gym equipment. The steps leading to a three-storey, beige-bricked Victorian house. I join him at the door where he's fiddling with a ring of many keys.

All being well, this silence of mine will soon seem ominous.

There follows more palaver as Suitboy breaks off the fiddling to have a good old rummage in his pockets. He produces a second ring of keys. Now he's selecting and testing key . . . after key . . . after key . . . Finally, that degree in Estate Agent Studies pays off. 'There you go,' Suitboy says, opening the door with the air of a craftsman who's done me a quick favour.

I check out the hallway. There's a rickety coffee table shoved against the wall, its surface covered in flyers and envelopes. A clip-framed poster of a Monet above it. Mushroom carpet, obviously. Prominently scuffed skirting board, obviously. Someone's mountain bike under the stairs, again obviously. And, as I follow Suitboy up the stairs, the smell of air-freshener and boiled vegetables. Obviously. Exactly the kind of stairs I used to traipse up and down ten years back, when everyone I knew – bar Carol and me – was buying one-bedroomed conversions in three-storey, beige-bricked Victorian houses.

We climb the stairs until there are no stairs left. Now, who'd have thought it? Suitboy gets the right key first time. Throwing out a sleeve in a be-my-guest flourish, he ushers me inside.

What could I have bought back in Falkirk for the same price? A five-bed exec new-build villa with sauna and indoor heated swimming pool. A castle with a helipad. Falkirk. This being an unfavoured part of London, what I'm going to get for my £170,000 is a one-bedroomed conversion at the top of a run-down, three-storey, beige-bricked Victorian house. A four-windowed flatlet where the kitchen is in a corner of the main room. A bathroom where you'd swing a kitten and kill it. A bedroom so small that it's a wonder it's got a window. All of it done up by someone with a few back issues of *Life & Style* and a season ticket to Homebase. The blond laminate flooring. The recessed halogen lights. The plain white walls. The High Street minimalism that will soon be carbon-datable to now, as passé as a middle parting.

This is where I'm going to end up after thirty-nine years on the planet. Eight years of marriage. Sixteen years of education. Eighteen years of hard toil. This box.

'Recently renovated, as you see,' says Suitboy. 'And no chain, of course,' he says. Triumphant at being able to add to the list.

'So when can I move in?'

'Straight away.'

'This afternoon?'

'Ah, well, you see, there'll have to be some paperwork and legal . . .'

Too much bother to explain that I was joking. Sort of joking, anyway. I smile and nod. 'End of the week?'

'That could be doable,' Suitboy says, and I catch him sizing me up. His gaze falling as he takes in the unkempt crumpledness that comes from living out of a suitcase and sleeping last night on Russell's concrete sofa bed. I must look to Suitboy every bit the washed-up old geezer who has screwed up in ways he just knows he never will. Someone who deserved whatever it is that's befallen him. Aye, a right loser. A loser who had it coming when he was kicked out by his wife or chucked out of his job.

Which is, coincidentally, what's just happened to me. This being the start of the week after the week when Ivan gave me the sack. And Carol came into the kitchen to tell me the marriage was over.

'Shall we adjourn, then?' says Suitboy. 'To the office?' he explains.

'What a good idea.'

2

7.58 p.m., Monday 15 April

RICHARD

'Ali? . . . Ali? . . . Al-i . . .' I do the last one in a sing-song to
make it sound gentle and or chummy.

'Yes.'

I think it's fair to say that the sing-song didn't work, and
probably quite justifiably so, because no matter how gentle or
chummy the intended effect, a sing-song delivery can easily
come across as rather irritating. But, mitigating circs, the
schedule's already gone to pot. Not that we've got any sort of
rigid regime, like in that book that's all the rage, which would
have you do everything with military precision – 6.15, end
bath, 6.19, into sleepsuit, 6.21, final cuddle, 6.22 lights out –
but we do have a sort of semblance of a routine and it is
Bongle's bedtime, and she has been in there for quite a while,
but of course it's only natural to want to wash away the
headache that comes from a hot, crowded Tube. Although
when she said she was going to have a bath, I was slightly
taken aback, not so much by the minor unconventionality, I
suppose, as by my assuming she'd splashed out on a cab,
assuming this for no reason actually, other than that I think
but only think that I heard a taxi draw off down the street as

Ali came in, and then because of realising that her having a bath really would mess with Bongle's own bath-and-bed routine. What a business, though, and all for a dental appointment, although surely even I can't begrudge the poor girl a dental appointment, nor the doubtlessly astronomical fee plus the fifteen quid I've just shelled out to Joanne from next door, but not to worry, and come to think of it, I would have had to have paid Joanne fifteen quid or so, no matter what time the appointment was for, unless Ali took Bongle along with her, which would be, of course, completely impossible.

'Um, Ali? When do you think you'll be finished?'

'Richard. I really. Don't. Know.'

Whoopsee – the Delivery Deliberate. I take heed and proceed with caution. 'Fine, fine,' I say to the shut and possibly even locked door of the en-suite in an unconcerned way, or at least I trust it came across as unconcerned, while also trying not to wonder if it's entirely normal in a relationship to have one party locking the en-suite door, thereby preventing other parties from gaining access while the first party is having a soak. Not wondering about this is helped no end by the sudden arrival of an image of Bongle downstairs, leaning out of his podule thingummy, more than precociously I'd have to admit, and falling out of it head first, his skull cracking on the carpet like an egg. I quick-march out of our bedroom, down the stairs and into the sitting-room lounge, half of which has been occupied by Bonglabilia, all of it costing a packet and all of it with a life expectancy of, oh, three or four months – play mat, gonks, toys, music boxes, sheepskin rug, changing table, inflatable doughnut, wigwam and podule thingummy. Bongle himself is still sitting contentedly in the middle of the last item – a plastic construction of a bright red not found in nature – like a solo astronaut, surrounded by a circle of instruments: a bright blue steering wheel, a bright green handle that makes a rat-tat-tat sound, a bright yellow button that squeaks, a bright red something-or-other on the end of a bendy bright yellow stalk, and a bright blue telephone, which Bongle now picks up, studies and, with the air of someone who has assessed what *this* tricky little item is all about, shoves in his mouth.

'Come on, then,' I tell him because I've finally decided to use my, and take the, initiative. I reach down, get a good hold under Bongle's armpits and lift him out and up so that he's peeping over my shoulder, my left shoulder, the one that's already smudged with nostrillular drool. 'Bedtime for Bongle.' And let's just hope that he's not too fazed by having his bath in the main bathroom for once instead of the en-suite, as well as three-quarters of an hour late. 'Good night, room. Good night, toys. Good night, stairs. Good night, exciting hall light. Good night, mirror. Who's that little boy in the mirror, do you think? Who's that lovely little boy? Who's the lovely boy in the mirror?' Bongle's gaze drifts over his own reflection but when he sees mine he makes his 'hoo hoo' noise, then he gives the me in the mirror a gummy beam, and then, with a sort of thrilled shyness, buries his head back in my shoulder.

When did Bongle first cotton on to mirrors? You know, I just can't remember. Like I can't really remember, not with completely confident, finger-on-the-buzzer certainty, when he, for example, first tried baby rice, or smiled or . . . anything, really. Oddly enough, I can still speak Newborn Pediatrics pretty fluently but perhaps that's a tribute to the strange hauntingness of the lingo – dilation, muconium, latch, posset, hindmilk – that sounds part *Star Trek* and part *Farming Today*. But as for the day-to-day stuff, the ordinary, everyday, all-the-time, heart-filling wondrousness . . . well, it's like work, where I could recite the entire contents of a current issue but would be racking my brains to tell you what was on last month's cover . . . I suppose because with babies it's like a sort of archaeology in reverse, each moment with them being so intense and full that it simply replaces the moment before it, layer piling on layer piling on layer. So, much as I try to memorise each moment, try to photograph each memory with my very much non-photographic memory, I'm struggling to recreate any convincing picture of Bongle as he was at any point in his short past, or, more mundanely, to recall what he could or couldn't do a month ago . . . a week ago . . . yesterday . . . Although that's not strictly true because of course I remember that yesterday was the day when he saw his first squirrel, in the park, a scrawny thing shivering halfway up a tree trunk.

I've given Bongle his bath, then dried him (paying particular attention to the creases in his skin, those folds among the chubbiness which look like he's been wearing elastic bands), on his own bed for once, and am just coming to the end of hoiking on a new nappy when Ali appears at the door, looking like she's stepped out of a brochure for a health spa in her dressing gown and a towel turbanned round her hair, and Bongle lets go a burbling splurge of diarrhoea.

'Feel better?' I say, turning to Ali to let her know that it's her I'm talking to.

'Yes, thanks,' she says. 'Shall I make up a bottle?'

'That's all right, love. I've got one ready. You go downstairs.'

'Okay.' Ali smiles – a quick smile but one that I actually for a moment feel in my chest, as well as, oddly enough, my toes, a tingling in both areas – then turns and heads downstairs.

'And don't you go spoiling this new nappy,' I tell Bongle, having disposed of the new nappy's soiled predecessor and hosed down its owner, while basking in a sudden, out-of-nowhere rush of heartfelt gratitude at the absurd-good-fortune-squared of having not only an Ali but a Bongle. 'It's ten past eight and it's getting very late,' I chant in a whisper into his ear and he cackles. 'Ten past eight and getting very late.' I cram him into the blue stripy jumpsuit that serves as the Herr Professor von Bonglestein's PJs, thinking as I fiddle with the poppers and pull the material taut over his nappy that he really needs a new lot of sleeping equipment, so that'll be another king's ransom I'll soon be handing over to Mothercare. Not too much protest from Bongle at being zipped up into his boy-in-a-bag sleeping-bag bag (the frolicking-bears one, not the one with the ducks because that's in the wash after The Incident first thing this morning), and soon he's propped up on my knee, eagerly sucking down another bottle of formula.

This putting Bongle to bed is, I realise, the first thing I've done, in the sense of having actually achieved anything, since I gave him breakfast. Granted, there were things that took up time at the office but none of it seemed to involve anything that could be thought of as real work, so that by the end of the day I hadn't really had a moment to myself yet still had nothing to show for it by way of progress on the actual issue, endless hours having been occupied on the phone, replying to emails, or just listening – to Bob getting antsy about this month's schedule, having, without any apparent awareness of the irony of his doing so, spent an inordinate time banging on and on about his latest theory that the Pyramids – or was it the Sphinx? – are or is much older than however old it or they is or are usually thought to be, and to Shirley getting antsy because she wasn't going to be able to see her chap, the MM, all week, as per usual, her chap, the MM, being an important, busy and, above all, married businessman, Shirley being that old-fashioned thing, a mistress.

Twenty past eight, by his Winnie-the-Pooh clock, so I bet myself that he'll be done by twenty to . . .

Not surprisingly I suppose, on reflection, this turns out to be a rather ineffective distraction and I soon find myself, despite the recent smile, fretting over Ali again . . . But then I remind myself, gazing off into the middle distance while Bongle continues to suck at the bottle, of Ali back in Aylesbury, Ali walking down the street to meet me, her long hair curled at the bottom like handles, and then Ali, but this time, for no particular reason I could tell you, more recently, only four years or so ago, Ali decorating the old flat when we'd just moved in, Ali wearing a headscarf and old leggings, and looking, well, the usual words – gorgeous, stunning, breathtaking.

And then, and I can only guess that it might be something to do with that span of four years but, for whatever reason, there now arrives the thought that has a bad tendency of arriving at unguarded moments such as these, the thought that thirty-nine over seventy is basically four-sevenths, which it will be, officially, far, far too soon, and whichever way I look at it, and I've tried lots, from a percentage (57 point something) to a journey home to a 24-hour clock (coming up to Oxford and going on half past one, i.e. half past thirteen), it has begun to seem just a tad too far advanced in its . . .

'Little Jakey okay?' whispers Ali at the doorway again, still in her dressing gown although turbanless by now. She runs a hand through her hair as though she's lost something in it, which is quite possible, given that it's every bit as thick and bouncy and nearly, with a little discreet help, as blonde as when we first met and it sometimes curled out at the bottom like handles. At the rugby-club disco, Aylesbury, 1993, March the sixteenth, it was, round about nine o'clock, nine-fifteen. I know that some people actually try to deny that there's any such thing, but there definitely is such a thing as love at first sight, and I should know that there is because it happened to me when I fell head over heels the first time I ever laid eyes on Ali – Ali standing across the room at the rugby-club disco, in a group, laughing, Ali at twenty-five, wearing a blue dress that was, I've since come to suspect, just a touch staid for a rugby-club disco, which only goes to make the memory all the more enchanting. And that's exactly what she was. And still is, of course. Enchanting. As well as gorgeous, stunning, breath-taking et cetera. Even when she's a bit out of sorts. Because she can't stop being Ali, can she? Anyway, so naturally I fell in love with her there and then, on the spot. Who couldn't have fallen in love the moment they caught sight of Ali in her blue dress? Why hadn't every man in the room already gathered round her in a beseeching, imploring scrummage? That she remained unmolested by any spontaneous wild mêlée of

inflamed rivals, far less, as was indeed the case, anyone at all, far, far less, able and apparently willing to chat to me, so driven was I by the sight of her that rather than do my usual silent yearning from afar, I walked over to her in a sort of trance and, still in the trance, introduced myself, asked her what her name was and offered to buy her a drink, seemed then, and seems, if anything, even more so now, a truly extraordinary stroke of preposterously good luck. And now as Ali stands in the doorway and Bongle lies cradled in my left arm, I sort of see this scene from the outside, as if I've somehow floated out of my body and I'm standing or hovering beside myself and I'm looking at the three of us and seeing this for what it is – everything I could have wanted. Every bit as if a fairy godmother had floated down and given me three wishes and flourished her sparkly wand and – ta-ra – granted them all. Although I'm not sure what the third wish would have been, not counting world peace.

'Fine, fine,' I tell her, mouthing the words rather than speaking them because Bongle's coming to the end of the bottle and beginning to drop off. Twenty to, according to the Winnie clock. I win. 'See you in a minute,' I whisper, raising my eyebrows and smiling, although I think too late for Ali to register before she turned and went. I'd better ask how she got on after I've laid Bongle down in his cot. Not that she was talking funny so it couldn't have been too serious or nasty.

He's drifting off, straining now to keep his eyes from closing, rather as Sophie Godfrey once acted being drugged by villains at the Stow Amateurs production of . . . some play. I can't remember. As Bongle's eyes, his enormous, liquid-blue

eyes, begin to close, I rock him in my arms and begin one of my home-made ditties, under my breath, whisper-singing.

'The Bongle man. The Bongle man.

Bongling and smongling whenever he can . . .'

Where do they come from, I wonder, these songs and chants and nicknames? Because he has also been not only Bongle and related Bongular titles but, among others, off the top of my head, Sniffly McGinty, Drooly O'Driscoll, Stinky Stonky and Stinky McGee, each one commemorating a key stage in his life so far – runny nose, onset of teething, and the unfortunate side effects of moving on to formula milk, when his once-fragrant poo suddenly turned stenchy, although of course I couldn't tell you with any confidence when those stages took place . . . You'd think, would you not, that nature would have sorted that one out, that your own child's ordure would always be sweet-smelling and nice rather than a reeking mess that makes the eyes to water and the gorge to rise . . . But it's a sweet-smelling little boy that I'm singing to sleep now, and there are times, and this is one of them, when I look at him and I just can't resist it any longer and I have to let my heart burst for love of my baby boy, my miraculous little baby boy . . . and then I remember again why the usual policy has to be to resist the bursting, because it's just too much and I have to swallow hard and take a deep breath before I can finish the song.

'Bongling for me. Smongling for you.

His name is Mister Bongle Boo.'

7.58 p.m., Monday 15 April

EWAN

This is me wandering back to the bedroom.

I perch on the mattress of the bed I've just assembled. The only other surface being the floor. I look at the two suitcases and the one bulging bin liner. Everything I now own. Apart from the bed and the mattress.

To think that I started this month still in possession of a job and a salary and an office. The co-owner of an unimpeachably trendy loft in an unimpeachably trendy area of central London. Married to unimpeachably trendy Carol.

And now it's halfway through the month. No job. No marriage. No loft. Instead, this: one very small, crappy flat, two suitcases, one bin liner, one bed and one mattress. Plus the oversized beanbag I bought with the bed in the main room. And, round the corner in the kitchenette nook, one dinky fridge containing one bottle of milk, one carton of orange juice and the bottle of Laurent-Perrier champagne that Russell handed me this morning as a moving-in present. But that's it.

I'll have to acquire a few things, I suppose. Pillows, bed-linen. Rig up a pole as a wardrobe, maybe. Maybe not if I can use the suitcases as cupboards for all the clothes. A TV. Possibly. A radio might be enough. Maybe a bedside light. Anything else? No. No, that should do me.

I get up and fetch out a few things from the bin liner. A pot and a pan, a couple of plates, two mugs, two glass tumblers, a thin package of crockery wrapped in a tea towel. I take this small haul into the kitchen nookette. A kettle, I need a kettle. Likewise a corkscrew . . . I wander three paces back into the main bit of the main room. Its sole occupant the oversized beanbag.

Implausible, I know, but there was a time with Carol and me when the conversations we had weren't only about the latest Baines & Hart catalogue or the mosaic tiling for the shower. Very early days, of course. Before the loft.

Easy to blame the loft, so I used to do exactly that as Carol and I, slowly and surely, drifted apart. But then I realised that it was the loft that was keeping us together.

Nine paces and I've reached the window . . . Seven paces between the east and west walls. So no danger of agoraphobia. I pace back to the east wall and sit down, my back against it.

No, me and Carol, we weren't husband and wife. We were co-managers of the loft-renovation project. What was our last conversation about? Window boxes. Window boxes. Not counting the conversation where Carol eventually sat me down on the sofa (big, cream, Conran) and told me that she'd been seeing someone else and that she thought it was time, no hard feelings, to call it a day.

That was on the Tuesday evening. Wednesday morning, Carol gave me the two-page printout that was her proposed separation agreement. Friday afternoon, Ivan called me into his office and sacked me. Of course, he didn't call it that. This was a suggested parting of the ways, one based on what he was sure would be the mutual assessment of our respective directional differences, with a grateful acknowledgement from him and every other member of the board of the contribution I had made, and a cheque. The postscript hinting that it would be advisable for me to clear my desk, retrieve any personal files from my computer, hand in my security card and leave the building by the end of the day. This at five o'clock.

By six, I was at the bar of the White Lion, being handed a beer by a furious Damien.

I went in for a lot of rueful head-shaking and brave smiling, judging that to be about right for a man who's just been fired from his own company. (Except that it wasn't my company. The company that I'd founded with Robin and Tim had died about a month after we merged with DMX. Just as I'd predicted to their impatient annoyance before we merged with DMX, i.e. got taken over and shafted by DMX.) Fortunately, I'd kept the Carol thing to myself, otherwise I'd have had to summon up a far more dramatic performance.

Still a bit of a performance, though, because in truth I didn't feel anything at all at that point. Just . . . blank. It would take a wee bit longer for it to sink in how much of my life I'd wasted. But it was an undemanding audience. Damien, Caro, Sam, Emma, all from the old days. All lamenting. All sloping off as soon as they decently could.

This laminate floor is, I can now appreciate, unbearably cold. Like sitting on concrete. I reach over for the beanbag and haul myself on board. Change of scenery too.

So I got myself back to Russell's in Hampstead on the Friday night, couple more drinks with him and a night of welcome unconsciousness on Russell's brick-mattressed sofa bed. Daundered out with Russ next day for brunch, which led to a pint in a gastropub with sofas, which led to a late-afternoon session back at his, watching the results come in. With increasing fervour after he produced his precious weekly gram. Thence to a party he knew about and an energised evening in Hammersmith. (Russell evidently very keen on showing how action-packed and glam is his bachelor's lot. Not at all lonely and tragic. Not in the slightest the sad, solitary lot of a congenitally single loser.) Got up on Sunday afternoon and went with Russell to the pub to watch football, and that was the rest of Sunday gone. The coke ditto.

Not quite a lost weekend – a weekend off from life.

Monday I bought this place with less fuss and thought than I used to devote to buying a vase. Monday evening, I went on a spur-of-the-moment visit to, as it turned out, Barcelona. Where, as it turned out, I stayed for the rest of the week because I had, as it turned out, a three-night stand with a young (thirty-one, but let's be realistic) girl from Derby called Siobhain. Surprisingly flexible.

And there was me with my dim but fond memories of a sex life. A marriage which saw off passion early on and replaced it with interior decoration. Carol becoming one of those who likes to be in bed, contacts out, specs on, pillows plumped up, book at the ready, by, in an ideal world, 7.30. Me conveniently turning into more of a night-owl. Putting in heroic hours at work. Lots of 'work' dinners and 'business' trips. Lots of late 'meetings'.

So it's only now that I'm back and I've moved in here that I'm really able to think about what's happened. And what I've been given. (1) Freedom from a marriage that had declined into pretence years ago. (2) Freedom from a bunch of asset-stripping bastards and a job I had come to loathe. (3) Quite a lot of money. I squirm deeper into the beanbag and put my hands behind my head.

Half the cash from the loft (bought in 1994 for £120,000 with a shared and mostly-paid-off mortgage, sold, immediately, for £760,000). Plus a knock-down fifty grand from Carol for all the fixtures and fittings, the car, the et cetera. Plus the handsome kiss-off from DMX I'd been aiming for, and arriving, I reckon, in the nick of time too . . . Call it £620,000. The Christmas bonus of any City numpty, but enough to buy this flat and have enough left over to give me an annual income of, let's say, a teacher, without having to do any work for the foreseeable future. Or, just feasibly, play my cards right, ever again.

Suddenly, I get this tingly rush.

It's one that I recognise. I've felt this before. I cast around to identify when. Some time early on with Carol, still at the gobsmacked stage? No. Sex? No. Wedding day? Very amusing. Football, maybe? No, not even the likes of Narey's goal against Brazil . . . And then I see the view from a train, a train rattling along an embankment, an anonymous embankment covered in the regulation foxgloves and cow parsley. The sun streaming in through a vague cloud of dust onto faded blue upholstery dotted with buttons . . . I was going home from university, Finals over, and it was dawning on me that I wouldn't have to sit another exam in my life, and then that this was the real start of my life, and then that this life of mine was all at once wide open with possibility.

So. What possibilities are there now? What do I want to happen next?

I have no idea except that it's going to have to be a complete change of direction. The nearer to 180 degrees the better. See if that works.

I look out at the patch of blue sky between the houses opposite and my window-frame. It's working already. Here I am doing nothing. With nothing in my diary. In an empty box. And it's great. Nothing but peace and qu—

zzz. zzz. zzz.

I look wildly around the empty room before I realise what's going on. Then, with a sigh, I haul myself up and out of the beanbag and go over to the beige apparatus that evidently is the entryphone and pick it up.

'—eezing out here, for God's sakes,' says the beige handset.

'Russell,' I say and I press a beige button. I hear the front door slam, so hard that I can almost see the walls here, two flights up, tremble at the impact. Then there's a rapid, violent pounding on the stairs. Then there's a furious rapping at my door. At a leisurely pace, I replace the phone in its beige cradle, amble off and open the door.

Russell is occupying a fair fraction of the stale and scruffy landing. Standing there for the paparazzi. With his long black overcoat, his charcoal-grey suit, his immaculately white shirt. Blending in like a deb at a dog track.

Russell narrows his eyes and does his Mafia shrug. 'Ba da bam,' he says.

I do the Mafia shrug back. 'Ba da boom.'

'Ba da bing.'

'Well, Russ, this is a surprise. But it'll be good to catch up, get all the news since we last met. This morning, wasn't it?'

'Your mobile was off.'

'I killed it. Took a hammer to the bastard.'

'So I thought I'd take a chance like they did in the old days, swing by. See if you needed any help with the flitting.'

'Really? Well, it's all done and dusted.'

'That is excellent,' Russell whispers, doing his Monty Burns. 'You not going to invite me in?' he asks in his normal voice. 'I mean, this landing does have a certain naive charm but . . .'

'Please. Be my guest.'

'Why, thank you.' Russell comes in. He takes off his coat and looks around the empty hallway. Finding nothing by way of a peg, Russell holds the coat out at me, pinching the collar disdainfully. He lets the coat fall. I let it continue falling to the floor. We both stand there, staring at it like it's just died.

'Ziss time.' Russ wags the index finger that was recently pinching the coat collar. 'Ziss time you heff gone too fah. So. The new gaff.' He looks around the empty hallway with the kind of instinctive enthusiasm that really needs the owner to do some vigorous hand-rubbing to complete the picture. 'The new pad. The new bachelor HQ. And in an interesting area, I'll say that for it. Very, uh, *street*. Makes Peckham look like Pitlochry.'

'Oh, that's very good. You've been working on that.'

'Hardly your scene, though, is it? Or are you all excited about living with the poor people? Where's my drink?'

'Still in the tap. Come through. Make yourself at home.'

I wave a hand towards the floor. I make the long, arduous trek to the kitchen nook, open the fridge, take out one of the fridge's two occupants, open the champagne and fill two tumblers. If I sit on the beanbag now I'll have used 90 per cent of my possessions in one go.

Russell's standing in the middle of the empty room, looking round as though he's trying to monitor a busy fly. 'Too much clutter,' he says. 'You want to get rid of some of this shit.'

'Here.'

'Too kind. Mm. Right. I'm thinking knock through that wall into the hallway because I'm thinking one big space, I'm thinking a big blue sofa over there, maybe an armchair there, I'm thinking TV and sounds over there, and I'm . . .' Russell marches through to the bedroom and marches back '. . . thinking clean and simple for the chamber of love. Yes, yes, this could be *cool*. Coffee table here. Yeah, *big* screen over . . .'

'Eyen't gonna happen,' I say in my crap hillbilly. 'I've decided. No, I've got my beanbag. That's going to be it.'

Russell nods and purses his lips. 'Minimalist, huh?' His nodding begins to quicken as his Positivity Machine cranks back into action, the pistons picking up pace, teams of burly-chested stokers shovelling coal into the furnace, bells clanging, funnels puffing out steam. But then the contraption stalls and judders to a halt. Russell stops nodding and frowns. He looks completely nonplussed for a moment before he tries to recover his poise with another Mafia shrug. 'Whaddaya gonna do?' he says.

For maybe only the third or fourth time that I can recall in the two decades I've known him, Russell — Russell the enthusiast, Russell the smoothie, Russell the unruffleable – seems distinctly downcast and ill at ease. I can think of various explanations for this. (A) Unbeknownst to either him or me, Russell craves emotional certainties in his emotionally volatile world and my marriage was one of those certainties, the loft in Shoreditch a domestic refuge from the usual maelstrom of flings and affairs, and he can't adjust. (B) He's looking around the barren landscape of this flat and hearing only the sound of his own bluff, the bluff about how great it is to be not-quite-so-young, free and single, being called. (C) The sight of this tiny, empty flat strikes him as so powerfully bleak that even he can't muster up enough positivity to conquer it.

I go for (C). Which would, you would have thought, be pause for thought. Except for this overriding rule: Russell is always completely wrong about everything. Russ being the living embodiment of the hapless hero in a how-not-to-do-it cartoon. The man who will put vinegar on a bee-sting. Doggy-paddle out to a rip tide. Dance on thin ice in hobnailed boots. If you ever get lost in the Sahara and stumble across Russell and ask him for directions and he points confidently due south, then you make sure to go due north, to the oasis and the Mid-Sahara Hilton, with its free bar, nymphomaniacs' convention and, on the very top floor, a powerful telescope through which you might just make out the figure of Russell still urging folk south, towards sand, more sand and certain death.

'So,' he says with a lame attempt at vim and verve, 'what's it to be?'

'Now, or for the rest of my life?'

'What, like we're *girls*? Now, you fool.'

32

'Go out, I think. Unless you want to sit on the floor and chat.'

'Go out it is.'

Ten minutes later we've reached the Ridley Road market. It's being hosed down by a crack squad of cleaners, recent arrivals from Albania and Moldova with PhDs, darting about their support vehicles like infantry.

Russell nods at the pub on the corner. 'Wouldn't put too much on your chances of survival in there,' he says.

'And you'd fit right in, of course.'

'We both know that's correct, my friend.'

'Russ, the last time anybody dressed like you went into that pub was to head the murder investigation.'

Russell seems happy to accept this harsh truth with good grace. 'I come here,' he says, doing his hoarse Godfather. 'And you show me.' He crosses his hands in front of him. 'No respect. So. Where we going?'

'How about we walk and take pot luck?'

'That is one option. And a daft one. However, there are a few places just up the road which are rather good.'

'How do you know these things?'

Russell taps his forehead and makes the grumbly sound that has to come before his West Country. 'Oi nose woh oi nose. So. What do you want? Turkish or what?'

'What.'

'Oakily doakily.'

Past a sudden thumping cacophony of house music from the halal butcher on the corner, Russell leads me up Kingsland Road then right along a dark side-street to a tiny café.

'The Kingston Traditional Caribbean Home-Cooking

Eaterie' announces a sign above a window smothered by pot-plant greenery and decorated with a gold, green and black flag and a poster of Bob Marley. 'I dunno,' I say. 'But I think it might be Jamaican.' We squirm through a pair of doors and sidle towards a table beside the pot plants. Only now do I take in how steamy it is in here. And crowded, what with there being about ten other customers in a place the size of a boxroom. Also, thanks to the heavy dub hammering out of the speakers above us and the pot-clanging, counter-slapping, shrill banter between the chef and the waitress, noisy.

We squeeze into a table and the waitress comes over. Annoyingly, on both counts, Russell starts flirting with her and, merely glancing at the small laminated card that serves as a menu, orders one jerk chicken, one goat with rice and peas and two Red Stripes. Then flashes the waitress his full-on smile-with-raised-eyebrow combo. The waitress lifts her head in acknowledgement and twitches her mouth, before sashaying away with a slow-mo wiggle of her hips. Russell gives me an expectant look, one that invites me to judge how just how cool one man can be.

I twiddle a finger against my cheek. 'Thank you for ordering for me, Uncle Wussell.'

'Not at all, my precious.' He leans back in his chair – a small and flimsy number which, particularly with Russell perched precariously on its wooden frame, looks like it really should come with a sloping, inkwell-holed school desk – and blows me a kiss. Finishing, unfortunately, before the waitress returns with our beers. She plonks a can and a glass down in front of me then turns to Russell. Slowly, carefully, she pours his Red Stripe and hands him the glass. 'You see,' I think I hear her say as she holds his gaze. 'Good head.' She pushes herself away from the table and sashays off.

'How's the wife?' I ask, raising my voice and hoping the waitress hasn't gone out of earshot.

Russell gives me a brief, sarcastic, ha-ha-very-funny smile. 'Which one? In actual fact,' he says, looking very pleased with himself now, 'she was round earlier.'

'Round where?'

'The surgery.'

'Who was?'

'The new one.'

'Oh. Right. Her. When?'

'Earlier. Half-fiveish. Just after Vanessa had gone. Thank Christ, because you should have seen what this one turned up wearing.' Russell gives me an expectant look.

'Okay, Russell. What was she wearing?'

'The following items, from the feet up. Stilettos. Black stockings. A coat. A smile. End of list.'

'No knickers?'

'He *shoots*,' says Russell, doing his Jonathan Commentator. 'He *scohhz*. Not a knicker in sight. Naked nude.'

'Ahuh. And then you were a sex god.'

'And then I was, indeed, a sex god. First I sat her up on the desk and—'

'Oh, no, please, just you pile ahead and tell me all about it.'

'So you don't want to hear about how I—'

'No.'

'Or how she actually sobbed with joy when I was—'

'No.'

'Or how she got into the chair and begged me to—'

'So that's why you've just popped round. You've just had your shag, she's gone off home to the hubby, and you suddenly found yourself with time on your hands. So you thought you'd just come over to see me and have a good old boast. Didn't you?'

'No.'

'It's never enough for you just to have the shag, is it? Like when you dragged me to that terrible pub in Fulham.'

'That was a complete coincidence. I had no idea she worked there.'

'All those girls of yours that we just happen to bump into when we're out. In otherwise inexplicable venues. Also, maybe some people might be of the opinion that it could be tactless in the circumstances to bang on and on about your alleged sexual adventuring.'

'Oh, forgive me, my friend, forgive me, how thoughtless of me . . . How long you been wanting out of that marriage?'

'All eight years?'

'Uh huh. And how many affairs did you have during that marriage?'

'Only a couple.'

'And one of them lasting a good year.'

'More off than on.'

'And how many affairs have you just had during your gentleman-of-leisure travels?'

'One. Hey, you're the one who was being all worried about me. Isn't this a bit of a – 'ow you say – turnaround?'

'Anyway, you're back on the market, you're going to be having affairs yourself. Not nearly as many or as sophisticated and skilful as my ones, but still.'

'I really don't think so, Russ,' I say, sincerely, because I'm under no illusions about my new life. Although, Jesus, after those long, long years with Carol, I really could do with some *sex*. Yes, a rampaging singledom of carefree shagging and, let's be candid, a bit less vanilla, that'd be great. Just as it would be great if there was a Heaven or if Falkirk won the European Cup. 'I'm going to be just as sad and lonely as you.'

The waitress sashays back, brandishing two full plates. 'Chicken?' she asks.

'Thank you,' I say, hoping that Russell ordered this for himself and his smile is a bluff.

The waitress smiles too, at Russ. 'I thought you were the jerk,' she says to him. 'Your goat, sir.'

'Nice and spicy, I hope,' says Russ, flirting just that little bit too long, I'd have thought, but the waitress pretends not to mind.

'Oh, you better like it hot,' she tells him, then raises an eyebrow.

'You know it, girl,' he says back. Next he'll be adding 'innit' or 'jeh nah ah mean' after every sentence. 'The hotter the better.'

She gives him another raised eyebrow, nods once, then, taking her time about it, wiggles away.

'It's a privilege to see you in action, Russell. The master at work.'

'Look and learn, my fine friend. Look and learn.'

'Oh, is that how it's done?'

'Let's see what happens, shall we?'

'Aw naw, Russ, please. Not the card trick.'

He does the Mafia shrug, holding out his hands as though they're carrying a large plate. 'No respect. Yes, the card trick.'

'Excellent idea. Being given your business card and some shit about her needing oral expertise . . . Yeah, you're right, chicks must love that.' Because that's Russell's great downfall. He can read the magazines. He can buy the stuff in the magazines. He can go to the places the magazines write about. But he can't change the, let's be charitable, uncool nature of his profession. Especially compared to mine. Even now that I don't have one.

'Indeed they do,' says Russell. The dentist. 'Just like this one earlier. Do you know, she . . .' He stops and frowns. 'Jesus, this is hot.' He sniffs and blinks in an astonished sort of way.

'Your little minx has spiked your food.'

'No, she thought I was having the chicken, remember? Christ . . . No, she's on for it, trust me. Fucking hell, though.' With the hammy self-control often seen in chilli victims, Russell has a mouthwash of lager then stares boggle-eyed into the middle distance. 'So,' he says at last. 'You any nearer on deciding what you're going to do?'

I shake my head, trying not to spit out the fire that's raging in my mouth. Calmly and sensibly, the recommended way of responding to the alarm bells in my head, I reach for my lager and blow air out through pursed lips.

'. . . Hey,' says Russell.

Never again. Never again will I ingest anything that makes it nigh-on impossible to speak. '. . . What?'

'You know what you need?'

'. . .'

'Parties,' Russ says as if it's a punchline.

'. . . Parties.'

'Parties. You want to get out there and work the party scene.'

I blink back tears and cough. It might have been my imagination but my ears seemed to pop just then. 'Why?'

'Parties. Go out. Have fun. Cavort. Meet ladies. Parties.'

Half a glass of lager left. I ration myself to swigging half of the half. Russell and his parties. He's like an eighteen-year-old. The alternative being an earnest assessment of the chances of me getting invited to parties, forbye meeting any ladies, forbye cavorting with them, I fall back on patter. 'You're forgetting the party-poopers,' I manage to say.

Even as patter, it is, I admit, a lame point. Party-Pooper A being people we've just met at a party asking, out of the blue, in the middle of us being hilarious or fascinating, 'Which part of Scotland are you from?' With a cheeky tilt of the head. Thereby signalling that they've cunningly detected the Scottishness of the accent but not the exact regional variety. Though to the English there are only two varieties of Jock accent – the Glaswegian whine or the nice one on voice-overs. And then the inevitable and dreariest possible conversation about them being an eighth Scottish actually because their grandad came from Dundee. Party-Pooper B is Russell's alone – people he's just met at a party calling him 'man'. Allowing Russ the possibility of the double – 'Which part of Scotland you from, man?' Though that still exists, like some exotic sub-particle, only in theory. People meeting Russell at parties being too busy coping with hearing a Jock voice coming out of a black face. Mind you, the shit he's had to put up with over the years, ever since his adoption made him the sole member of Falkirk's Afro-Caribbean community, some middle-class twat trying to be cool with the mans isn't too much of a burden.

All of which explains why Russell can now say 'Party-poopers, party-schmoopers' with the air of having just won the argument.

I'll let him think that he's won. Just to be nice. I take another sip of lager. Surprising that there isn't a sizzle as it hits my mouth.

'Say what you like,' says Russell. 'But you're going to have to get out there.'

'Russ, I don't *have* to do anything. That's the point.'

'Uh-huh. But not having to do anything is no reason not to.'

'Eh?'

'You must have some sort of a plan, surely?'

That's exactly what I don't have and don't want. My only plan is to have no plan. No dates in the diary. No appointments. No schedule. No nothing. I've retired, for God's sakes. And not just from work. I do the Mafia shrug but not the accent. 'Not really. See what turns up.'

'See what turns up? See what turns *up*? You don't have a job, you don't have a marriage, you're thirty-nine years old and your social circle seems to have dwindled to me and, let's see, who else, oh, that's right, nobody. I'll tell you what's going to turn up. Nothing. That's what's going to turn up, my friend. Absolutely fuck all. You have to get out there, make things happen. You can't spend the rest of your life sitting on the floor in that poky little flat.'

I remember the people in the desert, marching off under Russell's assured instructions towards the middle of the Sahara. 'Funny you should say that.'

3

6.38 p.m., Wednesday 24 April

RICHARD

That's my phone. And, all being well, that'll be Marcus
waiting for me downstairs. 'It's Callum in reception,' says
Callum in reception in his ridiculously camp Glasgow sing-
song. 'A Mr Johnson here for you.'

'So put all three factors together,' Bob says, unhindered by
the apparently negligible drawback of the person he's talking
to being on the phone.

'I'll be down in a mo,' I tell Callum in reception.

'Erosion caused by rainfall in a desert that last saw rain
13,000 years ago. A sculpture in the shape of a lion. A lion that
faces the constellation of Leo as it was 13,000 years ago.
Coincidence? I don't—'

'Sorry, Bob, I have to . . .'

'*Think* so. No, the only possible explanation is that the
Sphinx is thirteen—'

'Well, it's certainly intriguing, Bob, but I . . .'

'*Thou*sand years old. Which fits exactly with—'

'Absolutely, Bob. We'll have to continue this . . .'

'The end of the—'

'Some other . . .'

'Last—'

'Time. See you in the morning. Got to go. Bye.'

'Ice age, yeah, see you tomorrow,' says Bob, seemingly unruffled by the way the conversation, if that's the right word for it, has gone, presumably because that's the way all Bob's conversations go, which makes me think yet again, by the time I reach the lift and press the down button, that maybe Bob thinks that's the way everyone's conversations normally go – one person talking a lot and the other party backing off and finally running away.

. . . The lift bumps to a stop, the bump bringing with it, as the bump of a lift stopping always does, the sudden thought of sudden death, the lift doors slide open and there's Marcus perched on one of the reception area's trendily unsittable-in chairs.

'Richard,' says Marcus. The Handshake Manly. 'The head honcho,' he says. 'The grand fromage. Good to see you, Mr Fossett, sir.' Marcus starts back and looks at me suspiciously. 'Have you joined a gym?'

I catch sight of Callum in reception peeking up from his desk, no doubt alerted by the word 'gym', and giving Marcus a covert once-over. Don't bother, I want to tell Callum in reception, because I've seen Marcus's wallet photograph of Alexandra, Marcus's girlfriend, on holiday, in Barbados, at a bar, on a beach, in a bikini, leaning forward to mime a kiss at the camera, sunglasses holding back her long, tumbling, black hair – clearly not the kind of woman who goes to her bed with a jar of face cream and a Ruth Rendell, and exactly the kind of glossy, shiny dolly-bird you'd expect to see in the passenger seat of a red Lamborghini, although in fact what Marcus actually drives is a Mini, albeit a souped-up, wide-wheeled Mini with smoked-glass windows, state-of-the-art sound system and a miniature steering wheel made of what looks like highly polished oak.

Marcus ushers me out and, even though we're now in the middle of a fairly busy pavement, he holds my arm and stops. 'So, Richard,' he says. 'I have a confession to make. I'm afraid I've taken the liberty of booking a table. At The Groucho.' Marcus scrunches up his face and tuts. 'Bit boring, I know, especially for a media type like you, but the food's not bad these days and they do give you drink for folding money. What say?'

The Groucho! Well. Of course, I have been to The Groucho – for a morning-coffee meeting with a PR girl, when I sat on or rather lay back in an armchair and tried to imagine how this already-glamorous bar area, empty save for me, the PR girl and a waiter, would look with glamorous people in it and not just glamorous people but celebrities to boot. The Groucho, if you please. Wait till I tell Ali about this.

'Reservation's for eight. Hope that's okay. Which leaves us time to find a likely hostelry for a tincture or twain. What say?'

Memo to self: do not get drunk. Do not drink too much. Drink slowly.

'Great,' I reply.

'So, Rich,' says Marcus as he places the pints on the table. 'How's tricks? How's the wife?'

'Fine,' I say, although of course she isn't. My wife, that is. Not that she's anyone else's, it being the wife not the my that's inaccurate, Ali and I not being officially married. Not for the want of trying, on my part anyway, because I have asked her, several times – first occasion on bended knee with a ring in a box, in a nice Italian restaurant, second go after a decent interval, much more as-if-casually, on the sofa, and there was very nearly a third attempt relatively recently, at the height of the rosy spell that followed the sticky patch, a year or so back, when we were in bed, no ring, no box, but her holding the pencilloid pregnancy-tester and the pair of us staring in disbelief at the thin blue line, but I managed to stop myself from doing any blurting because the moment was big enough in itself, and certainly had not arrived, like a miracle, from nowhere, only to be spoiled, and then I realised that it would be spoiled and not enhanced by any question I might have been about to pop. One occasion since then, to be honest, my birthday, when I got squiffily amorous and very nearly said it, more or less as a joke, but didn't in any case because even I can take a hint and, do you know, I rather respect her reasons for not wanting to be a wifey, a missus, a her-indoors, although come to think of it I'm no longer entirely sure what they were, are. The reasons. Anyway, no, Ali isn't my wife – she's my . . . girlfriend? That sounds like we meet twice a week and snog in the cinema. Partner? Possibly, if we were in a law firm instead of a relationship. Companion? I'd have to kit Ali out in a parasol and a Paisley-patterned Gladstone bag. Strange that after at least two decades of huge amounts of perfectly normal people not being married but living with each other and bringing up kids and being in families the English language hasn't come up with a name for them, when there are words for other things that have appeared in the last twenty years.

House-husband, for example. Bottle bank, crack pipe, com-
pact disc, website, Internet. But nothing for people like Ali and
me. So she's my thing without a name, my back of the knee. I
suppose I do still have the odd fantasy about us having a
wedding day, updated to incorporate Bongle as a page somehow, back at St James, maybe, the pretty and pretty old
(sixteen something or other) church back home where Mum
and Dad were married, as commemorated in those curiously
small photos in one of the earlier family albums, the pair of
them standing in the black and white sunshine of August 1958,
both of them thirteen years younger than I am now but
looking grown-up and mature in a way I have never looked
and have certainly never felt – but basically, really, push comes
to shove, what difference would it make? Because of course we
are married, in all but name. We don't need no piece of paper
from the City Hall. Who was it sang that?

Carly Something . . .

King?

Carly King?

'Alison,' says Marcus.

'Sorry?'

'Your wife's name. Or, no, wait a minute, have I fucked
up?'

'No, no, you're right. Yes, she's fine.'

'And the little . . .?'

'Boy. Jake. No, he's great.'

'All good news. All good news. So, Richard, I don't know if
it'll interest you or not.' Marcus leans forward and glances
around so that for a moment I wonder if we're under some
form of surveillance. 'More of this anon, I fancy, but suffice to

say that I did have this offer, which I happily pass on for you and the wife and the little chap . . .'

'Yes?' I say because it seems that I need to say something at this juncture.

'Just this offer of a villa going free for the fortnight. In the Algarve. Pool, view of the sea, secluded, lovely bit of the coast as yet undiscovered by the great unwashed. Super place. Stayed there last year as a matter of fact. Took Alexandra.' Marcus shakes his head. 'Excellent place. Anyway, it's going free, in both senses, and I'm sure I could do something or other to wangle you flights for gratis to boot. What say?'

'Well, it sounds . . .'

'Hey,' says Marcus, and he leans back against the black planks of the pub's sort of medieval-looking seatback. 'What mates are for. Anyway. No need to make your mind up right now.' Marcus raises his glass. 'Let us drink and be merry. This one, then the Grouch, yes?'

'Same again?' Marcus rests his fingertips on the neck of the bottle and gives it a little waggle. 'Or something different?'

'I don't know,' I say. 'Could we manage another bottle?'

'Oh, I'm sure we could.'

'Well . . . Maybe something a bit cheaper?'

Marcus does a mime of shock and disapproval with a start back and a wince and a pursing of the lips. 'Oof,' he says, then he wags a finger. 'But that's what expenses are for. Same again, then. Or, no, wait a minute, did you hate it?'

'No, no, it was terrific.'

'There you are then. Another bottle of this,' says Marcus to a waiter who has materialised at his side like one of the people in *Star Trek* when they do that thing where they dissolve in a kind of tinkling, shimmery light and then reappear somewhere completely different, guns – that's to say, phasers – at the ready. Teleporting.

'Thanks,' I say and I take care with the old balancing act as I lean forward from the bar stool to collect the tall glass the barman is sliding towards me, a restorative vodka and tonic with a slice of, no, it's lime.

'Hi, there, babes,' says a girl, a strikingly pretty girl with enormous eyes, enormous blue eyes, a beautifully oval-shaped face, and a black dress that suggests, I'm afraid, a sumptuous figure, who has slinked up to Marcus, and she bends forward for an exaggeratedly pouty double air-kiss.

Marcus puts an arm around her waist. 'Well, hello there, gorgeous,' he says and I feel a wave of blasédom course through my system, because here I am in the middle of it all, sitting on a bar stool, at the bar of the Groucho, grasping a tall glass of vodka and tonic with a slice of lime. 'This is Richard,' says Marcus. 'Richard, this is . . .'

'Lucinda,' she says, though not to me, with a smile.

'Lucinda,' says Marcus, back to her, also with a smile. 'Lucinda's a great friend of Toby's,' he adds. 'Toby. Toby Armstrong. Great friend of Lucinda's.' Smoothly following up the possible glitch of her name with a double mention and a reassuring acknowledgement that he really does know who she is. Yes, very smoothly done.

'Right,' I say and I nod, as though I've got this Toby character placed.

'I'm upstairs with Paula and Johnny,' says Lucinda.

'Excellent,' says Marcus. 'I'll pop by later to say hello.'

'Mm. Do. See you in a little while,' says Lucinda before she does a pretend-pointed, sinuous twist, the kind an extremely camp man might do, and slinks away.

'Wowee,' says Marcus. He shakes his head. 'Lucinda.'

I'm not quite sure what I can say at this point so I give my eyebrows a bit of a raise, which feels a pleasingly suave sort of a thing to be doing, so I do it a bit more and then I wonder how to phrase the next, I'm assuming sort of required, contribution appropriately. 'So, ah, have you?' I ask.

'Oddly, no.'

I wince, with one of those winces that can be felt in the pit of the stomach. Of course. Alexandra.

'Lucinda . . . Lucinda, you see, is more of a Branston pickle job.'

I've just shoved a handful of Twiglets into my mouth so instead of saying 'Sorry?' what I actually say is something more like 'Oghy?' while Marmitey pebbles and nobules jut into my gums.

Marcus gives me a baffled look. 'I haven't told you the Branston pickle story?' he says, his voice cracking with mock outrage on the pick of pickle.

'No,' I say, slightly feebly, I can't help feeling, under the circs.

'Well,' says Marcus with one long, slow nod, down then up. 'In that case, you leave me no option, Mr Fossett, sir, than to tell you the Branston pickle story.'

I give him an encouraging look – more raising of the eyebrows, dip of the chin, rapid, small nodding, some goggling of the eyes – although hampered rather by doing this while also trying to sieve, through the ice and of course the slice of lime, some vodka and tonic into my mouth.

'The Branston pickle story,' Marcus announces. 'Copyright of my chum Peter.'

I bang the glass down on the would it be zinc counter. 'Peter Standman?'

Marcus sucks in air and holds his breath for a moment. 'No,' he says. 'Pete Miller.' He gives me a puzzled look. 'You know him? Peter Miller. At BKV.'

What, I wonder, would BKV be? Or perhaps it's something different. Beaky Vee, for instance. Biqué V, even. Or Vi. Or something completely different that I've misheard, and understandably too amid the room's growing tumult of what should be hundreds of but is actually about fourteen people chatting. 'No,' I say. 'I know Peter Standman.'

'Right . . . Should I know him?'

'No,' I say, and I hold my hand up with a little wave rather like Marcus himself did when I went through the motions of offering to go halves on the dinner.

'Right. So, yes, Pete Miller's Branston pickle story. You ready?'

'Ready, get set and go,' I say, bantering.

'Right. So. Yes, Pete Miller, he tells this story about the Branston pickle. Or in fact about this chum of his at the place he used to work. Before BKV. Can't remember. Anyway, this guy Pete knew was crazy for the lady he worked with. Right alongside her. Desk opposite. And he was completely in lust with her, right?'

'Right,' I say, although, to be more accurate about it, what I actually say, because I've collected, from a second and much longer sieving process, which, now that I think about it, meant that I had to have my head tilted right back and my lower row of teeth on the glass, as though I was about to chew it, a mouthful of vodka and tonic and lime and ice cubes, is 'Nng.'

'But he couldn't risk doing anything. On account of her being married and a colleague and him being shy. But all he thinks about is her, having her, shagging her. He's mad for her. Obsessed by her body. So, one time, they both get pissed at the office party, and everyone else leaves and they just catch each other's gaze and look into each other's eyes and that's it, they're snogging, okay, and then they're in the taxi back to his place and before he knows it they're back in his place, her on the sofa, him ripping his and her clothes off, and then they're going at it, over the kitchen table, her bent over the kitchen table.'

I keep smiling.

'And it's all absolutely excellent, okay, except that while he's shagging away the guy notices this jar of Branston pickle on the table and it's jiggling to the edge with all the shagging that's going on and it's about to fall so he has to pick up the jar so that when he's at the critical moment he finds that what he's doing is looking at the jar of Branston pickle he's holding and reading about the ingredients and the E numbers.'

Marcus seems to be looking for a prompt. 'Yes?' I say.

'Well . . . that's it.'

'Right,' I say. 'Of course,' and I do a little 'ha' with a sort of backwards head tilt to show that I get it, although I don't, not really, not that I could say.

'So the moral is,' Marcus says, as though it's obvious but perhaps, it occurs to me, tactfully offering me in the spirit of friendship an explanation under the guise of summing up. 'As with young Lucinda there, who is absolutely charming but one of those who are best off staying in the mind. Best kept at bargepole's length. Like so many of the ladies, don't you think?'

But how is that the moral? Where does the Branston pickle fit in? 'Right. Absolutely.'

'So, you're a West Country boy, aren't you, Richard?'

'Yes. Well, Gloucestershire.'

'Really? Whereabouts in Gloucestershire?'

'Stow. Stow-on-the-Wold.'

'Oh, *Stow*,' says Marcus. 'I know Stow,' and something about the way he says it makes Stow sound like a bit of a one.

It also leaves me slightly flummoxed. 'But I thought you were . . .'

'West Country, yeah. Zummerzet,' says Marcus. 'Ooh arr. Taunton. Or thereabouts. But I went to college in Cirencester for my sins, so I know whereof you speak. Lovely part of the world. Pure . . . England, don't you think?'

'Well, I suppose, in a . . .'

Marcus raises his glass. 'England,' he says in a very hearty fashion. 'To England.'

I raise my glass. 'England,' I say, with, curiously, a twinge of something rather though not quite like guilt, although why I really couldn't say, except that it seems that you're not really supposed to say things like that these days.

'Lovely part of the world,' says Marcus. 'Now, how's about another?'

I can't help noticing when a very beautiful woman wearing a very short skirt arrives at the bar three stools down. 'Have you seen Marcus around?' she asks the barman. 'Marcus Johnson?'

'. . . I,' I say, but she doesn't hear me. The barman goes up to her, juggling a small bottle of orange juice like a cowboy twirls his gun. He shakes his head. I take a breath before launching into what will have to be a spiel, asking if I can help her because as it happens et cetera, but I have to hold my horses because she's carried on talking. 'Only I promised I'd help him out this evening,' I hear her say to the barman. 'Some work thing he's got on.'

The barman shakes his head. 'No,' he says thoughtfully. 'Can't say I've seen him.'

'Well, if you do, give me a shout. He needs me,' she says with pursed lips, preparing for the punchline, which turns out to be a mock and exaggerated 'As if.'

'Excuse me,' I say after a preparatory little noise. 'I'm with Marcus. Richard Fossett,' I say, offering my hand for a handshake.

'Melanie Sharp,' she says with a bright smile. 'Pleased to meet you.'

'Marcus's's just popped down to the loo,' I say. 'He'll be back in a moment.'

'Oh, I see.'

'Yes . . . Can I get you a drink?'

'Er, yes. Yes, why not? Thank you. Glass of champagne, please.'

I turn to the barman and when I speak it's with a lower, richer and smoother voice than my usual. 'A glass of. Champagne, please,' I ask the barman and just after I've done so I realise with a bit of a jolt that that's the smoothest thing I've ever done in my life. 'So,' I say, cocking an eyebrow. 'What was it. You were helping Marcus out. With?'

She shakes her head. 'No, I've just remembered. I got it wrong. That's tomorrow evening. A couple of chaps in from Dusseldorf he's roped me into meeting for dinner. I'm here all the time, you see. Aren't I, Darren?'

'Sorry?' says the barman.

'I'm just saying, I'm in here all the time, aren't I?'

The barman nods, giving her a pitying look, as a joke.

'Hello there, gorgeous,' says Marcus, having materialised at the side of his bar stool.

'Hi, babes,' says Melanie, air-kissing him with an exaggerated pout.

'So,' says Marcus 'you've already met . . .?'

'Richard, yeah, yeah. And I was just telling Richard about the two guys you've got to see from Dusseldorf tomorrow?'

Marcus looks at her, smiling, nodding his head. 'That's right,' he says, to me now. '*Total* nightmare.'

'Yeah, see you later, babes.'

'Darling. Thanks. Ciao.'

'Ciao.'

'Ciao,' I say.

'Oh*kcay*,' says Marcus. 'What say we go on somewhere?'

Of all the things, curiously, what I'm being mesmerised by is the shimmering ball above me, one of those big shimmering balls made out of tiny, silvery, mirrory panels which reflect all the lights around them, the kind of big shimmering ball that'd hang from the ceilings of the venues in *Come Dancing* or that you often see in films set in a nightclub, which this place must, I suppose, be, at least sort of.

Marcus leans towards me, as far towards me in fact as putting his mouth to my ear. 'To Portugal,' he yells. At least I think that's what he yells. And he's raising his glass, so that would fit. I risk raising my glass in reply and mouthing 'Portugal' back though it's a little while after I've finished the mouthing that I know what that means.

During a brief lull in the racket, Marcus leans forward and beckons me close. 'Do you fancy going private?' he asks.

'Sorry?' I say.

Then the 'music' starts up again, so Marcus takes a deep breath. 'A private dance,' he shouts into my ear.

My heart starts thudding in time with the 'music' and all moisture leaves my mouth. The private dances are the ones where one of the girls leads the customer or customers past a small, presumably ceremonial, red rope slung low between two flimsy poles, then through a pair of overly long velvet curtains.

'No,' I say. 'No, thank you.'

'You sure?'

6.38 p.m., Wednesday 24 April

EWAN

This is a mistake. I shouldn't be doing this.

Why *am* I doing this?

Because I said I would.

Why did I say I that I would?

Because, one, the phone call caught me unawares and, two, it was easier at the time than to say no. And, three, I'm too much of a straight not to go when I said that I would. So that's going to have to change.

Okay. So why did I answer the phone in the first place?

Because the line had been installed about five minutes before, and I thought it was BT phoning up to confirm that it was working. Or something.

So why did I decide to have a phone line?

Because, one, it's easier having a phone than not having a phone, given that there's an answerphone to field calls and, two, whatever Russell says, I am *not* in a sulk from life.

Mind you, not having any contact with anyone ever again has its attractions. Obvious ones. Glaringly obvious if you're walking, as I am now, down Old Street towards Clerkenwell, retracing what used to be, every weekday for the last eight years and a lot of weekends, my walk from the loft to the office. Feeling like I'm doing a re-enactment for the cops. Heading for a painfully trendy bar that calls itself Umlaut. With two dots over the U. And it will be full of young people. With their haircuts. And their zips. And that Valley Girl shit. You're so this. She's so that. And I'm so totally like, blah. Ach, this is such a mistake. I should be back in my flatette. Sitting on my beanbag. Watching my new TV. Flicking the remote. What I should not be doing is approaching a dimly lit bar calling itself Umlaut. Or putting on a smile and waving a hello to the dozen or so young people milling around in the far corner.

'Hi,' I say. 'Hi. How are you? Hi. Hi. Hi there. Hi.'

There's Damien, whose birthday drinks this is. There's fat Yvette, whose phone call caught me unawares. Sam, Jez, Caro, Will, Tom − ex-colleagues. No. Let's be blunt. Ex-employees. Plus fat Yvette's girlfriend, Sue. Only a few unfamiliar faces, so I know for a fact that it's every bit as bad as I feared: most of the dozen or so are younger than Damien, and he's celebrating his 25th.

'Happy birthday,' I say to Damien. Perhaps I should have brought a present. A chemistry set. An Action Man. A card with a numbered badge and a ten-pound note inside. 'Let me buy you a drink.'

'Two drinks,' Damien says. This strikes me as slightly ungracious. 'It's a double celebration,' he explains.

What, he's lost his virginity? 'Really?'

'Yeah, see, thing is, this is also a leaving do.'

'Ah.'

'They fired me,' says fat Yvette. 'Made me redundant,' she continues. Redundantly, but I decide not to point that out.

'Why?' I say.

Fat Yvette snorts. 'Timekeeping. They said. *Time*keeping. I fucking ask you.'

No great surprise there. Fat Yvette's idea of an early start was before lunch. Fat Yvette, like the rest of them, blissfully prancing about, baby gazelles blithely unaware of the lions in the undergrowth.

'First you,' says Damien. 'Now Yvette. Where's it going to end?'

Nope, not a notion.

Oh, this is bollocks, I tell myself. Not for the first time in the two hours, going on a month, that I've spent listening to young people talk nonsense.

Complete bollocks. Exactly the kind of complete-bollocks occasion I will no longer be attending. Drinks after work. Birthday drinks. Work dos. Launches. Openings. Launches. Openings. All offering that slight charge of sexual possibility. Aye, right. Of course.

So. No more bollocksing around with colleagues and rivals and contacts and clients. Bollocks to all of it, and bollocks especially to this bezipped bohemia.

I sit there, nursing a bottle of Budvar. Unpeeling the label for something to do. Feeling like a pensioner at a rave. All the more so when I see that, next to me, Damien is taking out, from a bashed pouch, some cigarette papers, a torn cigarette, and a money bag of grass. And now starting to roll what looks to me very much like a joint.

'You can't smoke that here, can you?' I ask, wondering if there's been a change in the law I haven't heard about.

'That's correct,' says Damien. 'Fancy a walk?'

'Why not?' I say because the only answer I can think of is that I might miss out on some more bleeding from the ears and lager-nursing tedium.

So I follow Damien out into the street and up a narrow lane. I'm trying to act cool but the truth is that I feel . . . well, shamefully, a bit nervous, a little bit excited. I can't remember when I last smoked a joint and I can't recall ever smoking a joint not in someone's room at someone's party. My dope-smoking days, my dope-buying days, were when I was at college. Alcohol the drug of choice for most of my twenties. And since. Coke, of course, which has always been so very, very more-ish. Hence my rule – never buy, only mooch. Not too difficult. Especially with Russell and his strictly rationed gram a week of medically good gear. But Ecstasy, acid, mushrooms, amphetamines, ketamine, ice, crack, GHB, PCP – I haven't done any. So that's another thing that's going to have to change. Because I'm sorry to say that it's with a strong frisson of lawbreaking and living on the edge that I take a couple of puffs. Without coughing. Or being ambushed by Special Branch.

I pass the joint back to Damien behind a cupped hand. 'I didn't know you were a stoner,' I say, for the sake of saying something.

'Oh yeah. I smoke all the time.'

'What, so you'd have one of these with your cornflakes?'

'Weetabix, as it happens. Some days. Yes.'

'Really? First thing in the morning?'

59

'Some days.'

Damien passes it back. This time, I try a deeper puff, holding the smoke in, swallowing it. 'What about work?' I ask, a bit croakily. 'You didn't smoke in the office, did you?'

'Not *in* the office, no. I'd go to the fire escape or go for a walk round the block.'

'Wait a minute,' I say, turning to Damien, genuinely curious. 'You mean to say that you were off your face all day every day?'

'Not off my face . . . Gently lit.'

'Gently lit.'

'It's how someone described the Queen Mother,' says Damien. 'Apparently, that's how she lived. A gin and tonic early on, then kept topping it up until it was time for bed. She'd never overdo it and get obviously pissed. But there wasn't much of the time when she was completely stone-cold sober.'

'I never realised. About you, I mean.' I've had a few good goes at it and the lane's still empty so I quickly pass the thing back to Damien. 'I suppose it would explain how you never seemed to get flustered.'

'Maybe.'

'And never said much.'

'Mmm.'

'I just thought it was because you were so fixed on the job.'

'Well . . .'

'Not that you weren't.'

He shrugs. 'They're going to wind us up, aren't they?'

'. . . Yes.'

'That's why you got out, isn't it?'

'. . . Yes.'

'Big pay-off.'

My turn to shrug.

'Jesus, you jammy bastard . . . They're going to shaft the rest of us, aren't they?'

'You might be okay. Give you three months' salary, maybe.'

'Or fuck all.'

'Oh, you'll be okay, even with this DMX shit,' I tell him. 'You're good enough.' Uncle Ewan. 'This could be a big chance for you. Move on somewhere bigger maybe. Or even take some time out. Go travelling for a while.' Okay, this is me blethering but isn't that what young people do these days? Sling their possessions in a backpack. Dodge around the beaches and bars at the bottom of the map. Isn't that what anyone would do, given half the chance? You win the Lottery, you stay in the job? Please. Me, I toyed with the wandering notion. For about a minute. Didn't get much beyond the stage of wondering if all this might not have to involve a camper van.

Damien hands me the joint at the very moment that an undercover policeman disguised as a teenage girl rounds the corner. I hide the thing behind my back until she's passed us, then risk another couple of drags for form's sake.

'Not really an option,' says Damien. 'Not with my mortgage and child support.'

Possibly because of the distraction of the teenage cop, I need a moment before I realise what he's talking about. 'You joking?'

'No.'

'Christ. I didn't know you had, well, all that. A flat, okay, but, you know, kids and so on.'

'Kid. Girl. She's five now.' Damien takes a last suck on the joint, flicks it to the ground and squishes it underfoot. Thank God for that. We turn and head back up the alley. 'Winona,' says Damien. 'Her mother's choice. I get to see her at the weekends. Win, that is, not her mother. Not that . . .'

'Right,' I say into the silence. 'I see.' Meanwhile, what I'm saying to myself is, 'You lucky, lucky sod, Macintyre.' Damien has a five-year-old girl. Extraordinary. And this is his twenty-fifth birthday. No wonder he likes the odd spliff.

Not that the marijuana seems to have had much effect on him, other than to make him seem rather morosely thoughtful. I, on the other hand, seem to be wearing cast-iron shoes.

Picking up my feet as though making my way across a sticky ploughed field, I follow Damien back to the pub. I let Damien go ahead, out of some obscure sense of protocol, and then I find myself moving slowly, mindlessly, very contentedly, towards the bar. Which is fortunate because I really need a beer or, even better, a glass of water, and that's because my mouth seems to be coated with sand. I clutch hold of the counter and ask the barman, who has five rings in his left eyebrow, for water.

'You okay?' he asks as he hands me a bottle and a glass with a slice of lemon in it.

For some reason I drift off for a moment, with the thought that this is exactly the kind of thing that would outrage folk back home. Look – bottled water, and it's going to cost me thirty shillings.

'Fine,' I say, staring at the barman's eyebrow. 'Fine.' What's the point of that, then? And how sore must it be to get done? Does he take them out at night? Now, why would . . .

'Excuse me. Is this . . .?' A girl. Late twenties, rather good-looking, although the nose is a bit snubby, quite small but nicely almond-shaped, ice-blue eyes, a few freckles around the cheeks that mean no harm.

'Oh, no. No.' I say. I reach out in a mock-gallant beckoning gesture. And I wonder if I did that prattishly. Then I wonder if I've just had my first outbreak of marijuana paranoia since that weekend in Amsterdam. (With Carol – the early days, of course.) Then I wonder if wondering about the paranoia is itself a symptom of dope paranoia. Or if this whole train of thought isn't inevitable. Or if wondering whether or not this whole train of thought is inevitable isn't itself . . . 'Be my gueght.'

'Thank you. Vodka tonic, please,' calls the girl to He-Who-Has-Rings-In-His-Eyebrows.

Yes, attractive. Nothing much going on breastwise but slim. What could be a Nicole Farhi jacket. Black skirt. Prada shoes. Maybe Prada. 'Good idea,' I say suavely. Or perhaps it was really smarmily. But I've started so now I'll have to finish. 'I'll have one too. Let me get for them.'

I concentrate very hard on the ordering of the drinks and the paying for the drinks. I manage to do both without undue mishap. Not counting a possibly extended fiddle with my wallet.

'So who are you meeting?' I ask, successfully, nodding, also successfully, in the general direction of everyone else in the room.

'Paul,' she says.

'Ah, Paul,' I say.

'Paul's my friend,' she says, with an air of explaining everything.

'Well,' I say, competently, thanks to the water. And then I think, why not? 'Lucky Paul.'

'Friend. Not boyfriend or anything.'

'Oh. Don't you have a boyfriend, then?' Christ, I must sound like a pederast.

She turns to me and gives me a come-off-it smile. 'No,' she says. 'No boyfriend. You?'

'No. In fact, I've never had a boyfriend.'

'Really?'

'Hello,' I say, offering my hand. And definitely emboldened by the grass to give it a go and chat up this girl. Born when I was halfway through secondary. The trouble is, despite the Barcelona windfall, I still have no idea how to do this. As is already painfully obvious. Having last done this when I was halfway through secondary. 'I'm Ewan. Ewan Macintyre.'

'Nice to meet you, Ewan. I'm Nicola.'

'Nicola. That'gh a beautiful name.'

'Thank you . . . I'm sorry, I'd better go and look for Paul.'

'Oh, Paul can wait.'

'Oh, can he?'

'Yes,' I say. 'He can.'

Because I am physically unable to say anything more, I hold her gaze. She has interesting blue eyes. They really do sparkle. Sparkling eyes, I think. One of those phrases which remain just phrases until you come across an example of the phenomenon that has inspired the phrase. And now I find myself recalling, very vividly, a boat trip in Greece, with Carol, who was seasick, and, this being the early days, I cradled her head on my lap. Next thing I knew she'd thrown up over my trousers. I just sat there, astonished, having thought, until that moment, that seasickness was a metaphorical thing. Not actual vomiting. Arrived at the island in my boxers, pretending they were trunks. Flecks in the iris, probably. Maybe it's a new kind of contact lens. Then I realise that I'm still holding her gaze here, the smooth act surely degenerating into a jerk's full-on failure. I were her, I'd give me a look and head off to Paul sharpish. Find someone a bit more normal to talk to.

But she doesn't. In fact, she seems to be holding my stare. This must have been going on for some time. But instead of looking away and doing an apologetic laugh, I give her my smoothie's grin. It's got to be the grass that's to blame for this heedless smarm. 'He can,' I say, hoping to pick up the thread which I might well have lost here. 'Don't you think?'

God, I'm good. Because this is working.

'Okay, then,' she says, with a wary half-smile.

'Cheers. Nicola,' I say, offering my glass for a chink.

'Cheers. Ewan,' says Nicola, chinking it.

I encourage her to do the talking. Textbook, but there's going to have to come a time when I'll have to use words together too. The very notion seems ridiculous. God, the state of me . . .

So when Damien goes past, I hold up an excusing finger, prattishly, to this Nicola and grab him by the elbow. 'Waw the heh . . .' I give it another go. 'What. The hell,' I whisper, 'was in. That joint?'

'Kind of skunk.'

'And did you put. A lot in?'

'No more than the usual.'

'How much is that?'

Damien shrugs. 'The usual.'

'Quite a lot?'

Damien considers this for a while. He looks up at the ceiling, down at the floor, and then at nothing in particular. 'Yyyyyes,' he says eventually.

'Jeevuf Chrithe,' I say.

'I think we should go.'

I snap out of it. 'Where?' I ask, brilliantly.

'Um, your place. Unless you live somewhere like Cornwall or Aberdeen.'

'Dalston,' I say, still not quite believing my luck. Also, still marvelling at the younger generation. The morals of alley cats.

She smiles back. 'Dalston it is,' she says. 'We'll cab it.'

I do a salute. Only a flicky one, a couple of fingers springing away from my forehead. But still – a salute. 'Right you are,' I say and hope to Christ that was a normal thing to say.

I finish my glass of water with a harsh gulp, then follow her outside. Where I take in huge lungfuls of unfresh air in an attempt to clear my head.

That seems to work. To the extent that I can see and hail a cab. And open the cab door in time to usher in this Nicola. And remember to get in myself. Oh yes, this is going awfully well.

It goes even better when she puts a hand on my knee and sidles closer so that we're sitting there hip to hip. I insinuate an arm behind her and rest my hand lightly against her waist. We're like a couple of teenagers at the movies. Then she strokes her hand up my thigh and lets it rest heavily on my groin. And it's only now that it occurs to me that I'm about to tick a box in my shamefully short carnal CV. Ever had sex with someone you've just met? Answer, soon – yes.

The cab turns right into Ridley Road and begins to ne-gotiate the potholes and worryingly solid-looking discarded boxes.

'Here on the left,' I say, with some difficulty, what with my mouth still feeling like it would if I'd just eaten a pack of cream crackers.

Nicola wheechs out a note and hands it to the cabbie through the sliding glass window behind his head. The one that cabbies open to talk shite at you. Feeling like a spectator of my own life, I get out and watch her, still inside, go through the fankle of getting the change then giving some of the change back as a tip. But you don't pay inside the cab, I think. Not in London. Edinburgh and New York, yes. But in London you always get out of the cab first. More stoned drivel, I note to myself. But less stoned is the next thought – that my knowing this kind of thing and her not shows up the age difference. In rather a satisfying way. Her the naif, yet to be schooled by maturity. Me the man of the world, showing her a thing or two. Her in a short skirt. Could be a gymslip. White socks.

'Hello again,' she says, done with the cab at last.

'Thiff way,' I say.

It doesn't come as too much of a shock that it's her who starts the kissing and as soon as we're inside the door of the flat. A bit of a surprise, really, that she didn't fondle my rump as we climbed the stairs. The way she's been going, she should be twirling her moustache or reaching round to unclasp my bra.

She breaks off the kiss. Maybe because it must have been like kissing an unused sponge. We go through. Her instinct for these things honed by recent studenthood, she heads straight to the kitcheny bit and the fridge.

'Got anything to drink?' she says. Without waiting for a reply, she kneels down, opens the fridge door, pulls out two bottles of Budvar and opens them.

'Tell you what,' I say. 'You fetch a couple of beergh.'

I join her in the kitchen nook, less to be sociable than to down a few more litres of tap water. She hands me a bottle then marches to the window, takes in the view – of rooftops, houses and street.

'London,' she says. 'Bloody London. It's so crap. Compared to, I don't know, Madrid or Lisbon or Berlin or Paris or anywhere. Glasgow,' she adds, giving me a wee look. One that involves a slight lowering of the head and a lifting of the eyebrows. Oh, well. 'But London. Mediocre, second-rate, rubbish. So bloody English.'

But she's English, isn't she? Maybe she isn't. Or maybe calls herself half-Welsh or something, the way English people do. 'Nah,' I say, risking speech now that I've had the water. 'London isn't English. Like New York isn't American. Because,' I say, surprised at both my sudden desire to blether and ability to do so. 'The thing is about London and New York is that they're both . . .'

'And the endlessness of it all. Don't you think?'

Now why is this happening? Why this brittle pause in the action? She's getting cold feet. Or she's wittering with nerves that have come on. All of a sudden as we approach the crunch. Or she's acting sophisticated. Or it's a token effort at playing hard to get. Or something else completely different and completely unfathomable. Woman – the eternal mystery.

To prove just this, she puts the bottle down on the floor and comes back towards me, half-smiling. Comes right up, throws her hands behind my neck. 'Let's go somewhere,' she says. 'Paris. Let's go to Paris.'

'Now?' I say, keeping up my own half-smile. Partly genuine, because I'd very much like to give her the benefit of the doubt here.

'My friend Sylvie has a flat in the seizième.'

The half-smile's still there but the doubt is growing.

'With a wonderful view of the city.'

'Really?'

'And a spare room with this huge double bed.'

'Really?' The doubts decreasing. The chill fading.

'And opposite the bed, these mirrored wardrobes.' She goes on tiptoe to brush her mouth over my ear. 'Floor-to-ceiling mirrors,' she whispers. Then she starts to kiss my ear. Pecking at my ear with soft kisses. I reassure myself about my scrupulous hygiene, then I close my eyes and put my hands on her waist, then her hips, then her arse.

Which seems to go down quite well. Because the next thing she does is pull her head back and ask, with a quizzical variant of the half-smile, 'Where's the bedroom?'

'Ah, well. Third on the right, up the stairs, first right, along to the end of the corridor and it's the second on the left.'

'That door there, then?'

I prepare to be cool. 'Where you can thee the bed, yeff,' I say in a low drawl.

She holds out her hand. 'Come on.'

She leads me to the bed then pushes me, not with obvious force but effectively enough, onto it. I lie there, propped up on my elbows, not moving. She comes towards me and stands between my dangling shins.

'Take off my jacket,' she says.

'Oh, all right then.' I sit up, reach forward and cumbersomely remove her jacket,

'Now take off my blouse.'

I fumble with the buttons. Her bra is black. Her breasts, as predicted, look to be respectable rather than remarkable. Not melons but pears. Not that I'm compl—

'Take off my skirt . . . Zip's on the side.'

Slowly, unsurely, I ease the skirt over her hips and down. Somehow, her tights have started to unroll themselves. Ah. Stockings. Which I've always found a bit over-the-top, the fuss and palaver of them, but never mind. She steps out of the skirt. Now she holds my gaze while she reaches behind her back and unclasps her bra.

She lifts her legs even higher. Her ankles rest on my shoulders.

Gascoigne's goal, Euro 96. Gascoigne lobbing Hendry. Taking it on the volley. The schoolboy glee of the celebrations.

Her hands move round to clasp my arse.

82 World Cup. Hansen and Miller colliding. The Russian winger given a clear run in on an invisible Alan Rough.

The clasp evolves into a gentle clawing.

Argentina 78. Hammered by Peru. Drawing with Iran . . .

I feel one of her hands sliding further across.

We're on the march with Ally's army. We're going to the Argentine . . .

I feel fingers sliding even further across.

Ally MacLeod. The stricken face of Ally MacLeod . . .
Good Christ.
The stricken . . .
No use. David Narey's about to score against Brazil.

4

RICHARD

'. . . Are placed exactly to reflect the three stars of Orion's—'

'Just a mo, Bob, I think that's . . .'

'Belt, but the really interesting thing is that it's Orion's—'

'My phone so I'd . . .'

'Belt as it appeared in the sky—'

'Really better . . .'

'Thirteen thousand years a—'

'Go.'

'Go.'

''Scuse me, Bob.'

I hurtle across the office, banging my hip on Shirley's swively chair and knocking over on Shirley's desk a card of an angel playing something like a mandolin, playing it in an oddly sly manner, it occurs to me as I watch the card fall into the waste-paper basket (memo to self: retrieve sly angel from Shirley's waste-paper basket), only to reach my cubicle just as the phone stops ringing. Breathing heavily, I look at the phone for a while, then at the toasters flapping across my computer screen. Then I grasp the edge of the desk and let out a groan that, rather to my surprise, turns into a sort of keening whimper, not unlike the sound le petit homme qui s'appelle Monsieur le Bongle sometimes makes in his sleep and my heart grows sore.

Technically, it's half-ten in the morning but effectively it's the afternoon, given that today started at twenty past five, when I came to, head throbbing, eyes gritty, mouth a scorched wasteland, brain and body utterly exhausted but wide awake. I suppose it could conceivably have been a car horn that wrenched me from unconsciousness, or something else, someone shouting in the street, for example, but it was probably nothing, just the usual reasonless violent awakening of drunkard's dawn, one of the crappinesses of middle age that nobody seemed to warn me about, along with the sudden appearance of the odd grey chest hair, or, more appallingly still, puboid. But whatever the cause or lack of cause, it had me sitting bolt upright, on the sofa, still wearing my suit and my shoes, at twenty past five in the morning, and slowly realising that, what with that being the telly in the corner and that being the mirror over the mantelpiece, and this being a sofa I was sitting bolt upright on, I had been sleeping in the sitting-room lounge, and by design too, it appeared, judging by the note I then spotted on the coffee table beside a neatly folded blanket and an unused pillow – *Gone to bed. You sleep here. A.* Evidently, I had obeyed orders – longest way up, shortest way down, no names, no pack drill – but I had absolutely no recollection of having done so. Or of getting home. Or of being wherever it was I was before I got home.

Then slowly it came back, memory cells coming fitfully back on-line – Marcus . . . The Groucho . . . the, ah, gentlemen's club. (Which, I immediately vowed, Ali must never ever find out about. Ever.) And then, and then, yes, a taxi and another club, a disco-y sort of a place possibly in the Marble Arch area, or possibly not . . . and women . . . Marcus and me chatting to three women, young women with very big hair and very short, spangly skirts, at a bar, and me talking about . . . cricket.

Jabbering on and on and on about bloody cricket, or to be more specific, my own cricketing career at school, my celebrated cover drive, and then, more specifically still, the memory of this arriving with unusual and ghastly clarity, backing up my explanation of how I'd keep my eyes on the ball and my left elbow high but straight, left foot advancing to the pitch of the ball, with a, oh God, oh God, oh God, oh blimming flipping hell, demonstration of my technique. The three women moving off very soon afterwards. I'd Bobbed them.

I'd had plenty of time this morning – two whole hours, as it turned out – to remember quite a bit more about last night, wince-making episode after wince-making episode, while I stumbled about, fetching water, going for a pee, and then while I lay on the sofa, head throbbing, eyes clenched, mouth still a scorched wasteland despite the water, brain and body yearning for sleep, before I heard Bongle wake with an outraged yelp and the day could officially begin.

'Ad dropped from page eight.'

With a bit of a start, I have to admit, I lift my head from my desk where it was resting for a moment and see Shirley at the cubicle entrance. 'Sorry?' I say.

'Twenty by two ad dropped from page eight.'

'Ah,' I say and I do a wise nod. 'What was the ad for?' I ask because it seems right for me to ask something at this point.

'Um, Kirkpatrick Plant Hire, I think.'

'Kirkpatrick Plant Hire. Right. What size was the ad?'

'Twenty by two.'

'Twenty by two? For the love of Mike, how are we going to fill that kind of space now?'

'Well, I . . .'

'I mean, what are we supposed to do?' There's a cracked falsetto at the end of that question so I have to clear my throat. And then, from nowhere, I have a sudden brainwave. 'How about,' I say with some deliberation, 'we put in a really big headline and a huge intro, maybe even increase the type size of the copy?'

Shirley frowns in an uncertain sort of a way. 'I don't think . . . It's Barry's concrete article which came with a couple of spare photos. So I was thinking more that we could add in one or two of those.'

'Right . . . Good idea.'

'. . . Are you all right, Richard?'

'Yeah, I'm fine, thanks. Just a bit knackered.'

'Oh, right,' Shirley says in a hurry, and looking away, and I think I know why – because the next bit might have been the bit that would have to go unsaid, the bit about, though of course it actually wouldn't have been on this occasion, Bongle keeping me up during the night, because obviously any Bongle reference must have about the same emotional impact on Shirley as a recently dead person's name to his or her kith or kin, because, you see, Shirley has *no children*, nor, at her age (forty-one? forty-two? forty-three? who knows?) and in what must perforce be an unprocreational relationship with her married business-man friend, will she ever. Have any, that is. Children. Not that she goes on about it or even ever mentions it but the stark fact remains, and it remains there between us like an unremarked-upon large pink elephant standing in the middle of a room, the stark, brutal, cruel and utterly unmentionable fact that I have Bongle and she doesn't, and the odd thing is that it's only now that I do have Bongle that I have begun to fully appreciate, to appreciate fully the tragedy of this for Shirley, because it was only by Bongle appearing on the scene – out of the blue, after all those years of Ali being uncertain about the whole business, before perhaps the advancing years or something got to her and she was suddenly so keen, and that was it, first time of trying or thereabouts – that I discovered this new part of life, like I'd walked through a door I didn't know was there into a room I didn't know existed – no, not a room, a whole country, an entire new world – and I could suddenly see why they use babies in adverts, just like in adolescence and it dawning that there was a reason for all the slurpy, slushy kissing and so on and so forth in *Plays for Today* and suchlike. So – not to mention the war.

'I'd better get back,' says Shirley. 'See if I can lay hands on an extra photo.'

'Right you are.'

Shirley leaves with a smile and a flutter of her fingers, closing the door, which is thoughtful of her, and also does the much-needed service of preventing any view of Shirley's fine, full behind, which must be looking particularly full and fine in what threatened to be a tightish black skirt. To say nothing of the blouse. Even less about the contents of the blouse.

An extra photograph to illustrate an article about concrete . . . I gaze at the flapping toasters and wonder if Shirley ever lets herself be haunted by her alternative life, the one where she got married and had kids. No, that's unbearable . . . Then again, this really isn't the career I thought I'd have. At this point, I'd very much like to have an indulgent laugh at the funny little ideas I used to have about what I'd be doing when I was big, but to be honest they don't seem outlandishly ambitious, those ideas, because it wasn't as if I was hell bent on being an astronaut or captain of England. No, and, in fact, it's my actual CV that seems to belong to someone else. The chap whose CV lists not Cambridge but the Poly, not London but Aylesbury, not *The Times* or the *Telegraph* but *Bricks and Brickmen* . . . Well, on the other hand, if it hadn't been for Aylesbury and the *Courant*, I'd never have met Ali, would I? Or, come to that, Frank, so I'd never have got the deputy's job here – deputy editor, indeed, although, yes, granted, fair enough, it is true that job titles at *Bricks and Brickmen* are awarded with Ruritanian grandiosity, so that everyone has a job title with epaulettes in a magazine whose editorial team consists of the editor (self) and the deputy editor (Shirley) and whose art department, e.g., consists of Patrick, who pops in twice a week in his capacity as art director – nor would I have replaced Frank when he retired . . .

There's a knock on my door and a millisecond later the production manager has marched in. 'Proofs,' he says, plonking, with Bobbian carelessness, a pile of proof pages on my desk.

'Thanks, Bob,' I say, rather desperately pretending to be very busy doing all this concentrated reading of the cellophaned brochure about coloured cement that's lying on top of my mail, but when I try to focus on the type I go slightly dizzy and have to close my eyes for a mo to recover.

'I was going to say,' says Bob, hovering, oblivious, 'about the fact that the Pyramids' alignment relates to Orion's—'

'Sorry, Bob, I . . .'

'Belt but Orion's—

'Sorry, Bob, but the . . .'

'Belt as it appeared in the night sky of guess when that's right thirteen—'

A wave of something that could conceivably precede nausea washes over me. 'Really, I . . .'

'Thousand years ago, which means that—'

'Oh, Richard, could I grab you for a minute?' It's Shirley back in the cubicle doorway, leaning against the door in a way that, alas, involves an outthrusting of her left hip. 'It's that headline.'

'What headline?'

'The headline that was giving us trouble before.'

What on earth is she talking about? Ah. Well, talk about impenetrable. 'Sorry, Bob,' I say, tapping the cellophaned brochure in a businesslike fashion, then scraping back the chair. 'It's that headline again. I'd better dash.'

'I thought you might need rescuing,' Shirley whispers as we walk towards her desk.

'Thanks,' I reply, also in a whisper, although we're surely out of earshot, but then there's something infectious about a whisper, like a yawn. And, I'm afraid, sexy. 'I did.'

'Well, now that you're here,' says Shirley, in a normal voice now, and nodding at her computer. 'Do you think the headline's okay?'

I peer down at her screen, trying to pay no attention whatsoever to the ripe swell that's stretching her blouse. 'Something to build on. Very good. Which piece is it for?'

'Barry's one. Concrete.'

'Right. Something to build on. No, that's good . . . Though maybe we could liven it up a bit.'

'Sure.'

'How about an exclamation mark? Something to build on! More . . . oomph. And' – the thought arriving in a flash, inspirationally, from who knows where or how – 'it sort of shows we're making a pun.'

Shirley frowns. 'Yes. Yes, it does do that . . . I'll give it another think, shall I?'

'Good idea, Shirley. Well,' I say, after a bit of a pause when I just couldn't help noticing the swelling blouse mere inches away from my shirtsleeve. 'I'd better . . . um . . .'

'Yes,' says Shirley and having said that she seems to straighten her back, thereby making the swell even more noticeable to the extent that it's in danger of turning majestic.

'. . . Yes,' I say. 'I'll . . .' I pat the top of her chair and force myself off and away and back to the cubicle and festering with what has clearly turned into a randy as well as nauseous hangover and one that has now produced an unusually clear picture of Shirley sitting at her desk but divested of the blouse, just sitting at her desk, wearing a bra, a black bra that has to jut some way from her ribcage, coping as it has to with the ripe . . .

Patting about like a blind person, I reach for my raft, I mean of course chair, and plonk myself down, with a hint of a bounce so therefore also a bit of a lurch in the old breadbasket.

I do some deep breathing and stare at the toasters flapping by . . .

Okay . . .

So now I will keep breathing and I will find one of the many bright sides of my life to look at. For example, what the villa in Portugal, courtesy of Marcus, will be like. Ali and Bongle in Portugal, in a villa . . . And, sort of in return, I cover a story that I would have covered anyway had I known anything about it which I wouldn't have done had it not been for Marcus, so that makes it an all-round, bang-on, one hundred per cent stonker of an arrangement. I get excellent inside info and – who knows? – a scoop, at the expense of having to take the family on a free holiday to a villa in Portugal.

Ali in her yellow bikini. Ali going brown. Ali even in her black one-piece swimsuit . . .

That Branston pickle story. It's only just occurred to me. His friend's colleague? There was no friend's colleague. It was just a whatsit. One of those whatdoyoumacallthems.

'Sorry, Richard?' says Shirley and then she taps on the open door.

I turn my head, very, very carefully, in her general direction. 'Yes?'

'Sorry to be a pest, especially when you're feeling a little fradge but we do need to clear a couple of pages.'

Urban legends. 'Ah,' I say. 'Right. Which ones?'

'Seven, ten and eleven, sixteen and nineteen, first off.'

'Right.'

'Then five, thirteen and fourteen by lunch if poss.'

'Right.'

10.28 a.m., Thursday 25 April

EWAN

So I walk her to the station. Being polite. When we reach the market — another day's hard selling of halal meats and competitively priced household cleansers already in full swing — she takes my arm.

We reach the station. She lets go, heads off to the ticket machine. Comes back, smiling.

'Well . . .' she says. 'I'd better . . .' she does a head-flick in the vague direction of the ticket barriers '. . . go,' she says. She leans up to give my cheek a peck. 'Thanks for having me,' she says.

'It was nice knowing you,' I reply. I give her a smile.

She nods her head. 'Bye, then,' she says. She turns, walks towards then through the ticket barriers.

I gaze at her clothed back as she makes her way to the stairs. Her head doesn't move but she does put a hand in the air for a moment. Like a schoolgirl who's not very confident of the answer.

Then she goes down the stairs. And disappears.

I head back to the flatlet.

. . . She didn't even try to give me her number . . . Because I was crap?

. . . Nah.

Then . . . wow. Tick that box. Tick several boxes, come to that. One of them not figurative. Because my sex life really has been that bland and uneventful.

'Hey.'

It's a guy who's sticking his head out the window of a clapped-out Volvo parked outside the house. Guy's fairly clapped out too – hippie, bald, rat-faced, thin. Sixties, in his and casualty of the. And wearing, I see, now that he's clambering out of the car, flip-flops. He locks the car, manually of course. 'You're a new guy from upstairs,' he tells me.

'Hello,' I say, only because it's far less bother this way, and I offer my hand. 'Ewan. Ewan Macintyre.'

'Noel,' he says. 'Noel, yeah?' We shake hands. 'Better known as Grassy. Grassy Noel. Get it?'

I nod.

'Fancy a cup a tea?'

On the one hand, can I be bothered? And I do need a shower. Quite badly. On the other hand, cup of tea from a clapped-out hippie, that'd be another box to tick. 'Aye, okay, then,' I say. 'Why not?'

As host, he guides me in through the front door and up the stairs. We stop a flight short. Three keys later, he opens his door and beckons me into . . .

A small, intermittently furnished rug warehouse. The floor layered with rugs. Rugs in long cylinders propped against the walls and every piece of furniture. Rugs piled on every piece of furniture. Clapped-out Hippie Man goes through to the kitchen – a kitchen! – and I take a seat on what I guess to be, beneath the rugs, a sofa.

'So what,' I call through, 'is it that you do, er, Grassy?'

'Rugs,' comes the fairly muffled reply. 'Rugs, mainly. Want one?'

'No, thanks.'

'You?'

'Nothing much.'

'I hear you, man, I hear you.'

No surprise at that because here he is back from the kitchen. With two not terribly clean-looking mugs. Containing, I now see, weak, milky, grey tea. 'World's Best Dad,' says my mug. I peer across at his. 'I've Been On *The Big Breakfast*,' it says.

I nod at it. 'So have you?'

'Eh?'

'Been on *The Big Breakfast*?'

Grassy narrows his already-tiny eyes as he mulls this over. Then he shakes his head. '. . . Nah,' he says. He sits down cross-legged on some rugs and rug-embroidered cushions and leans back against a stack of rugs. He takes one sip of tea then reaches over to an elaborately decorated box, doubtless from the duty-free at Goa. 'Fancy a smoke?'

I think he means a joint. It's quarter to eleven in the morning. My head's still 80% wool after last night.

'Sgood gear,' he says, passing me the joint which he has already assembled, with a conjuror's flurry of fingers, and lit.

I take the thing. It looks like a handmade tampon. I roll the end to and fro between my fingers, discreetly removing as as many molecules of his spit as I can. I take two tentative puffs, stifle a splutter and pass it back. 'Where do you get it?' I ask eventually, to ask something.

'Smine,' he says. 'Smy own.'

'Right,' I say, things really ticking along now. 'You grow your own?' I look around at the very minimum of greenery you'd expect in a hippie den. Ivy trailing down the side of the small and rickety rug-filled bookcase. Cheese plant looming out of the rugs at the window. Fern on the little table that's wedged between some rolled rugs. Nothing that looks illegal. 'Your bedroom?' I say, not brilliantly, I know but, fair's fair, the back of my head has just disappeared.

'No way, man.' He gives me a knowing smile and nods. He'll give me a wink at this rate, I think. Just before he taps the side of his nose, winks and passes back the joint.

Determined to do it right, I take three puffs, holding the smoke at the back of my throat each time and swallowing it. Textbook.

. . . Jesus Christ, here I go again.

'Tho . . .' I say, before I lick my lips. '. . . You grow your own . . . but not in your flat?'

'Sright.'

'. . . Where?'

'Nah, sorry, man. Wild horses, you know what I'm saying? Yeah, wild horses.'

'. . . Go on.'

'Nah.'

'. . . Tell me.'

'Nah.'

'. . . Where?'

84

'Nah.'

'Unless it's, like, you're the mastermind . . . of a vast criminal operation . . . a Mr Big . . . and the whole project is on such a scale . . . vast aircraft hangars . . .'

'Nah. Small-scale.'

'. . . Right . . . Where?'

He hands me the stub and spreads his hands wide. 'All over, man . . .' He taps his nose again. 'And that's all I'm saying. You know what I'm saying?'

'You want smore tea?'

'. . . What?'

'Tea?'

'Umm . . . yeah.'

'Chuh. Jackie.'

'What?'

'Jackie.'

'Jackie who?'

'Jackie. A ex-wife. Jackie. Her I've been telling you about.'

'Right . . . Jackie . . . What about her?'

'She was the one got me into them.'

'. . . Into what?'

'Rugs.'

'. . . Right . . . No, thanks, I'll pass.'

'. . . You sure?'

'Oh, go on then . . .'

'. . . But I solved that one when I met this guy over in Rotterdam who helped out with a seeds.'

'. . . Right.'

'He'd done a whole genetic-engineering thing. You know, like . . . wheat. Compared to wild wheat. You know what I'm saying?'

'. . . Right.'

'Asically, a problem here is with a climate. Not enough sunlight for not long enough.'

'. . . Right.'

'Sept hemp, at's always been grown here. Hemp ropes, they built a fucking British empire on hemp ropes. An' a medicinal thing going way back. Sept hemp's got, like, almost zero THC. So Jan's trick was to cross good old English hemp with proper gear. Someing like skunk.'

'. . . Right.'

'So it could grow here. Naturally. No UV, you know what I'm saying?'

'. . . Right.'

'So he's got iss hybrid now does pretty well outdoors.'

'. . . Right . . . Where?'

'Nah.'

'. . . Where?'

'Nah.'

'. . . Where?'

'Okay.' Grassy pushes himself upright and goes back to the kitchen, returning a moment later with a small bundle of papers held together by a frayed and greasy strip of tartan ribbon tied with a little bow. 'Iss'll give you an idea.' He hands me the bundle. 'Go on,' he says, with a benevolent air. The wise man showing his raw disciple the way of enlightenment. 'Untie a ribbon.'

I take a good swig of the noisome but strong coffee and

shake my head. Surprisingly, this seems to work. At least to the extent that I can untie the ribbon. I take out a page, any page, and focus on the soiled piece of paper in my hand. A rip at the top. Bottom left, a smudge of old jam. Or possibly blood. In the middle, a scribbled diagram. An intersection of two streets, it looks like, with an X marked beside a tree, crudely drawn, like a car-freshener pine. I give the page a ninety-degree turn to read the scribble on one of the inter-secting streets. 'Thstlwt Rd,' it says.

Grassy leans forward to take a peek. 'Ah,' he says. 'Istle-waite Road. Nice one. Go on. Take another.'

I pull out a second sheet. Even grubbier. A scribbled diagram of an intersection marked beside a box that has 'ELEC' written above it. One street is labelled 'Grn Lns', the other 'Stk Nwngtn Ch St'.

'Oh, yeah,' says Grassy. 'Nice one. Corner of Green Lanes and Stoke Newington Church Street. Take another.'

'I don't know if it's got the same excitement now that you've explained the code. How much time do you save by not writing the vowels?'

'What you're holding,' says Grassy, ignoring the question like he's on *Newsnight*, 'in your hands are fifty-four maps. I suppose you could call them.' Grassy pauses for dramatic effect. 'Treasure maps. With each X marking a very special spot.'

I flick through the pages. 'Right. So you've got crops of marijuana plants growing alfresco all over London and these are the maps for each site.'

Grassy looks crestfallen. '. . . Yeah.'

'Each site being somewhere that's, let see, accessible yet secluded, open to sunlight but hidden from view?'

'. . . Yeah.'

'Maybe protected by thistles or nettles?'

'. . . Some.'

'Corners of disused gardens? Maybe uncruisy bits of wood-land on Hampstead Heath?'

'Not on a Heath, nah. No parks, no heaths. Too busy, open access, you know what I'm saying?'

'So how many plants have you got?'

'Nah, mainly it's a railways. Embankments an' that. Nice little patch near Finsbury Park, bit outside a station, line diverges, you know what I'm saying? Drayton Park, ass another. Right beside a station, little patch of trees and shrubs they've let go wild, five in there. Yeah, nice one. Yeah, like the man seems to have got into wild gardening these days, let nature run free. Yeah, suits me.'

'How many plants in total, then?'

'Old dears' gardens. Back bit of a garden of a hospice up Stamford Hill. Little bit at a side of a A2 turn-off. Back of an old factory place in Homerton. Ucking *round*abouts, man.'

'Roundabouts?'

'Roundabouts. Two roundabouts.'

'Which two roundabouts?'

Grassy gives me another of his winks. 'Sall in a maps.'

'So how many plants in all?'

'Ucking King's Cross was another good one until a JCBs moved in. Embankment down Mildmay Grove, one there. Takes a bit of work, though. Fifty-four sites, keep them all going. Checking them for males. You don't want male plants, see. Pruning. Watering. Yeah, lot a work.'

'So how many plants?'

'Grow a cuttings here, plant them May, Juneish. Three, four munce growing time. Prune a buds. Harvest in September. Hang dry for a couple a weeks. Upside down. Like a good piece of meat. Test it. Like a good cheese. Use a fan leaves for tea. Ninety-three.'

'Fifty-four sites, ninety-three plants? Not exactly efficient, is it?'

Grassy shrugs. 'One or two at a time, they don't get noticed. Small-scale. Cottage industry. You know what I'm saying? Organic.'

'Right . . . Grassy?'

'Yeah?'

'How come you're telling me all this? I could be a cop.'

'Yeah, like you're a cop. I dunno. I truss you. Sides, you're the first person I've spoken to for three days.'

'Really?'

'Yeah. Three days. Since I bumped into Rocky. Mate of mine.'

'Do all your mates have nicknames?'

'Ass just it. You get to my age, you get to find there aren't so many of a mates around.'

'. . . What age would that be?'

'Have a guess.'

'No.'

'Go on. Have a guess.'

'No, seriously, just tell me.'

'Have a guess . . . What you think?'

Well, I could be honest . . . I decide to be smooth. 'Fifty-eight?'

'. . . Fifty-one.'

'Ah . . .' I nod and smile while I marvel anew at Grassy's creased face. The blotchy skin. The scanty, wispy, dirty-grey hair. The tiny bloodshot eyes with bloodhound bags. 'Fifty-one. Right . . . So what happened to all the mates?'

Grassy frowns, looks around like he's mislaid something. His life, for example. He shakes his head. 'Guys leave. For a country. Leave a country. Couple've died . . . Dunno . . . Happens.'

'Well, that's good news . . . Christ, is that the time?'

5

7.35 p.m., Saturday 27 April

RICHARD
No bath tonight so, having cunningly extended a nappy change into a complete clothes removal, I put Bongle down on the bed and proceed to shove, with not much but nonetheless some force that I'd really rather not need to use, his arms and legs into his PJs, the ones with Winnie-the-Pooh and Tigger, not the skiing bears nor, alas, the new white all-in-oner which lasts a maximum of one night before it has to go back in the wash but makes him look like an angel. Despite my goings-over with the wet-wipes, the wisps of his hair are still stiff with vegetabloid motes and there's a farmyardy whiff about his nether quarters. Ah, well, on with the show, which, without bathtime, isn't the usual show at all – something that's really no good to man nor beast and is certainly no good to the Bongle boy, who needs his routines, his props and beacons in this still-strange world where giants loom down at you and plonk you on your back and cram your limbs into a jumpsuit covered with upside-down tigers and bears.

I fumble around his undercarriage to do up his last popper. There are times, and this is one of them, when, staring down at the Bongler, fidgetting about his person and mauling him around the place, that I have these almost-memories, like a hint of a dream that's already floated off, from the time before my earliest official memory (a black-and-white image of me sitting behind Dad in our first car, so dating back to 1965), of lying flat on my back, helpless, looking up at the world, possibly while someone enormous yanked and tugged me into my clothes. Ah. Extra button. Nothing for it but to undo the whole shooting match and start all over again. Despairing at this incompetence, Bongle yelps and squirms. I hold him, gently, very gently, down with my right hand and strain with the left to get the upper-thigh popper popped, and Bongle gives in to the misery of this, his face collapsing into one of his envelope-mouthed bawls. Leaving his sleepsuit not comprehensively popped, I zip up his boy-in-a-bag sleeping bag, pick him up and hold him with his mouth howling into my chest. 'Oh oh. Oh no. Oh dear,' I whisper as I give him the gentlest of jiggles. 'Oh dear oh dear. Oh you poor little fellow . . . Oh no. No no . . . Hush hush . . . hush shush shush . . . there now . . . Shush shush . . . oh my darling . . . my darling boy . . . my darling little one . . . hush now . . . there now . . . yes yes . . . hush hush . . . yes . . . hush hush.'

All this upset just to get him tucked up in bed and, with a little help from two spoonfuls of Calpol, asleep before Joanne gets here because the less Joanne has to do the happier everyone is. Joanne. It seems completely and utterly preposterous, absolutely, entirely ludicrous that for the next five hours we will be placing our little baby in the care of an eighteen-year-old, whom I wouldn't dream of letting drive my car. Or even wash it. So how on earth can we conceivably hand over this most precious of bundles-in-a-bag to the care of someone who probably thinks the number for emergencies is 911, assumes that bleach is full of vitamins and knows that it's a sign of rude good health when a baby's face goes purple?

But that's just what we do only a few minutes later, or, more accurately, just what Ali does, it being her job as boss of the household to oversee the staff and it being my task to make sure the aged and poorly rustbucket hasn't expired in the twenty-five, twenty-six hours since it last coughed and wheezed itself into action, thereby escaping the scene of the crime.

I don't mind, to be honest. Well, I do mind about the aged and poorly, naturally, because who wouldn't mind having to drive a J-reg rustbucket rather than a decent car with a newfangled number plate and some of the more recent additions to the usual family-car repertoire – CD player, air-conditioning, doors that open without sounding like an industrial accident. What I don't mind is my assigned role of designated driver. Although, yes, I suppose a drink's always handy at Peter's parties, for a bit of the old Dutch courage and as a useful prop during those occasional moments when I'm not holding an audience rapt with delight at my sparkling wit and merry repartee, but sober or squiffy, it makes no difference to the invariably main feature of Peter's parties, viz., that they are occasions to be endured rather than enjoyed.

On the bright side, I've managed to start the engine at only the second attempt so it's with an air of relief that I nurse the old girl with some gentle pedalwork and sage application of what I think might be another period piece, the choke, when there's the sudden racket of machinery going awry as the passenger door opens, followed by the sight of Ali lowering herself into the passenger seat, with some difficulty, what with the tightness of her black dress that shows off the curvaceousness of her figure, which, let me just add, has not only recovered from the pregnancy and the birth and so on and so forth but has recently seemed to ripen into a new and almost scarily sexy womanliness. Her dress rides up a little as she wriggles on to the seat – oh, most fortunate upholstery – but I can't quite see if that's a tell-tale darkening of the hosiery or merely the shadow of . . .

'Right, then,' she says, which I take as my cue to commence driving. 'And let's remember. This is a party we're going to. Okay?'

'Got you,' I say, making do with a nod instead of the full salute. 'Party.'

'For once, let's try and enjoy it, shall we?'

'Absolutely,' I reply, still wondering if that we was a straightforward we or the kind of we doctors use to soften the blow when they really mean you. How are we feeling today? How's our tumour coming along?

I crunch down the gears as we come up to, fingers crossed, a terrible tailback, staring ahead, giving myself instructions – self to buck up and be jolly, mingle and not show up or be in any shape, way or form a burden on the host's sister. Whereas, truth be told, in grim reality I'm just hoping that it will be over soon, also praying that nobody will whisk Ali away so that I can tag along with her for ninety-nine or indeed a hundred per cent of the time. I smile. 'So has Peter told you yet what the occasion is?'

'Why does there have to be an occasion? Why can't he just throw a party because he feels like it?'

'Yes,' I say and is all I should say, but the tailback's disappeared, I'm sorry to say, and I'm too busy nicking into the inside lane and trying to remember the best route to take after the tunnel – a shame that Ali gets seasick walking past a puddle, because it would have been quite fun to have gone as per the invite – to stop there. 'But Peter's parties are usually for something, aren't they? His birthdays, your birthdays sometimes,' and, wittering now as I realise I'm making a bit of a bish here, 'a promotion or before he goes off somewhere or . . .'

'No, they're not,' says Ali, ready to put her dukes up.

'. . . Great parties, though,' I say with a lamentably poor impersonation of enthusiasm, further boosting the score on the bishometer with the 'though', thus implying that I haven't conceded the point, which of course I haven't but which of course Ali should think I have. Conceded.

Much to her credit, Ali restrains her reply to an almost conciliatory humph, one of those Ali noises which carry such complexity of meaning that mere Earthling letters can't cope. 'Ffmfnf,' she says, or however one could transcribe this puff of air through the nose with a subtle bass accompaniment from a throaty snortette.

'. . . Traffic looks pretty good,' I say.

'Touch wood,' she says, and she gives me two light taps on the head, showing that the incident is over, the moment has passed, and everything's okay again. So it's in a companionable silence that we head east to the motorway, where, with a bit of luck, we'll spend an hour queueing for the Blackwall Tunnel.

. . . Alas, no, and all too soon we've arrived at Peter's,

where there's an exactly rustbucket-sized space between two immaculate silver vehicles evidently designed for use on the Moon.

So there now follow several minutes' hard labour of getting the rustbucket into its vacuum packaging. If a genie appeared now and granted me one wish, I'd ask for power steering. Ali went tight-lipped early on, during the sixth or seventh reverse, and now there's the clear and present danger of her going into contemptuocity, if of a quiet, serene, reflective kind.

Eventually, I pull up the handbrake and turn off the ignition.

'I'll walk to the kerb from here,' says Ali, sweetly. And rather petulantly, I'm afraid, as, I'm afraid, always, I wonder if she knows that she says that every time. Then she's gone, and although I'm off the mark pretty smartish, I manage to catch up with her only at the door.

'My favourite sister,' Peter announces with a smile. 'And Dick. How are you?' He shakes my hand, and it's all as if he were introducing himself. 'Come in, come in, things are just getting under way.'

Which can't be true because not for Peter the merest twinge of hostitis – not for him the anxiety of waiting for an empty room to fill up, of failing to prevent himself beginning to wonder if a nearly empty room will stay nearly empty all evening, because, as always, this evening bash was preceded by an informal teatime bash when half a dozen select chums gathered to help Peter prepare for his party, along with, it should go without saying, the crack squad of Oriental white-jacketed caterers, so that by the time Ali and I walk into the one big open-plan room which takes up the entire first floor, not counting the hall we've just come from, a full half-hour before the advertised kick-off, it is to find the joint if not already jumping, then, at the very least, bouncing.

After a small, brown waitress in a trendily collarless white jacket has proffered a tray of drinks, from which Ali has taken a glass of champage and I have taken a glass of orange juice, I do a quick, furtive surveillance, enough to appreciate that the gathering has, as per first impression, already evolved into a proper party, the kind you might see in, for example . . . well, some drama on the telly that involves people standing around in the background at a glamorous party. I sip the orange juice to cure the dryness in the mouth inevitably caused by the trepidatious nervousness caused by Peter's crowd. You would think that one of the few advantages of having a brother-in-law who worked in the City would be the dullness of his life and his friends. This is not the case, though, with Peter, who has fashioned a job for himself apparently designed to be the exact opposite of his father's – the late Mr Standman having worked long and hard in a blacking factory for an implausibly tiny wage, whereas Peter's fantastically remunerative work-load consists solely, so far as I can gather, of flying first class to five-star hotels in parts far-flung. As for his social life, that, rather gallingly, I have to admit, features a rich and varied range of achievers – some financeular types, yes, but of a noticeably bohemianish hue, and outnumbered by advertising types, high-flying media types, and so on and so forth, so there's not one pinstripe to be seen. Which is fine, of course, but still, just a bit . . . intimidating is probably too harsh a word, I decide as Chris, who's one of the select chums, a friend of Peter's from way back – well, as way back as Peter's friends go – comes up to us and makes something of a performance out of kissing Ali on each cheek.

'Hello, lovely,' he murmurs to her while smiling at me to show that this is all innocent and just good fun. 'Looking scrumptious, I must say.'

Ali laughs, her short, high, tinkly laugh and tells him to stop it.

'And how's Richard?' says Chris.

'Very well, Chris. How are you?'

'Yeah. Come on then, lovely, you must know. What's the occasion? What's the big surprise?'

Ali looks at him with coquettish pretend-wariness. 'If I knew, it wouldn't be a surprise, would it?' The next thing Chris says I don't quite hear, because he's turned to talk only to Ali now for some sort of a confab, leaving me suddenly feeling a bit of a pill on my own. I put on a relaxed face and stand there holding my bittily thick orange juice.

Time passes . . .

Still here, sipping orange juice . . .

Just standing here, sipping away . . .

Then I catch, by accident rather than anything else, the eye of a neighbouring youngish chap wearing a diarrhoea-brown T-shirt that has a sort of roughly etched Union Jack on it and having about him the drifty air of one who might be un-partnered and might not know many people here.

'Hi,' he says, not quite sheepishly.

'Hello,' I say, with a mad smile. 'Nice party.'

'Yeah,' he says.

'. . . Have you . . . come far?'

'Er, no. No, not really. Just down the road.'

'Really? Whereabouts?'

'Bermondsey.'

'Ah. Bermondsey . . . Flat?'

'Sorry?'

'Is it a flat you live in in Bermondsey?'

'No. More of a warehouse apartment. Kind of a live-work space.'

'Great.' I nod enthusiastically, which takes up five more of the seconds that will have to have passed before Ali returns. 'We're north London,' I say. 'Stamford Hill. Well, Tottenham. South Tottenham. A bit further out than we used to be in Stoke Newington, but we wanted more space and a garden and the schools aren't too bad or rather they could be a lot worse, and the . . .' The young man is looking around him. I take a last quick swig of orange juice. Time to win back the audience. 'So,' I say, quite loudly. 'So . . . What is it you do?'

'Me?' The young man looks rather startled by this turn of events whereby someone makes conversation with someone else by asking them a question about their job. 'Consultant. Mainly R-and-D.'

'Ah, R-and-D.'

'Yeah, R-and-D. Mainly.'

'And what does that involve usually?'

'What you'd expect. Basically getting the synergy right for brand development.'

'I see.'

'Trend-spotting. Cool-hunting. You know.'

'Right.' This is far too like one of those conversations I have with cabbies – not the conversations where I can't think of anything to say about Arsenal but the ones where I just can't decipher the words because we're in a car and in traffic and because – a fact often overlooked by garrulous cabbies – there's an almost-closed glass panel between his words and my ears, and I end up making what I hope are appropriate 'ahs' and 'I knows' and 'mmms', perhaps agreeing – who knows? – to the reintroduction of slavery.

'Basically surfing the *Zeitgeist*, hoping to catch a wave.'

I force a laugh. 'I'm not sure there's much of a wave left by the time it reaches Tottenham.' Which was, I reflect, rather smooth of me.

The young man, however, looks perplexed. 'Tottenham?' he says, with the air of someone who can have no idea why I've mentioned the place, before that is abruptly replaced by a sort of a concessionary inclining of the head. 'Well, you say that but give it a few years and you're looking at Tottenham being majorly cool.'

'No. Tottenham? Really?'

'For sure. First you get the inevitable slump when the burbs are caught between the pastoral idyll and inner-city buzz, and that whole Metroland ribbon becomes ghettoised.'

'You mean . . .'

'Inevitable. You see it happening now. You have two paradigms, yes?'

I do some steadfast nodding in the manner of someone who really is in charge of the brief here.

'The cottage and the apartment. What you don't have is even a post-ironic embrace of the whole Terry-and-June thing. Which shows how you're either going to get a centrifugal energy, flowing down the line to rural-based contractees, or a centripetal imperative, spiralling in towards the vibrant urban centre. Which'll leave a chasm where currently you find wannabe embourgeoisification at its peak. Give it ten, twenty years and that whole swathe of city suburbia, all that entre-deux-guerres middle-scale owner-occupation, your Crouch Ends, your Hampstead Garden Suburbs, those'll be abandoned ghettoes. Give it thirty, forty years and the cycle will have moved on, and those'll be the happening areas, like Hoxton or Bermondsey now.'

'I see,' I say, thinking it wisest to stick with the serious nodding as well to buy time for the next thing that I'm going to say, which turns out not to exist. '. . . I see.'

The young man looks around him. 'Any idea where the bogs are?'

'Oh, right, well, ah, yes, they're through there. Oh, or up the stairs.'

'Cool. Er, you want to join me?'

'Ah, no. No, thank you.'

'Sure? It's quality chop.' He raises his eyebrows expectantly.

I raise my eyebrows too and opt for a vague smile-and-headshake combo.

He gives me a wary look. 'Cool. So, I'll catch you later, William. Must dash.'

William? William? Where did he get that from?

And that was drugs he was inviting me to do with him in the loo. Drugs. Here, in Peter's house.

William?

I stand there, on my own again and even, I very much fear, more scandalously in what is an increasingly crowded and jovial bash. I do some scanning of the room for Ali and try to look happy and comfortable and not at all bothered about standing on my own at a party in a conspicuously Johnny-no-matesian way.

That Union Jack pattern on his jersey, the trendy way it has been turned into no more than a collection of fussily intersecting stripes, if that is indeed the idea, strikes me as very much a young person's thing, whereas I, apparently unlike him, am old enough to remember a time when the Union Jack wasn't just used by football hooligans and Nazis and when people could, as I did, as a child feel genuinely sorry for all the people in the world who couldn't be English. How did that happen . . .?

Quarter past nine, so Bongle really should be asleep by now, unless Joanne has completely scuppered the bedtime routine. And only, say, three hours to go.

Oh, well. Time for a top-up of the old vitamin C.

I mean, it would have been bad enough taking such an appalling gamble when Bongle wasn't mobile or mobile to the extent that he could topple, when the only fears were that he'd choke on his mush or forget to breathe during his sleep. But now that he's getting curious and can do something about it (to the extent that he can crawl, stand up, though wobblily, and poke his fingers into things) there are so very many new images to choose from – Bongle eagerly making his way to a somehow-unstairgated stair, hurtling down, landing on his head, cracking his skull like an egg, or tugging at the cable of, say, the TV and the TV crashing down onto his head, his skull cracking like an egg, or Bongle crawling to a socket we've forgotten about and haven't covered with one of those little white plastic guards, being intrigued by the three neat holes, seeing if his fingers can fit in there, getting excited because it seems that they might, all three fingers, pushing the fingers in as far as they can go, and next thing, BLAM, he's been hurled through the air or, probably much worse, he's stuck there, juddering, his normally wispy hair spiking out like a cartoon cat's, the fatally unguarded socket shaking the life out of him, and it can only get, as far as I can see, worse, because then there will be roads to be crossed and bikes to be ridden and pools to be swum in and gaps to be jumped and walls to be climbed and . . .

'Oh, Richard,' sighs Ali, who's whatdoyoumacallited herself to my side. 'Come *on*. Don't be such a lummox. It's a party.'

She looks around confidently, and, impressively soon, has somehow kicked off a conversation with a man whose name I haven't forgotten but only because I didn't quite hear what it was when he said it. Teleported. He's twiddling his swizzle stick around an opaque cocktail which also contains a thin spiral of lemon peel. I wonder who cut that lemon peel, if Peter could possibly have done it, spending hours in his stainless-steel kitchen, fashioning delicate twists with some small sharp knife, or perhaps if there might be an implement now for fashioning thin spirals of lemon peel, a chunky item, it would doubtless be, in pewterian metal, with levered handles like bolt-cutters, available from trendy shops for a hilarious sum. Too easy for Bongle to get his hands trapped in, with those levered handles, and there would have to be a sharp surface as well, so all he'd have to do would be to pick it up, turn it around for a look-see, and run a tiny, fat, seemingly boneless finger up the sharp edge . . . All of a piece with Peter's kitchen, though, with its Bongle-high, sharp-edged surfaces, its . . .

'Oh, but that's marvellous,' I hear Ali saying, and thank goodness she's here and not being dragged off somewhere that isn't by my side, or, slightly more accurately, slightly in front of me. I remind myself to smile and look interested and tune back in.

'. . . just finished a new series,' the man in front of me is saying. 'Should be out in the autumn.'

'Well, that's great news for us, isn't it, Richard?'

'Absolutely,' I reply. 'Great news.'

'Yeah, well, it's only TV. Pretty good TV, I like to think but . . .'

'Oh, definitely,' says Ali. 'We watch it every week. It's *so* good.'

The man does a little head-nod to the side, acknowledging the general truth of this point while reserving the right to retain a few minor quibbles. 'Hey,' says the man, perking up. 'Do you know where the loos are?'

'Up the stairs, first right is the best one,' says Ali.

'Well, if you'll excuse me . . .'

'Lovely to meet you,' Ali says, beaming. 'Well,' she says, to me now, no longer beaming, but rather as if she's just returned from a long winter walk. 'Better pay attention to the credits in the future.'

'Mm. Absolutely.' I take a sip of my allotted glass of champagne. My mouth fills with soft, smooth foam. All the things that Bongle doesn't know about yet. The wondrousness of expensive champagne, e.g. The sky. The stars. Running. Chocolate. Make-believe with toys. Setting soldiers up to defend a fort, or a cowboy stockade with a covered wagon inside, the soldiers lined up on the ramparts and a regiment of sentries waiting behind the stockade's shut double doors . . .

'Please, Richard,' says Ali with a heartrending, imploring look. '*Please* can you make an effort? . . . After all, how often do we get out? Hardly ever. And how often do we get out to a party like this? Where there are really interesting people?'

'Wow. You're looking fan*ta*stic.'

It's a man called, I think, Brian. Or maybe Barry. Barry? Brian. Brian, yes, Brian. Who's smooched up to Ali, squeezed her round the waist, planted a comedy kiss on her cheek, and now noticed me.

'Hi there,' he says, showing the kind of big white teeth that go with that sort of coiffure.

And before I know it, far less before I've had time to reply, this Brian or Barry has led Ali off and away to meet some chap called Charles, and I find myself standing next to a chap who's wearing a blue, zipped cardigan. I didn't know they were in again, although they must be for someone like him – tousled, stubbled, spiky-haired, only five years at the very most younger than me – to be wearing one.

'So what do you do?' he asks, having introduced himself, thereby having me introduce myself.

'I edit,' I say, fully aware that this doesn't sound like a real job. 'I'm an editor . . . Of a magazine.'

'Really?' He looks at me expectantly.

'No, a trade magazine.'

'Ahah.'

'. . . It's for the domestic construction industry.'

'Right.'

There's a pause while he rummages in his jacket pockets, pulls out a cigarette and lights it. 'What's it called?' he asks eventually.

'*Bricks and Brickmen.*'

'. . . Right . . . Now, you wouldn't know where Peter keeps his ashtrays, would you?'

'Um, maybe over on the table?'

'Good idea. Would you excuse me?'

He slopes off in a somehow trendy way, leaving me clutching my drink and praying that Ali won't look over to spot me not mingling, but there are enough people here by now to offer pretty good cover if I keep my head down. Only too easy to imagine what she'd be saying if she were standing here now and not, thank the good Lord, ensconced with that group of men in the corner. 'For God's sakes,' she'd say. 'Richard. Don't be such a lummox.' A jokey nudge in the kidneys. She's right, though, I mean, what's so difficult about it? It's not like I'm having to climb Everest or fight Mike Tyson.

I glance around me and try to see if there's anyone here I could conceivably latch on to. The few people I know – Peter, Ali, that Chris, Peter's chum Whatshisname . . . Malcolm? Michael? Malcolm, I think – are all busy being popular. There's one chap, though, in the kitchen area, who seems less scary than the other blokes, probably because he's bald with a gingery sheen to his head, and he's grappling with one of Peter's enormous and complicated corkscrews in a contest which the enormous and complicated corkscrew seems to be winning. And he's not surrounded by laughing and bantering people. Perhaps he's even here on his own. I count to seven, then force myself to move towards him. What'll I say? I have no idea . . .

'Having a spot of bother?' I ask.

'Sorry?'

'Having a spot of bother? With the corkscrew.'

'Oh. Yes. Ha. Yes.' He gives a small cough into his fist.

'Well,' I say, suppressing a rush of panic. 'That's Peter for you.'

'Who? Oh, Peter. Yes.'

'Him and his hi-tech equipment. You should see his vacuum cleaner, it's so hi-tech it's got a life of its own, whizzing around the place like it should have eyes, like the Noo Noo.'

' . . .'

'The vacuum cleaner on the Teletubbies.'

He smiles apologetically.

Ah. So this chap doesn't have children. That scuppers my next line, which is a real blow because I'm always amazed at how eagerly chaps as well as chapesses open up in conversations about kids. And, new as I am to the parentular experience, I'm already not quite sure how to talk to people who don't know what the red Teletubby's called or where Spot is. (Po, and, in the basket, for the record.) I'll have to go for the so-what-is-it-that-you-do? option. 'So,' I say. 'What is it that you do?'

'Ah, I'm a, well, a journalist.'

'Really? Me too. Who do you work for?'

'The *Sunday Chronicle*.'

'Ah. The *Chronicle*. Gosh. Impressive.'

'Well, I don't think . . .'

'No, really. Impressive. I mean, you know, the thing I edit is only a trade magazine.'

'Ah.'

'. . . For the domestic construction industry. *Bricks and Brickmen.*'

'Ah. That's very . . . interesting.'

'So which bit do you work for at the *Chronicle*?' I ask.

As he says, 'Well, I've got this wine to deliver so . . .'

Then he smiles and moves off.

Twenty past. Say two and a half hours to go.

7.35 p.m., Saturday 27 April

EWAN

'Got yourself a telly, then.' Russell nods at the screen.
'Wossis?'
　'Football.'
　'Ah, I *see*. That's not Arsenal, is it?'
　'Correct.'
　'Sorry?'
　'It's not Arsenal.'
　'Okay, so who is it, then?'
　'Rotherham.'
　'*Rotherham?*'
　'Rotherham.'
　'Rotherham . . . And Rotherham are playing?'
　'Walsall . . . Highlights. I got cable.'
　'Walsall versus Rotherham. Walsall, Rotherham.' Russell
nods sagely.
　We both gaze at the screen. A midfield scrap. The ball
squirts out to a wardrobe-sized defender. Who hoofs the ball
up and up and over a small grandstand.

I pass Russell the joint. He holds it twattily, between his fourth finger and his pinkie, his hand cupping round his mouth. Then he takes several long, noisy sucks. 'Where the hell am I going to sit?'

'Try the floor. Good for the posture.'

'Well, thanks. I come here,' he says switching to his hoarse Godfather. 'And you show me. No chair.'

'Fortuitous. God, that pisses me off.'

'Hi no unnerstan.'

'The commentary. Fortuitous. A fortuitous corner, he said. When he means fortunate. Except fortuitous sounds fancier. Never minds that fortuitous means by chance, nothing to do with good luck or bad. Just by chance. But they all do it now, football commentators. Like a couple of years back when they all started to say intervention when they meant a tackle.'

'Ewan, my sweet, sweet, sweet young friend, you really need to get out more. When were you last outside this luxurious new penthouse apartment of yours? Not counting getting the milk.'

I shrug. Not the Mafia shrug. Just a shrug. That, after all, has been the idea. Not to rush about like a blue-arsed fly. Not to start the day jolting awake to the alarm. Not to spend the day shoving a mouse around a mat. Not to be a slave to the phone and the Inbox. Not to waste any more of my time on swine and fools. It's taking a bit of getting used to. But I'm getting the hang of it. Practice will make perfect. And the joints certainly help. This latest joint in particular, I think before my thoughts wander to consider the fact that I have been out. Not far and not often and not for a couple of days, but I have been out. Enough to appreciate that the market is one mental place. Particularly mental on Fridays when the Muslims are out in full force and regalia. The women in their Darth Vader kit. Eighteen-stone temptresses, so seductive they can bare only their eyes to the world. And every day of the week, the enormous West African preachers with their gold trappings and ultra-smart retinues. The two lots seem to remain invisible to each other. Just as well, all things considered. There being nothing like religion to turn a man into a maniac. But even without the prospect of the whole market, pop. several thousand, erupting into a brawling, knifing, shooting bloodbath, there's just the basic, inescapable fact of all that unshakeable faith to cope with. Religion filling the air. Like a smell. A sickly-sweet smell, it would be. The kind you can feel in the back of your throat. . . . I'd like to set up my own stall. Russell standing behind me as my retinue. Handing out subscriptions to *Nature*. Full military back-up. 'YOU'RE ALL WRONG,' I'd say, easily booming the message out over their tinny racket with my state-of-the-art mega-megaphone: 'YOU'RE ALL SO WRONG YOU MIGHT AS WELL BE MAD. WE ARE ACCIDENTS OF EVOLUTION IN A GODLESS, MEANINGLESS UNIVERSE. GOT THAT? SUPER. THANK YOU AND GOODBYE. PLEASE STAND WELL CLEAR DURING THIS AIRLIFT OPERA-TION.'

'I *have* been out,' I tell Russell.

'Don't get sulky with me, young man.'

'I'm not getting sulky, I'm just saying. I have been out. I've met people. I've talked to them.'

'Really? Who?'

'You really want to know?'

'I really want to know. Because I don't think there's going to be too long a list.'

'Asif,' I say.

'Who's Asif?'

'Guy with a stall in the market. Sells vegetables at pre-decimal prices.'

'Asif doesn't count.'

'The woman at the newsagent's. Don't know her name but she has to do everything one-handed because she's always on the mobile.'

'Doesn't count. Especially if she's always on the mobile.'

'Oh. Yes. The hippie downstairs. Grassy.' Of course. I knew there was something. Grassy downstairs. In fact, I've spent parts of a few evenings with Grassy downstairs. And through Grassy downstairs I have acquired (a) this big bag of marijuana (£80 for the ounce, which I think even Asif would think reasonable) and (b) working knowledge of the others in the house. Although I've yet to meet Mrs Longname on the ground floor. Or the middle-aged woman I've seen fleetingly, scuttling in and out of the basement with a battered briefcase and a suit that's obviously an old favourite. Clearly living a life of excitement and adventure behind a DSS counter.

'The hippie downstairs. See? Your list amounted to one. So?'

'So what?'

'So what *have* you been up to? I haven't seen you for going on a fortnight.'

'I've been surveying my options,' I say.

'Surveying your options. You don't *have* any options. Here. I'll finish that off, if you don't mind . . . Right. We're going out.'

'Where?'

'Anywhere. Just to get you out of your box.'

At which point I can no longer resist the temptation to play a trump card. 'Well, just to show that you are, as always, completely wrong, I have been invited to a party tonight.' Because I have indeed.

Russell's eyes gleam. 'Excellent,' he whispers in the Monty Burns. 'What party? Where party? Who party?'

'Down in Shoreditch. The Zed Bar. Hosted by my ex-co-workers.' A work wake, in fact, hosted by Caro, Sam, Damien, Emma, the lot, to commemorate the passing of their jobs at DMX. Which is one good reason we won't be going.

'Ahah,' says Russell. 'Your old stomping ground. I'm thinking brown colour scheme. I'm thinking suede upholstery. I'm thinking website consultant. I'm thinking young website consultant with a cut-off top showing off her flat young tummy.' Russell gazes up at the ceiling. 'Right,' he says, having snapped out of whatever pornographic nonsense he's been projecting up there. 'Come on.' Russell stands up, then grabs my forearm and hauls me up from my beanbag. 'Get your coat,' he says. 'You and I, my fine young friend, are going out on the pull.'

Pistons clanking, bells ringing, wheels whirring, Russell's Positivity Machine is up and running. Just for a moment, I consider going. Only because the prospect of seeing Russell try to chat up fat Yvette's Sue does have a certain appeal. 'And is there a *Mister* Fordham?' I imagine him saying suavely, doing his Roger Moore raised eyebrow. 'Come, come, let's neither of us be . . . naive.'

But no. 'No,' I say.

'Eh?'

'No,' I say. 'I'm not going.'

'Are you in*sane*? This is exactly what you should be doing. Going out. Getting out. Getting off with young ladies.'

'No.'

'No? No? Is that all you're going to say? No?'

'Yes.'

'Right. Well, I completely understand, because, a party, there's every chance you might enjoy yourself and even you might get talking to a nice young girl with a jewel in her tummy button who would take you home and then you be a-rockin' and a-rollin' all night long. Yes, absolutely, spot-on, great decision, much better to watch Rochdale versus Hartlepool. No, really, that's super, excellent choice.'

'Sit yourself down, Russ, and I'll make another joint. Get stoned, watch the rest of the football.'

'Okay, okay, so not Shoreditch, then. But somewhere. Come on, Saturday night, and I'm in the mood for lurve. Look. What about . . .' Russell rummages around in his jacket. 'This.' He waves the large piece of elaborately italicised card he's evidently been rummaging for. 'Let's not forget,' he says in his crap Leslie Phillips, 'that I can always be welied on to have a lahge stiffie.'

'You've been keeping this one on the bench? Oh, boy, even you must think it's a stinker if this is the first of you mentioning it.'

'Fackin ell,' says Russ, peering at the invitation. 'I addint realawahwahwahised.'

'What?'

'It's ownly a fackin bout trip.'

'What?'

'Onna fackin rivah. Right,' says Russ, normally at last. 'We can just make the final one, if we get a move on. You know, this could be a bit of a giggle.'

'Well, you go off and giggle on your own. I'm staying here and skinning up. Come on, you Rotherham.'

'. . . There's a line in it for you.'

'. . . Seriously? You've brought some?'

'Seriously. Right now. If you come out.'

Ten minutes later and this is the pair of us striding through the hosed-down remains of the market. Russell confident he'll soon be hailing a cab. Right. As though in Dalston black cabs aren't as frequent as unicorns. So it's either going to be five hours by bus or friendly neighbourhood Maniac Mini-Cabs near the everything-a-pound shop.

Miraculously, there is a black cab trundling down towards us. Might as well have been a Maniac Honda though, with the cabbie's almost visible BO.

We take the chance of a snarl-up near Covent Garden to get out a couple of streets early and breathe some oxygen. It's only now as we trudge towards the Embankment that I wonder if the line of cocaine – and the promise of more – really might not be worth this.

We cut down by the Savoy, go through some remarkably tramp-free gardens, and sprint over the racetrack at the Embankment. Arriving at a roped-off bit that seems to lead down to a jetty. A boy in sailor's costume salutes us.

'Good evening, gentlemen,' says Sailorboy. 'May I see your

invitations? Thank you, sir.' Sailorboy beckons us, with a flourish, over the unhooked rope.

We follow the jetty down until we reach a gangplank. Waiting here is another youth in a surely bogus uniform.

'Climb aboard, gentlemen,' he says. 'You're just in time. Just the two of you, is it? The step just here, sir. That's it. And you, sir. Just a jiffy and we'll be off.'

I find myself sitting in a boat. Sitting on a well-upholstered banquette and being given a glass of Pimm's by a young girl in a starched white jacket. But a boat, nonetheless. A disarmingly small boat. The river reachable by hand. Bogus Officer Youth jumps in and climbs the few stairs to the driver's bit above us.

Russell gives my glass of Pimm's a hearty biff with his. 'Cheers,' he says, with a broad grin as the boat edges away from the jetty.

'Where the hell are we going?'

Russell smiles by way of a reply. The Man of Mystery. He leans back, his legs splayed, his arms resting on the boat's lurching sides. 'Last time I did this was before the *Marchioness*.'

'Oh, well done for mentioning the *Marchioness*.'

'*De rien*,' says Russ, throwing up an arm with Gallic flair. We move off towards the South Bank then veer left, picking up impressive speed. We zoom under Waterloo Bridge. The wind picks up. I'm suddenly aware of what I'm wearing – of course, my own new uniform: thin white T-shirt, thin grey jersey, thin breeks. I look over at Russell's long black overcoat.

'Look!' shouts its owner, all cool lost. 'The Gherkin! The New GLC! The Tower! Hey! Tower Bridge!'

'Russell!' I shout back.

'What!'

'Shut up!'

'No! Hey! Take a look at all of this! Look at it! Fackin ell!'

We're hurtling downriver. Me hunched, clutching my Pimm's in a cold fist. Russell gazing around at the waterside warehousing that has done so much to alleviate the suffering of oppressed developers and estate agents. Well, I should be grateful. If it hadn't been for all those City schmucks wanting to live in lofts, I wouldn't have made such a hilarious profit from the Shoreditch pad. Luck? I don't think so. You make your own luck in this life. I knew what I was doing. I knew what would happen. And it happened. Suddenly, everybody wanted to be the guy in the Halifax ad. Lofts were in.

Russell's still gazing around at the riverside real estate. Shaking his head in wonder. Too overwhelmed to speak, thank God. We zoom on, past what seems like mile after mile of scrubbed brickwork and blue balconies. The boat slapping the choppier water. Russell still looking around him like a child at his first theme park. We career past Rotherhithe, round the ninety-degree bend south. Canary Wharf looming to the left while we bounce along to somewhere just shy of Greenwich. Where the boat slows and draws in to a jetty.

We clamber out and get another salute from Bogus Officer Boy.

'Up to the left there, sirs, and first right. You'll find a map on the reverse of your invitation.'

So now will come the trudge to what is bound to be a banker's lofty-styley apartment. Commanding a view of the back of the neighbouring block of lofty-styley apartments.

'That was just *amazing*,' says Russell, shaking his head in wonder as we walk up the jetty. 'Amazing. Amazing. I had no idea about how all that waterside devel—'

'Correct me if I'm wrong,' I say, with some urgency because I've just realised an awful truth. 'But this *is* the south side of the river, isn't it?'

'Aw, aye, but . . .'

'South of the river. Russ. You know the rules.'

'You and your rules. Anyway, I thought you were supposed to be breaking all your rules?'

'Only bad things happen south of the river.'

Russell shakes his head, not in wonder. 'Anyway, this isn't south, this is . . .'

'SOR, Russell.'

'No. It's Docklands.'

'Docklands? *Dock*lands? Brookside.'

An unerringly accurate punchline, which wins me this one, because we're not walking along the Disney-Dickens lane between two polished warehouses that I'd been expecting. No. What we're walking along is a raw new street with a fenced patch of scrub on one side and on the other a block of new-builds. Which existed only as drawings until, what, two years ago. But now here they are, in Millennium Waterfront Close or whatever the hell this place is called. Pointless tiny balconies on the first floor, above the garages occupying the entire ground floor. Looking a lot less inviting than they did in the drawings.

The map tells us to turn right and find number eight. And here's the door, beyond the brick lawn, tucked away at the side of the garage, with an 8 on it. Russ gives the bell a short blast. Perhaps half a second later, the door is opened. By, it soon turns out, a surprisingly imposing woman – tall, pretty fit, mid-thirties maybe, probably good-looking underneath the make-up that she's wearing like she's selling it. A silvery dress, low-cut to reveal a freckled bum of cleavage. Long, thick, chestnut-brown hair that must cost her a hundred quid every second Thursday. Looking on the bright side, she's not a Sloane, so she should spare us any grabbing and hoiking of the hair from one side to another.

'Well, hi,' she says. 'Gatecrashers. Yummy. Come on in.'

'Why, thank you,' says Russell with what he thinks is his winning smile. He goes side-on and begins shuffling past her. Very slowly. Their shoes are almost touching. His chest approaches hers. 'My, my,' Russ murmurs. 'Quite a tight fit.'

'Yes, I noticed that,' she murmurs back, apparently fixated by his mouth. 'The tightness of the fit.'

I stand there in the doorway with saintly calm and a sinking feeling. What sort of a party is this going to be, where it starts off with (1) a boat and (2) this pair of eejits trying to be suavely dirty? The slight dread, growing less slight by the moment, is that I'm about to walk into a room full of horny middle-aged saddos throwing their car keys into a pile.

Russ leans forward to whisper something in Orange Door-lady's ear and slides a little white card into her hand. Finally, he manages to squeeze past her. I follow. Finding lots of space.

We walk up some stairs into a room that seems to take up all of this first floor. Minimalist, school of Ikea. The new-build as loft-lite. A stainless-steel kitchen area at the back. Just like the Dalston flatette, only bigger, more expensive and worse. Nigh-on empty of furniture but full of people. Lawyers and lawyers' wives, by the looks. Most of the men are in regulation kit – dark suits, white shirts. A few of the shirts with ruffled cuffs. Couple of Hoxton rebels in student garb. The women . . . well, the women are mostly glossy. Mid-thirties, most of them. Some younger. Including a couple of luscious corn-fed princesses in wafty blouses and this year's distressed denim, bejewelled belts slung low over their toned hips. All of them posing like extras in a gin advert.

A wave of tedium washes over me. I should have stuck by my new no-parties rule. How many parties just like this have I walked into over the years? Except there would have been shoulder pads and wide lapels in the Eighties. The men would have had more and higher hair ten years ago. And the non-existent decor is a recent addition. But, oh God, the inevitability of it all.

I turn to Russell to ask him for the wrap, but he's busy handing over his overcoat to a small Filipina and removing invisible specks from his immaculate dark suit. I check my own clothes again. These breeks, they're just about good enough for doing the garden. In fact, I'd probably look more respectable if I put the breeks straight on the compost heap and did the gardening in my pants. This isn't quite as bad as turning up to a non-fancy-dress party as a pirate, but it's halfway there. Then it occurs to me – hey, fuck it.

'Russell, my man!'

It's a lantern-jawed rugger-bugger. Tiny head topping a gym-inflated body. Topping his head, the kind of curly ginge that can't help but look pubic.

'Oh, hi there . . .'

'Chris.'

'Chris. Good to see you again.'

'Keeping well, Russell?'

'Keeping very well, Chris.'

'Excellent news, my man.'

'Chris!'

'Tony! Sorry, Russell, a spot of talking shop to do. Good to see you.'

'And you.'

'Catch you later.'

I turn to Russ and say, my teeth meeting and my mouth barely open, 'That counts, duzzin it.'

'Oh, that counts.'

I hail a passing white-jacketed Filipino and snaffle two glasses of champagne, hand one over to Russell. 'Did you recognise him at all?'

'Nope.'

'He recognised you though.'

'Yip.'

'Who *are* all these people?'

Russ takes a sip of champagne. 'No idea.'

'I see. Do you know *anyone* here?'

'That guy there.' He nods towards one of the chaps in a dark suit and a white shirt. One of the ones with ruffled sleeves. 'The guy whose party this is.'

'Host, I think is the technical term.'

'Quite so. Anyway, Pete, he's a mate.'

'Anyone else?'

Russell scans the room. 'Nope.'

'Right.'

'Well, one or two.'

'Right. So who's Pete?'

'Patient. Gum problem a couple of years back. Very nasty. Fortunately, I was there to save him.'

That this chap is a feature of Russ's social life only goes to show how much of that social life I don't know about. All of it going on while I discussed soft furnishings with Carol. 'Christ, you go on about me having no mates,' I say. 'There's you chatting up your patients. Asking them if they fancy a couple of beers or a game of squash. Like they're going to talk about their busy diaries when you've padded their gums with cotton wool and you're holding a big fat needle and a slow drill.'

Russell shrugs. 'He's a great man for his parties. On the naff side, I'll grant you but they have proved to be . . .' Russ gives me a meaningful look. 'A happy hunting ground.'

'Oh, really.'

Russell does a little conspiratorial head-flick. 'She's over there.'

'What you talking about? Who is?'

'The current sobbingly grateful recipient of my carnal expertise.'

'You mean Coatwoman?'

'Eh?'

'Coatwoman. The one who turned up at your place of business wearing a coat and nothing else bar a smile.'

'The very same. That's her over there. The bottle-blonde in the little black dress.'

Russell nods in the direction of a group by the opposite wall. Three women. Number of these three women who are bottle-blondes: three. Number of these bottle-blondes wearing little black dresses: three.

'The one on the left,' says Russell with heroic patience.

'Talking to the twerpy-looking twerp in the blue cardie. Pete's sister. Alison. Met her at his last do.'

'Here. Didn't you say Coatwoman was married?'

'I may well have done. Because she is. Well, sort of.'

'So where's the hubby?'

Russ shrugs. 'Somewhere here, probably. Ah dinna ken whit he looks like, ken, neebur.'

'What's that supposed to be?'

'Fife.'

'Jesus, that's even worse than the Welsh one that goes into Pakistani. . . . What were we talking about?'

'You really are completely off your tits, aren't you?'

'No, Russell, as you know, I've had just the one tiny line.'

'I was referring to the chain-smoking of marijuana cigarettes.'

'I may have had a couple. Hardly out of it, though. No. I'm . . . gently lit.'

'Gently lit. You're a human bonfire. We were talking about the hubby. Me not knowing what he looks like.'

'Oh, right, you being the cool customer. So he could be any one of these blokes?'

'Not any one. Three or four I've met here before so I know they're not him. But you are right. I am a cool customer.' Russell leans towards me and, completely unpleasantly, whispers in my ear: 'Baby, I be so cool, I be ree-*fridg*eraded.'

I wince away and flick pretend-spittle from my ear. Then I take a look over Russell's shoulder. 'So the cuckolded husband could even be the guy right behind you who's overheard us and has begun to stare at you.'

Russell swivels round, knocking an elbow of the blousy

princess behind him and spilling her drink. 'Oh, I *am* sorry,'
he says, producing a starched tablecoth of a hankie. 'Let me
wipe that clean.'

The spilled-drink routine. What an eejit. Nobody falls for
that. And this one's having none of it. 'That's quite all right,'
says the princess frostily. She takes the hankie and starts
dabbing at her admirable chest. Then turns her back on us.

'Can't you just *smell* the sex?' says Russell out of the side of
his mouth.

'No. A lot of perfume and a lingering hint of seaweed, that's
what I'm smelling.'

Russell shakes his head. Russell the Wise. 'No, this is a lot
livelier than Pete's usual. All these bored couples, desperate
singles. Place is *buzzing* with sex.'

I look around a room of bourgeois dullards. I'm assessing
the best way to escape – taxi? swimming? – when there's a
small commotion at the other end of the room.

'Some order, please, ladies and gentlemen,' someone calls out.

It's Russ's new best friend, the host. Standing at the
pointlessly balconied window. Tinging a pen against his flute
of champagne.

'Thank you, ladies and gents, thank you . . .'

The party falls into a dutiful hush.

'Thank you. I'm afraid this is the part of the evening when
I make a speech.'

'Shame!' someone shouts.

'No!' yells someone else.

Window Man holds his hands up as though in surrender.
'You're too kind. Now, I've gathered you all here this
evening . . .'

'To unmask the culprit!' yells a wag.

'. . . For a special reason. Now, I know some of you might have begun to think of me as a confirmed bachelor.' A couple of twats jeer. Happy to go along with it, Window Man places his left hand on his hip, does a limp-wristed, ooh-get-her flounce with his right.

Laughter.

'And I know this caused you all to ask yourselves one question.'

'Who's his boyfriend?' shouts out a chap in front of me who looks like he'd be useful in the line-out.

'How could someone so eligible as me. So handsome.'

There are shouts of scorn.

'So brilliant.'

More shouts. Plus a few whoops.

'So wonderfully successful.'

By now it's a collective response, the vague 'Way!' when a goal's scored.

'So fabulously wealthy.'

'Way!'

'So famously excellent in bed.'

'*Way!*'

Window Man holds up his hands to calm us down. 'How could such a catch manage to avoid being snapped up? While so many of you, my very good friends, coupled up and settled down, I walked a hard path alone, the path of loveless solitude and empty despair . . .' Window Man pauses for the ironic 'Aww' that follows. 'And yes, of long years of celibacy.'

There's much laughter at this, so that I have to put Window Man down as a notorious swordsman.

'Yes, I had to make do with a life of needlepoint, charity work and early nights.'

More laughter at this, though fading and there's the cheering prospect that he might be about to overplay it.

'But no more.' He holds out a hand in a stop sign and he looks at the floor. Getting serious. Unfortunately, the room has followed his cue and become silent. 'I never thought it would happen to me,' he says. 'After all this time . . . But it has happened. It happened last month. When I met Jocasta. Jocasta?'

Window Man looks straight at me. Suddenly, I feel very conspicuously at the centre of everyone's attention. Eh? What is this? How am I Jocasta? Then a door opens behind me and someone is walking past me and through a crowd of dropped jaws and unblinking eyes.

They're staring at the vision which has just brushed past me. A vision with a perfect profile. And perfect blonde hair – straight, past her shoulder blades, and not out of the bottle. A vision of youthful loveliness, wearing a short, tight, white dress. I watch her perfect legs and arse walk her away from me and up to Window Man's side.

She turns and faces the room. She is perfect. She is what girls are supposed to look like.

'Everyone? This is Jocasta. Jocasta, this is everyone.'

Window Man's a prat but the perfect girl copes admirably. She gives a semi-rueful smile then raises her eyebrows, takes a breath and says, 'Hi, everyone.'

'Hi, Jocasta,' call back several less thunderstruck members of what is now no longer a party but an audience.

'And it was love at first sight. This beautiful lady.' Window

Man puts an arm round her waist and pulls her towards him. With enough force for her left ear to be squashed against his chest. 'God knows what she sees in me . . .' He pauses with a horrible smile of false modesty. 'But she must see something. Because, well, I asked, she accepted and here we are. Engaged to be married.'

Applause, whoops and cheers.

Oh, for fuck's sake.

Russell's powdering his nose. So this is me, on my tod. Maybe muscle in on someone's conversation for the hell of it? . . . No. I'll finish this drink then bugger off back to the flatlet. A spliff and an early night.

'Oh, I'm sorry.'

I turn round to find a woman dabbing at my sleeve with a tissue.

'Well, thank God it's champagne and not red,' she says. 'And only a bit, so it shouldn't be disastrous.'

'I'm sure it'll be fine,' I say, watching as she attaches white flecklets to my jersey with each dab.

'Well, at least let me buy you a free drink. Waiter,' she calls, not actually snapping her fingers but near as damn it. 'A glass of champagne for the gentleman. I'm Eunice,' she says, offering a hand. 'Eunice Trimble.'

Ooshah. That is one terrible name. 'Ewan. Ewan Macintyre.'

'Well, very nice to meet you, Ewan.' She tilts her head a little and gives me what I suspect she thinks is a maverickly winning look. I'd guess that she's of an age with me. Mixed race. Half-Malaysian, at a guess. Milky-coffee skin, brown, almond-shaped eyes, a long, straight nose, full mouth. Shoulder-height so about five eight. Most striking of all, she's got this old-fashioned hair, the kind that an actress might have worn in a *Tale of the Unexpected*, a big black clump of it balancing on her skull and the rest toppling down in brittle, aerosoled curls. The kind of hair that doesn't necessarily bode well. On the other hand . . . Well, on the other hand, she does have the air of being completely on for it.

'So what do you think about Peter's news?' she asks. 'Incredible, isn't it?' She nods towards Window Man who is busy being awfully amusing to a semicircle of chums.

I shrug. 'Never met the man. Only thing I know about him is that he's an arsehole.'

She throws her head back and releases a cascading tinkle of laughter. 'Ahahahahaha. Well, then,' she says, the tinkle of laughter abruptly replaced by, with a little jerk of the neck and a sideways squint, a quizzical look. 'How come you're here?'

'I came with him.' I gesture towards Russell, who's returned and been nobbled by a clump of blokes. 'The guy in the dark suit and the white shirt. Russell.'

'Ahhhhh.' She draws it out and down the scale. 'You're a friend of Russell's. I don't know Russell. So how do you know Russell, Ewan?'

'Well, Eunice,' I say, naming names clearly being the thing to do round here. Although if I were her, I'd go for anonymity every time. 'Russell and I met at Heaven but we also go to the same hairdresser and . . .'

She smiles. 'I don't think so.'

'Worth a shot. And I bore myself with the usual answer because I get asked that all the time. "So, how did you two meet?" Like we're a couple, one of those odd, not-obvious-why-they're-together couples, and people genuinely want to know how on earth they've contrived to have a relationship when by rights they should never even have met.' I pause to think of an example.

And she says, 'So which part of Scotland are you from?'

'. . . Ah, Falkirk. It's a town between Edinburgh and Glasgow.'

'I *love* Scotland.'

'Great.'

'Do you know Oban?'

'No, I . . .'

'Oban's lovely. And the Highlands.'

'Yes.'

'We used to go on family holidays when I was a little girl. Lock Lomond. Lockgilphead. Kyle of Lockalsh. Troon. Do you know Troon?'

'No, I've never—'

'Troon had this fantastic ice cream. What's that place called?'

'Like I say, I—'

'Margetti's? Margotti's? Margalini's? Something like that. Or maybe it was Largs. Oh, I used to love holidays in Scotland. *So* beautiful.'

Okay. Which do I go for? Maybe play the oppressed card? And/or go for an impressive riff on tartan being invented and the Romanticist idea of the Highlands' wild beauty starting up only after Culloden? Fuck it. 'Where do you come from yourself?'

'Oh, all over.'

Uh-huh.

'Mainly Kent.'

'Right. And how come you're here? Who do you know?'

She waves a vague hand. 'Oh, everyone.'

Right.

'And I used to have a thing with Peter.' She gestures towards Window Man. 'Yonks ago, though. And I should think ninety per cent of the women in this room have had a thing with Peter at one time or another. So this is incredible, really.'

This woman has a talent, I realise, for leading the way up conversational cul-de-sacs. I smile, as though encouragingly.

'I just hope she likes a bit of adventure,' she says, with a wee smile.

I give her another encouraging look. In the forlorn hope that this conversation might acquire some point by turning flirty.

'Because, let's just say,' she says, lowering her voice, 'that when Peter and I had our thing, yonks ago now, he did enjoy a bit of adventure. In the bedroom.' She pulls back and does a squinty wee smile. She's drunk. Excellent. 'And not just the bedroom because that's the point, he had this thing for doing it in odd places. Public places too. Parks, dark alleyways, his car. There's a lay-by on the A12, just past the Southwold turn-off, that I remember especially well. Do you know, we once did it on a train.' She has a furtive look to either side, making sure she's not under immediate surveillance. 'An empty carriage. I sat on his lap,' she says. 'And I just lifted my skirt.' She draws back suddenly and gives me an impish, twinkly grin – the naughtiest girl in class. 'What do you think?'

What bugs me is that this aren't-I-a-one? schtick of hers

clearly depends on me being shocked and tongue-tied. All in all, at a bit of a loss with how to deal with someone so wild and free. 'What do I think?' I say. 'All I know is that I've gone hard.' Which, under normal circumstances, would be the kind of terrible line even Russell might spurn. But worth a gamble, I reckon, with this Eunice piece. The state she's in. And me not giving too much of a shit.

'Really?' she says. Then she bites her lower lip. 'Oh, dear.'

'No, it's quite all right. Rather pleasant, in fact. The only trouble is, it can sometimes get distinctly uncomfortable. At its full size.'

She's waiting for me to give a non-serious signal, a wiggle of the eyebrows or a quick snort of ironic laughter. I keep a straight face and stare her out.

'Really?' she says, obviously agog.

Oh, this is so easy it's embarrassing. Which makes me wonder just what the hell is going on. What happened to the sexual desert I'd been braced for? Soon come, I have no doubt, but in the meantime . . . First the girl in Barcelona, then that Nicola, and now this Eunice. I haven't been on a roll like this since . . . No – bin the 'since'. Which is daft, considering this is me I'm talking about. Face, teeth, hair, model's own. I could have had so much more sex in my life. Why haven't I had so much more sex in my life? Where was my rampant promiscuity? What happened to my drug-crazed sexfests? Someone nicked my share. Mick Jagger. Warren Beatty. Christ, how come I've lived like such a square?

'So what are you doing after the party?' I ask. And cue negotiations about taxis and the venue being her place or mine. The only doubt I have is that potentially desperate edge to her, how she could easily be the kind of neurotic who mistakes a ride for a relationship.

She does another of her head-tilts. 'After the party?' she says. 'I'm giving my friend Amanda a lift home.' She checks her watch, gives me a smile, then puts a hand on her head and pulls up her hair. Which keeps rising. She pulls it further up and off. She holds the hairdo in one hand and gives her shortish, side-parted, black, normal hair a rub with the other. 'Is that the time?' she says. 'Goodness. Well, nice to meet you . . .'

'Ewan.'

'Ewan. And good luck with the penis.' She flutters her fingers and shimmies off.

Well. Damn.

Part Two

6

RICHARD

I stride into the kitchen. Ali is standing at the sink . . . doing the washing-up. She turns to face me – and dries her hands – as I approach her.

'Ali,' I say. I step forward and pull her firmly towards me. 'Ali,' I say, 'I'm going to take you. Now.' I hold her face in my hands and guide her mouth to mine. But just as our lips are about to meet, I delay, prolonging this longing, prolonging this desire for exquisite seconds. Our breath mingles. Our breaths mingle. Our breath mingles. We're panting. Our pants min—

Right. I prolong the moment of desire for exquisite seconds. Our breath mingles. And then . . . And then I cover her mouth with mine. 'Ali?' I say, with low, husky urgency. No. First I break off the kiss. Then I say, 'Ali' with low, husky urgency.

Then she says, 'Yes?'

And I say, with a fair degree of forthright masterfulness, 'Take off your dress.'

It's that Laura Ashley-type dress, my favourite, or one of my favourites, the one with a pattern of pinkish roses and a sort of Forties look about it. Not that Ali would normally be

135

wearing it for doing the washing-up in but still that's the dress which, responding to my tone of firm command, she now begins to take off, letting it fall to her feet and revealing, again not as per, I suppose, but stick with it, that she's been wearing nothing underneath. I step towards her, because I would have had to have taken a step back while she took off the dress, and cup her full breasts, then stroke them with my palms, giving them the gentlest polishing, then suddenly try to think about the garden in Stow, the long, striped lawn sloping down to the oak trees and then the river, and the wood pigeons cooing in the oak trees, cooing in the oak trees, as we come out of the tunnel and into the sudden brightness at Farringdon, rattling by the crowded platform and lurching to a halt and the doors about to open and it could be as many as a dozen more people about to get in and stand next to me here by the pole in the middle of the carriage's standing bit. Trying to make it look like the natural movement that it isn't, I swing my briefcase in front of me.

I take a deep breath to calm myself, not that I'm in any panicky sort of a mood, but then neither are the twinges at the dentist's unbearable, the point being that where both getting around London and being at the dentist's take the biscuit is in threatening at all times to get a lot, lot worse, very, very quickly, the twinge exploding into searing agony. I glance at my watch as a businessy-looking young man in a suit shuffles another half-pace towards me and register the sorry fact that it's nearly half past ten.

I'm still holding my briefcase in protect mode, my left forearm beginning to ache a little, my right hand hanging on to an unsettlingly warm patch of yellow railing, my right trouser leg coming into occasional contact with the left trouser leg of a small dark man with a bald patch who's making his move early for the door, my eyes studiously avoiding anywhere in the region of the two secretaryesque girls sitting down, one of them wearing a very short skirt, when the train stops, the doors open, three people step in and I realise with a jolt the sheer dodginess of the scenario, what with Ali being cast as the domestic drudge, although can I just say that the Ali-doing-the-washing-up arrangement was the furthest-fetched part . . . arguably, there being of course other not very likely aspects on consideration, to wit, the unresolved issues of her hands probably remaining a bit washing-uppy to the touch, despite the cursory towel-wipe, and the fundamental implausibility of her wearing the Forties-type Laura Ashley dress to do the washing-up in, far less nothing underneath. Although, come to think of it, there is something rather horny about housework – not the drudgery or the exploitation but the hair pinned back, the graft and the sweat, the stretching and the bending, the being down on the knees, the possibility of some sort of uniform being involved, perhaps one with a teensily short skirt and a white frilly bibby thing in front. Where could this little fetishette have come from? Not, I assure, you from Mrs Ferris, our woman as did back in Stow. She was the oldest person in the world and evidently stuffed her housecoat with pillows. No. I rather suspect Whatshername the actress a few years back, very good posture, long blonde hair and a distinctive, creaky voice, Adam Faith's girlfriend in that series called . . . Bongle . . . No, *Budgie* – could it be *Budgie*? . . . yes, *Budgie*, on, I think, ITV, when ITV was still considered in our house at any rate a little infra dig, a little milk-in-first, as

Walls was to Lyons, football to rugby, Ford to Rover, Pan to Penguin, or maybe that one was the other way round, so it was probably more by luck than cunning that I was watching *Budgie* in the first place, but just as well because out of nowhere there came a scene where this young actress with the straight back, creaky accent and long, blonde hair was doing the ironing, dressed, as I recall, or at least according to my memory of it, in a vesty top and knickers . . . Yes, that. But it's not as if Ali has to be doing the washing-up. Or, despite the above, honestly, any domestic task at all. She could equally be sitting on the sofa, or watching the telly, or . . . reading the paper. Or something else. It doesn't matter. Especially now when I should, even with the briefcase in protective mode, be concentrating on the long, striped lawn sloping down to the oak trees, the oak trees at the bottom of the long, striped lawn in Stow . . .

As chance would have it, there's no trouserular crisis, so when the train draws into Barbican, the Barbican, Barbican, I'm happy to squirm my way out of the carriage to join the throng waiting to go up the stairs. The kind of throng that might be pictured for a documentary about the rat race or even the population explosion but that always strikes me as the most civilised of gatherings, governed as it is by a collective benevolence that's encouraging, almost inspiring, each and every one of us politely and carefully respecting every one else's space, every bit as if there were some sort of force field preventing any unseemly contact, so as to render barging or argy-bargy of any nature completely inconceivable, and then up and over to the barriers and then out to the street and then, at quick-march, towards the waiting office.

Twenty to. So it'll be ten to before I get in, most probably. I suppose that, as starting times go, ten to eleven cannot honestly be regarded as, in any sense, early, but we've always been fairly relaxed about that sort of thing, promptitude and so on and so forth, at *Bricks and Brickmen*, ever since Frank's day, when Frank's day could start at noon and end by three, and include a two-hour lunch, not too much happening by way of any hold-the-front-page drama, or often any activity at all, in Frank's day. Not that it's as cushy now, with dark rumours abroad of a mooted rival about to burst upon an awestruck world with startling coverage of the domestic-construction scene conveyed with unparalleled expertise and glossiness, from a certain organisation with an HQ not unadjacent to the South Bank . . .

To be honest, I really don't know what I could have done to speed things along. Got Bongle dressed quicker? Easier said than done, and all the more so when the Bongle boy is in sprightly form and eager to play the chasing game instead of meekly accepting the irksome botherage that comes with some big fool trying to haul and maul you into your clothes. And yes, of course, I could and should have got up earlier, but it was a broken night and I woke up when Bongle woke up, with his usual cry at, doubtlessly because of the broken night, a very welcomely belated half past eight. So I slipped out of bed, leaving Ali to go back to sleep, her having done the up-in-the-night thing on two separate occasions, as opposed to my single shot at it, so it was only fair, and commenced Bongle duty – dealing with the noisome nappy with which the Bongle invariably greets the rosy-fingered dawn, carrying him downstairs for breakfast, giving him breakfast (Weetabix today), hosing him down after breakfast, reading *Dear Zoo* with him, the regulation four times, playing with his blue rabbit and his big yellow truck (the blue rabbit sitting in the big yellow truck and going for a more or less comprehensive tour of the sitting-room lounge), finishing up with several recaps of *Dear Zoo*. Only then could I start thinking about taking the sprightly one upstairs soon and dumping him on Ali, although it was already well after nine and I was still unwashed, unshaved, unteethcleaned, and in my PJs, so, all things considered, not quite ready to leave the house. So then we climbed up the stairs, because Bongle can do that now – climb stairs, that is, clambering upwards on all fours albeit not at hugely effective pace, as I had some opportunity to appreciate anew while I followed him one . . . step . . . at . . . a time . . . towards . . . mummy . . . and daddy's . . . bedroom . . .

And let me just stress that clambering on all fours up the stairs very slowly is but one of the Herr Professor von Bonglestrudel's many areas of expertise. Crawling – very good at crawling. Standing up, if a little wobblily. Clap – oh, yes, he can clap. Even throw a ball, trembling with the excitement of it all, brandishing his boingedy-boing ball high above his head as though it's the trophy he's just won, and then hurling it with all his might, the boingedy-boing ball flopping down and landing with a boing behind him. Answer to his name. So I suppose he's still, technically, looking at it with a cold, objective, scientific eye, at the level of an interesting pet. Ah, yes, but you can see it in his eyes, the way he's fizzing away, fizzing into life, trying to make sense of it all, and getting better and better at everything. And *it* just gets better and better, and my heart swells like a balloon, a balloon that gets bigger and bigger until it's stretched so tight that it surely has to burst. Because of Bongle, Bongle, Bongle. My darling, my sweetheart, my darling little one. With the constantly red, mottled cheeks. With the dribbles. The ears and the chin that so shamelessly copy mine. The orange gunk in his ears. The giggling. The practising sounds – 'nanananana', for example, or 'mehmehmehmehmeh', or, sometimes, often looking at me, honestly, 'dadadadadada'. The everything. So that just looking at him sometimes, it's so powerful that it comes to me and I know, I just know, that there has to be a point to all of this, that of course we are part of something grander and more amazing because it's so blatantly obvious, because there's the sheer miraculousness of this, that there should be such a thing as this living, breathing, giggling, gurgling Bongle.

. . . Funnily enough, it aches sometimes, as it aches now, I can feel it, yes, because it is a real physical thing, happening somewhere not quite placeable in the pit of the stomach, and not at all unlike how I used to feel when I went on those first dates with Ali, at the flicks or the King's Head or just going for a walk around Aylesbury or the park (walking in a park being something I'd done rarely before and never since, until, curiously, last year and the tours of our new neighbourhood and the teensy, forsaken park with Bongle in his buggy), when I fell for Ali hook, line and sinker, and I ached for her, or not for her so much as really just to be near her, and she could zap me with the slightest movement, and, all these years later, the aching's still there, and the zapping. Ali in her Forties Laura Ashley dress – zap. Ali in her jeans – zap. Ali reading in bed, face cream on – zap. Ali with a tan, somewhere hot, on holiday, wearing her white dress – zap, kapow, boom.

One thing leading to another, I'm soon conjuring up a scenario of us all on holiday, abroad somewhere, France maybe or even the villa Marcus keeps on mentioning in Portugal, but somewhere warm at any rate. The three of us splashing about in a pool. And one day – who knows, if Ali changes her mind? – the four of us . . .

But this is a daydream that's bounding with puppyish glee and gusto in completely the wrong direction and I have to be tugged back to reality, and the reality is that Ali's still recovering from Bongle and in no shape or mood yet to think about the conception far less the delivery and mothering of a second so soon after the first, and that I'm currently pushing at the glass doors and now waving an evasive hello to Callum in reception and now getting into a waiting lift.

There's no avoiding Bob, of course, but just as I'm about to come within range and he's about to start, his phone rings, thus proving that there is a God, so he can only hold a finger in the air and with whistly lips mouth an O as I walk serenely by, sauntering now to the cubicle where I plonk the briefcase on the floor and self on the executive swivelly seat, have a little swivel, gaze at the flying toasters and wonder what to do next.

'Knock knock,' says Shirley, standing Lollobrigidianely at the doorway in a white blouse and black skirt that reaches down past her knees but is nonetheless a little bit too tight to be safe, especially at her hips where the skirt really seems to be struggling to contain the extravagant curve.

'Who's there?' I reply, keeping the banter going.

'Um, me.'

'Um me who?'

Shirley crinkles her eyes and gives her head a little shake. 'Sorry,' she says.

'Maybe you could have said Shirley to start with and then Shirley shome mishtake or stop calling me Shirley or something.'

'Yes . . . Good weekend?'

'Fine,' I say, slightly economical with the truth perhaps but basically, overall, over the forty-eight-hour piece, accurately enough. And now that I have no choice but to utter the word, there stirs within me a profound sense of foreboding. 'You?'

Shirley takes a couple of steps forward. 'Well,' she says, in a vaguely conspiratorial way that makes me forebode even more. 'It was heading to be a complete wash-out, what with my QNI on Friday. And Saturday a write-off because I was supposed to be having a hot afternoon date with the MM but then he couldn't get away, some family do, so that was two days in a row just me and the Rampant Rabbit. But then he rearranged some golf thing on the Sunday and came round with a bunch of flowers and a bottle of really good wine.'

'Oh, that was good,' I say. The Rampant Rabbit. That, I'm pretty sure, is a vibrator. Shirley has a vibrator. The words are enough but far worse is the image, fleeting and blurred but nonetheless, of Shirley, dressed as she is but lying on a bed, her knees up, her skirt rucked up, both hands tucked down under her tights and over her, her, her groin, her mouth open, her eyes shut tight, her hair flowing back over the pillow behind her, an insistent buzzing noise the only sound in the room apart from her gasps . . .

'. . . plied me with wine,' I register as I tune back in. 'And then, well, we'll draw a veil . . .'

Yes, please. Yes, please, let's do that.

'. . . but suffice to say that matters soon came to quite a head,' says Shirley, and she nods meaningfully.

But what *does* she mean? Oral sex? Or the, argh, head of the, argh, penis? What? I really couldn't say. So I smile back. And then try very, very hard not to listen to the next bit.

'. . . why my tendons still ache.'

Not listening, not listening, not listening.

'You know those long tendons at the top of the thighs? The soft inside bit?'

Lalalalalala.

'Well, I can still feel those today. Just here.'

Actually, there's some part of me that's rather miffed by this. It's like I've found myself in the changing room at St Trinian's, and, slightly gallingly, some might say, can continue to gawp at the scenery because the scenery has failed to notice me, or has noticed me and dismissed me. Well, looking on the positive side, that is quite an honour, quite a badge of our friendship. Yes.

'. . . over the sofa,' says Shirley. 'And me still wearing my shoes.' Shirley gives me a knowing look. 'So that was Sunday. Oh. Incidentally. Simon was in looking for you.'

'What, you mean *the* Simon?'

'Yes. Thee Simon.'

'When?'

Shirley shakes her head. 'Half past? Twenty to?'

'What did you tell him?'

'I didn't tell him anything. He just walked in, saw you weren't here and walked out.'

'Right . . . I'll give him a call. Or anyway, Thingummy his secretary. Oh, God . . .' I gaze at the squadron of toasters.

'Oh, don't worry, Richard, it'll be nothing.'

'You're right. Yes, you're right. I'll give him a call.'

10.22 a.m., Monday 7 October

EWAN

I peer out through the murky windscreen of Grassy's decomposing Volvo. At a sequence of squat, stained blocks of flats made of asbestos and dried egg. 'Where the hell are we? Bratislava?'

'Coming up to Sidcup Road.'

'There is no such place.'

''Ere is.' Grassy does some slow nodding. 'Sih road at goes to Sidcup. Here.' Grassy proffers the moist stump of his joint. Only because it's the moist stump, I shake my head. He takes a last few violent sucks. 'Roach,' he explains, with a high croak because he's holding his breath, then he chucks the stump out the window.

We pass a row of pre-war semis with paved gardens. A row of shops. A vast pub advertising its karoake nites and meat raffle.

South of the river. Why the hell did I agree to south of the river? Because I wanted to break my own rules as well while I was at it. Only goes to show that some rules are rules for a good reason. Never go SOR – sensible, correct. 'God but this is a lovely part of the world.'

Almost to my surprise, Grassy detects sarcasm. 'Sall right. Some nice spots. In fack.' Suddenly, Grassy swerves into a space behind a bus stop and brings the car to an abrupt halt. He rummages round the debris at his feet – Twix wrappers, empty packets of Drum, a black banana, balls of tissue, some ruined socks, a street map of Brighton – and eventually fetches out from under his seat a very used-looking poly bag. I look for the logo. Spar. Of course.

Hugging the bag under his armpit as he might a small dog, flip-flops flapping, Grassy trots across the road. He seems to be heading for the petrol station on the corner, but then he slows down and stops below a very large poster of Elizabeth Hurley, in a ball gown, lying on her side, her head resting on a hand, smiling at us. As for Grassy, he seems to be appraising a wooden fence beneath her. Then he pushes at a couple of slats and sidles through the new gap.

I look around until my gaze settles on another advert, one at a bus stop down the road. The adverts being the only sights worth seeing in these parts. The one on the bus stop is for some chick-lit paperback. Regulation retro illustration of pert young woman sitting on a chair, her legs tucked beneath her microskirt, toasting the world with an outsize glass of yellow wine. The title an italicy scribble in pink. *Looking for Mr Wright*, this one's called. Shoutline below – 'For anyone who has ever been in love.' Young piece, in the city, has ghastly boyfriend, is chucked, falls in love with nice man, gets drunk with pals, gets nice man. I'm guessing.

Christ, as if love was the answer. Dearie, dearie me. As if.

All those books. All those songs. All that utter, utter drivel. Never doubted or questioned. No matter what. Because it's just one of those things people have to say to comfort themselves. The alternative being, er, the abyss. Love, love, love. Love, love, love. Love, love, love. It's ea-easeh.

Christ.

The view outside and inside being so poor, I close my eyes. And see, ironically enough, Carol, who's turned up out of nowhere. Carol a year after we got married, spring of 94, her dressed down in T-shirt and jeans because we're in the Bricklayers, the only visitable pub in the whole of deserted, forgotten Shoreditch. No shops for miles. No nothing for miles. All we have is the hunch. One, run-down area, full of ethnic retail outlets and dilapidated warehousing. Two, known only by a small but apparently growing bunch of young arty artisans because there's cheap studio space. Three, a short sprint from Officeland and the City. Give it ten years, we both reckon, and this'll be TriBeCa. Carol is giving me a beatific smile. We're clinking glasses because we've just paid one hundred and twenty thousand pounds for two thousand, two hundred square feet of nothing. A shell that used to be a sweatshop and is now the abandoned, derelict top floor of a knackered warehouse in the middle of nowhere. Lucky us. Because seven years later, that wreck would be a property-porn centrefold. And Shoreditch would be the most happening part of London, i.e. Europe. Good call, Macintyre. *Great* call.

'Nice one, man.' Grassy chucks the poly bag on top of the litter pile in the back seat. 'And we've had a nice little drop of rain.' Now he reaches just beyond my knees for the glove compartment. By rights, this should of course contain a neat stack of motoring documents and a tin of disappointing boiled sweets lying on sugared dust. This being the glove compartment of Grassy's Volvo, it holds an avalanche of shattered CD covers, loose Rizlas, Twix wrappers, a musky T-shirt, many broken biros and a grubby sheaf of papers held together by a tartan ribbon. He takes out a page. 'Bhnd grn fnc,' he writes with a barely functioning stub of pencil. 'Undrnth bllbrd.'

Grassy files the grubby sheaf between his feet. After some grinding and spluttering and barking by both vehicle and owner, we move off.

'You don't have to do this any more, you know,' I say, the very model of patience and calm.

'Yeah, but,' says Grassy. 'What mows people don't realise about iss game is at it's not just a job. Sa thingy.'

'Vocation.'

'Nah, swot I'm saying. Snot a holiday. Sa opposite. Sa fucking . . . calling, you know what I'm saying?'

'Aye, I think so.' I reach over to the pile of parking tickets and Twix wrappers on Grassy's side of the dashboard and extricate the map that's to blame for all this. I unfold it and peer down at the bottom right-hand corner.

'Smottingham now,' Grassy explains. 'Should be coming up to Mottingham Lane.'

'Right. Got it.'

'See at policeman on a left?'

'. . . Yes.'

'At's a sheriff of Mottingham.'

'Ah ha.'

'See a trees past a shops?'

I look ahead at two frail saplings bandaged in plastic tubes. 'Yeh-ess.'

'At's Mottingham . . .'

'Forest, yes, I see.' I assess the possibility that Grassy suggested this particular area so that he could make those jokes. Then it occurs to me that that's actually a better reason than the real one – we chose Mottingham because it was on the edge of this fold-out map of London. The bottom right-hand corner, to be precise. Why the bottom right-hand corner? Why not the top right or the top left or the bottom left? Why not, let's see, Manor Park or Willesden, or . . . Jesus, Wimbledon? Why not nowhere at all? Because that would have been what I would have done. Here was a chance to do the opposite. And I'd had several bongs of white widow. And I would have happily agreed to an amputation.

Well, what the fuck.

Grassy hoiks an abrupt left and stops with a jolt. 'We're here,' he says. 'Home again, home again, yeah? Clippety-clop.'

We get out. I look around. A cul-de-sac of semis. Regulation net curtains and crazily paved lawns. Christ, this is the burbs. Where folk talk about going up to London. To see the sights. Double-decker buses. Tube signs. People enjoying themselves. Grey pebbledash on some of the walls, just to rub in the reminder of Falkirk. Yip, I bet they all lead rich and thrilling lives hereabouts. Full of incident and intrigue.

I follow Grassy, who stops at a crocked gate hidden in the middle of a sprawling hedge and kicks it open. 'Fuck!' he shouts, hopping and glaring down at his flip-flops. I, meanwhile, stare up the crumbling path at the worst semi in the street. The kind you're not sure is council or not. Designed by a moron and built on the cheap in 1935. In resolute decline ever since. From the top. Pink tiled roof, red brickwork, a vivid red the shade of a nasty jalfrezi, couple of rotting windows on the top floor, one rotting bay window on the ground floor beside a flaking door tucked away at the end of a gloomy brick porch. What surrounds the house was possibly intended to be a garden but has long been home to some rubble and a lot of high, spindly weeds.

Grassy spreads his arms wide and turns to me. 'Sour house!' he says with boyish glee. 'Sour fucking *house*, man.'

'Good morning, gents!'

It's the estate agent, striding up the path towards us. He's a burly type in his early thirties. Wearing a spivvily blue pinstripe suit. Shirt and tie the same colour, an electric peach that reminds me of Angel Delight. He looks like he'd be much more at ease in a tracksuit, with a whistle, organising a scrum. But instead here he is, crammed into a suit and opening the door with a discreet biff from his shoulder. 'Here we are, gents,' says Pinstripe, then he beckons us in with a flourish.

A hallway whose wallpaper (faded roses, natch) peels up at the bottom like a naff Eighties hairdo. Living room at the front, kitchen at the back, and that's the tour of the ground floor complete. Up the stairs to mouldy shunkie and three small bedrooms, all empty except for assorted rubbish.

'Terrific potential,' says Pinstripe after the three of us have clomped back downstairs and started to crowd into the living room.

Grassy gazes around him with an expression of awe and wonder. 'Yeah,' he whispers, and he shakes his head in disbelief at the great good fortune of owning such a palace.

Pinstripe is smiling broadly. And actually rubbing his hands. This from the man who made such a show of defeat when he finally accepted our offer, an unfeasible £125,000, but still a few grand under the asking price. I feel an unwelcome twinge of anxiety. Maybe the search missed something. Maybe next door has planning permission for a sewage plant or a runway.

Do I trust my judgement? Even without the sewage works, there's still the police to worry about. But what, seriously, are the chances? Slim. As long as Grassy keeps shtum. But Grassy doesn't know anyone not to keep shtum to. Something else, then. The property market collapsing. Possible, but not likely. Is Grassy setting me up in an unfathomably elaborate con? Possible, but, given Grassy's guile, not at all likely.

No, I've assessed the risks. And there has to be some element of risk. Because that's sort of the point, given that what I'm breaking isn't just one of my rules but a law of the land. That's why I had to dare myself in the first place – Go on. Do it. Just do it – and that's why I haven't backed down since the evening of the bongs. The one which ended up with the pair of us kneeling over Grassy's map of London and deciding, because it seemed such a stroke of genius at the time, to go for the bottom right-hand corner. With his thirty-odd grand life savings, ninety-odd cash from me, we'd buy some crappy little place down in the godforsaken bottom right-hand corner and, as it were, do it up. Not quite Grassy's daydream of the little tucked-away cottage in Dorset with a thatched roof over the attic's hydroponic farm. Well, not the Dorset cottage bit, this crap semi in Mottingham being this crap semi in Mottingham. But he's going to get the hydroponic part all right. Because that's what this crap semi's going to be. A three-up, two-down marijuana farm.

It was late next day, the day after the evening of the bongs, and after a lot of coffee that I finally got it together to go back downstairs and exchange estimates. Mine: fifteen to twenty per cent return on the property the first year, minimum, follow the market after that. His: with tiny outlay for seeds, extractor fan, and a dozen UV lights, cultivate a total of, say, a conservative one hundred plants, four crops a year, a conservative three ounces per plant that allows for cock-ups, sell at £40 an ounce to the right man (and Grassy, plausibly, says he knows one of those). I'd obviously get two-thirds of the property profit. We'd go halfers on the crop.

'Eighty-twenty on a crop for me,' Grassy replied without pause.

'I'm the one making this possible. Two-thirds to you.'

'Done. Let's get a map.'

So, one way or another, I should make thirty-five grand on this place in a year. Easy. Unless we're arrested. Or Iraq invades and the Ba'ath party take over the estate agents.

Leaving Grassy and Pinstripe in the lounge, I wander through to the skiffle-era kitchen. The only things in it are a dead cooker and a Formica table that inspires a sudden, clear memory of me spooning in Rice Krispies, tapping my heels against a chair rung.

We'll fill a few skips and do some structural repairs, rewire the sucker. Then I'll do the painting and decorating while Grassy tidies up the garden outside and starts the garden inside. We're going to keep the front room un-net-curtained and ostentatiously normal. Maybe stick up a couple of framed

Vettrianos. But we'll use everywhere else. Even the mouldy shunkie. Thirty-five grand. For a little renovation work and, er, no, that's all. Not bad.

And I'm getting a bit of a buzz from this. Not just the criminality, though there is that. But also scheming again. Plotting property exploitation, and try saying that after a bong of white widow. Little daydreams beginning to flicker about building this up, owning several places, using them as farms . . . or just renting them out. Either way, getting good money for doing bugger-all. I look into the future and what do I see? I see one big fucking holiday.

I return to the lounge.

'Right then, gents,' announces Pinstripe, rubbing his hands. 'Shall we adjourn?'

7

8.35 p.m., Wednesday 9 October

RICHARD

I pop my head round the door, as though playing peek-a-boo
but very much not, because, snug under his blankets, his white
blankets, his heartrending, white, perforated baby blankets,
all cosy in his little sleeping-bag apparatus and his Bob the
Builder PJs (not, alas, the PJs in black-and-white check which
make him look so smart, as he holds my hand and we make
the slow ascent together, one considered step at a time, up the
wooden hill to bedfordshire, that I feel I should be replaced by
an audience of entranced and cuckling aunties), lies the boy
they call the Bongle boy, fast asleep, face pressed, as per usual,
hard against the thingummy, the long white padded-band
thing that goes three-quarters of the way round the cot's rungs
above the mattress and that after each wash I have to retie to
the cot's bars with unimpressive reef knots and that always
slips down, probably not despite but because of all those
fiddlily tied ties, and that is supposed to but often doesn't, not
really, prevent or even minimise head-bangage during out-
bursts of sudden Bongalian twisting and turning, which used
to look impatient and perhaps even aggrieved but have very
recently started to look like protests at some bad thought

that's seized the opportunity offered by unguarded slumber and attacked, thereby only backing up the manuals' predictions that the next and imminent stage is the arrival of witches and faces at the window and being suddenly lost and alone in a dark forest where there are bad men and big bad wolves and . . .

'Everything okay up there?'

It's Ali, calling up.

I tiptoe out to the hall. 'Fine,' I say in a sort of whispered shout. Then I tiptoe back in, for as long as I think I can, to watch him sleeping.

Busy as I am, trying to record the sight for posterity, I remember the time only as I reach the sitting-room lounge. Eight-thirty on a Wednesday, which is now up there in Ali's schedules with Sunday mornings, 10.15 to 11.30. Hesitantly, in fact only doing this because I can't think of a way how not to, I join Ali on the sofa, and, alas, it's a question for a thousand.

'Which of the following rivers flows through Paris?' asks Chris Whatshisname, the quizmaster. 'Is it A, the Danube, B, the Tiber, C, the Seine or D, the Rhine?'

'C,' I say.

'C,' says the mumsy lady on the telly.

'C,' says Chris Whatshisname. 'C. The Seine. Sure? Positive? Let's show the correct answer, for one thousand pounds.'

C.

'The next question. For two thousand pounds . . . Who was the inventor of the steam engine? Was it A, James Watt, B, James Watson, C, Isaac Newton or D, Michael Faraday?'

'B,' I say.

'B?' says Ali, incredulously.

'A,' says the mumsy contestant with a little smile.

'Sorry, A,' I say.

'James Watson was Crick and Watson. DNA,' says Ali.

'Yes, that's right,' I say. Ali gives me a look which I think isn't a come-off-it one but one whose extra little nod attached to it speaks rather of her wisdom in campaigning for me to go for an eye test. 'Sorry, I misread it. You're right, I do need spectacles. Steam engine, James Watt, A. Of course it's A.' I give her a little smile and a kind of shrug movement but with my hands held out like I'm a waiter at one of Peter's parties and offering a platter of sushi canapes, as I say 'A,' again, successfully it seems. Blimming hell, though.

'Now. For four thousand pounds. The next question . . . Who was the manager of last year's FA Cup winners? Was it A, Alex Ferguson. B, Gerard Houllier, C, Sven Goran Erickson or D, Arsene Wenger.'

'Oh, no,' moans Ali. 'That is *so* unfair. I'd have to lose a lifeline and phone a friend. On four thousand.'

It looks as though the mumsy lady on the telly is stuck as well. Like her, I purse my lips. 'I think it's D,' I say, risking it because Ali's already passed and choosing D only because I know that Arsene Wenger is the manager of Arsenal. The Arsenal. Arsenal.

It *is* D.

'Who'd be your friend to phone for that one?' I ask, during Chris Thingy's banter.

Ali looks off as she casts around. 'For football? . . . Oh, I'd . . . No,' she says abruptly. 'No. Do you know, I have no idea.'

'Bob,' I say. 'Bob would be mine because he knows everything about football. Football, Ancient Egypt, his motorbike. Any of those, I'd phone Bob.'

'Fifty-fifty's rubbish because they'd just take away two and I'd be none the wiser. Ask the audience, I suppose.'

'Cricket,' I say. 'I could be your phone-a-friend for cricket.'

'Okay. I'll add you to my list.'

The eight-thousand one strikes me as being very harsh for eight thousand but the mumsy lady seems confident and so does Ali, so I put in some thoughtful nodding before Quito lights up as the correct answer, then take the chance provided by the subsequent chat about the lady's recent completion of a mini-marathon in aid of a hospice to ask Ali if she'd like some tea and finally escape to the kitchen to make same.

It being so important to let the tea brew, I dally a while over the remains of the washing up, squeezing in a little going-over of surfaces with a J-Cloth for good measure, before sorting out a tray of tea stuff and carrying it, slowly and steadily and not rushing in any way whatsoever, only because this is a task that of course requires great care, back to the sitting-room lounge.

Where, calamitously, because I've reckoned without what must, I only now realise, have been a break for adverts at the cliffhanging bit before Chris Whatshisface gives the answer, it's still only the sixteen-thousander and the mumsy lady shaking her head.

'Oh, come *on*,' says Ali.

I glance at the screen. 'Which letters denote the metal lead in the periodic table?' it says. Blimming flip. I fuss about with the procedure of pouring out our teas and adding, with terrific care and precision, the splashette of milk into Ali's Sagittarius mug.

'C is the correct answer. Congratulations, Irene, you've just won sixteen *thousand* pounds.'

Biscuits. I could go and get some biscuits.

'Next question. For thirty-*two* thousand pounds. And, Irene, you still have two lifelines left. Which of the following authors was married to Catherine Hogarth? A, Anthony Trollope. B, Charles Dickens. C, Wilkie Collins. D, Oscar Wilde . . . Take your time.'

Ali puts down her tea and leans forward, as though the answer's written in tiny type somewhere on the screen. 'Wilkie Collins,' she murmurs. 'Wasn't he a bigamist? Wilkie Collins . . .'

'Could be Wilkie Collins,' I say, and then a thought arrives in my head, from nowhere, in a flash. 'Can't be D,' I mutter, as if mulling it over to myself. 'Oscar Wilde being not of the marrying persuasion.'

Ali does an impatient movement with her hand. 'Wilde married. Vivian Holland,' she adds inexplicably.

Do we *have* any biscuits?

Suddenly, Ali sits up and brings her hands together quickly for one loud clap. 'Dickens,' she says. 'Catherine Hogarth. His first wife. Dickens. B.'

Some time later, the mumsy lady decides it's B, it's confirmed as B, the business of a cheque being offered and withdrawn comes and goes and I haven't gone for biscuits and it's the next question.

'Who became Party Secretary of Czechoslovakia in January 1968?' asks Chris Thing after piling on the tension with inane banter, in exactly the same way, it occurs to me, as a dentist who prattles away about football or his holidays, thus delaying the arrival of the slow drill. 'Was it A, Vaclav Havel? B, Gustav Husak? C, Alexander Dubcek? Or D, Erich Honecker?'

It being, I think, just about acceptable to be stumped by a sixty-four-thousander, I blow out air as though stumped . . . which, come to think of it, I am.

'Has to be C, doesn't it?' says Ali but in such a considering sort of a way that I don't think she's really asking a proper question. 'Yeah, C . . . C,' she decides and I'm immediately overwhelmed by a rush of love at her braininess, although to be more accurate the rush is mainly of love but one that also comes with one undercurrent of awe and another of anxiety because there has to be stuff going on in Ali's head that I can have no notion of, not that this is a new anxiety, having been much, much more of an anxiety during our own apocalypse (in 96, three years earlier than the official date for the Armageddons predicted by Nostrawhatsit and the TV documentaries of my adolescence) though not to think about our apocalypse, yes, no, not that . . .

The mumsy lady, it turns out, is every bit as stumped as me. She goes for the fifty-fifty, phones a friend and bows out, happy to accept her cheque.

'Sixty-four thousand,' says Ali. 'Even thirty-two thousand. God . . .'

'You should go on it,' I tell her as I tell her every week. 'Really. You'd get the million.'

'Even thirty-two thousand,' Ali murmurs and then she inspects the screen again because it's the fingers-on-the-buzzers bit for the new contestants.

What I'll do, I'll wait until the next lemon-squeezy £500,

when it'll be an acceptable time to have lost interest and the best time to commence extended faffage in the kitchen, thereby avoiding the awkward squad between £1,000 and £16,000, then I'll go for the biscuits.

If there are any biscuits.

8.35 p.m., Wednesday 9 October

EWAN

'No, it's about you taking the car to the garage.'

'I don't have a car.'

'Don't you?'

'No.'

'Why not?'

'I can't drive.'

'Can't you?'

'No.'

'Why not?'

'Never learned.'

'Really?'

'Really . . . Anyway. What happens at the garridge?'

'You're not making this very easy, are you? So. You've taken your non-existent car to the garaahj. Okay?'

'Okay.'

'Okay. It's late and the door's locked but there's a light on inside . . . You knock on the door and you keep knocking until someone opens it. He's a . . . big guy.'

'Yes.'

'Dark.'

'Yes.'

'Swarthy.'

'No.'

'Okay. Dark. And wearing . . . blue overalls. Overalls stained with grease and oil.'

'Uh-huh.'

' "We're closed," he says, but you bat your eyes and tell him you'll pay extra if he can have a look at your car now.'

'I what my eyes?'

'Bat them. Isn't that the right word?'

'No, it's fine. Anyway, carry on.'

'Sorry for interrupting. So. Ah, yes. So, you get the car into the garridge, where another bloke appears. Young. Dark. Overalls covered in grease and oil.'

'Yes.'

'And the two mechanics have a look under your bonnet and sort it out.'

'You're not going to go on about the fan belt or something, are you?'

'No. Jesus . . . What I'm going to go on about is what happens when you discover that you've left your purse at home.'

'Oh . . . Oh, dear.'

'Yes. Oh, dear. And the two mechanics are not happy. One of them, the big guy, he turns to his mate and says, "Well, we'd better call the police. Unless," he says, "unless there is some other way we could be paid." And the young one looks you up and down and says, "Yes. Yes, you know maybe there is." '

'Oh.'

'The two of them come closer and closer. You find yourself pressed back against the bonnet of your car.'

'Oh, no.'

'The big guy starts to stroke your neck. His oily hand smudging your skin.'

'Oh, no.'

'He moves behind you and starts to unzip your dress. He pulls your dress down, over your hips. It falls on to your shoes. Then he unhooks your bra. And then he tugs down your knickers. You're naked. They look you over.'

'Yes.'

'Taking their time.'

'Yes.'

'Then the younger guy moves even closer. Then he starts to stroke your breasts.'

'Yes.'

'His oily hands fondling your breasts.'

'Yes.'

'And the big guy behind you. You feel him through his dirty overalls, pressing against your arse.'

'Oh.'

'Then the big guy puts his big oily hands on your shoulders and pushes you, gently but firmly, down onto your knees.'

'Oh.'

'Imagine that. The two of them.'

'Oh, God, no.'

'The young guy standing in front of you.'

'Oh, God.'

'The big guy behind you.'

'No. No.'

'Imagine that.'

'Oh, no.'

'The two of them.'

'Oh, God, no . . . No . . . No . . . No . . .'

'Here. Let me take that.'

'. . . Ta.'

'How do you . . . Ah. Got it.'

We lie back on the cushions, exhausted. Though why I should be I can't quite say. Apart from age, I suppose. She's so still that I start to assume that she's fallen asleep, but then she gives her head a shake and pulls herself up. Finds her regulation white, waffle-patterned (White Company, I think) dressing gown behind the sofa. Shrugs it on and runs her hand through her hair. 'Water,' she says. 'We need water.' Not, I think, putting it on, she wanders off with a luxuriant, languorous swaying of the hips.

I prop myself up and look around the room. Many things to draw the eye. The shuttered floor-to-just-about-ceiling windows. The alcove filled with silver-framed photos and rows of of bulky, shiny hardbacks, mainly on art and interior design. The large and long creamy sofa behind me. Lucas & Grant, at a guess. Beneath the unbanistered stairs, a water feature – a genteel trickle wetting an arrangement of small flat stones, which I think I recognise from the Marylebone Conran. Going for a quasi-Japanesey effect. Or maybe a domestic homage to Andy Goldsworthy. Though I'd bet on quasi-Japanesey. And the object that's currently drawing my eye – the abstract on the wall facing the ornate fireplace. A great big splodge of red in the middle, surrounded by wee twiddly spirals, and not quite touching the band of dark purple at the base. A sizeable number, about four metres by three. The signature's a meaningless squiggle, but it could conceivably be that of a big name. Hodgkin, even.

So who is this woman who likes to be told stories and skimmed with a vibrator and who's just sashayed off to the kitchen? Who could paaawsibly live in a place like this? Let's look at the evidence. The big, creamy sofa. The free-standing stairs. The alcove of expensive books. The charming jeu d'esprit of the fountain. The possibly priceless painting. Yes, it does look like our mystery owner isn't short of a baab or two. And has no kiddywinkles.

'Here you are,' says Eunice, back from the kitchen and handing down a bottle of San Miguel, slithery from the ultra-effective, space-age fridge. She tightens the belt of her dressing gown and sits on the sofa above me. Crossing her legs with ironic propriety and pulling the dressing gown's crossed fold tight over her knees.

'I don't know why I haven't asked before. Who's the painting by?'

'Ah, now that would be telling.'

Mildly irritating, but only mildly. 'That's right,' I say, nodding.

She laughs.

Please, I say to myself. Please don't say, that's for me to know and you to find out. Because that's what Carol would say now. Probably with an arch, knowing look, all raised eyebrows and one of her tight, wee smiles.

'It's one of mine.'

'Really?'

'Yeah, really.'

'. . . Well.'

'And I can also tell you why you haven't asked before.'

'Why's that, then?'

'Because we haven't spent much time in this room, really. Have we?'

'No. Fair point.'

'And because you're not *that* interested.'

'I don't know about that.'

Eunice does another of her laughs, a big, delighted one that has her throwing her head back. 'That's right,' is all she offers by way of explanation so I just let it go and stroke my knuckle against her smooth, glistening shin, the colour of milky coffee. Like the blue-black hair, contrasting very pleasingly with the white of the waffle-patterned dressing gown. Which I will soon be unfolding again. Oh, yes.

By the way, contestants on this week's programme who assumed that the mystery owner was rich and kidless would be wrong on both counts, or not quite correct. As far as I can tell, Eunice has some, but not enormous amounts, of her own money but much of her upkeep and this two-storey flat, with its chic fixtures and view of the canal at Little Venice, are supplied by Michael, an Irish businessman and, until last year, her husband for two decades and half her life. Also father to their two boys. And those sons aren't falling off the stairs or soiling the sofa because they're both at college.

A woman who did the conventional thing early. And has done with it, as a result. The folds of the waffle-patterned dressing gown have somehow fallen to either side of her trim, brown thighs. I crawl towards her but she places a hand on my shoulder and pushes back.

'Not yet,' she says.

'Not yet?'

'Not yet. You see, first, I thought we might try something a little bit different. What do you think?'

'Oh, okay, then.'

8

RICHARD

I just hope it isn't anything serious. Something . . . bad. But no, no, of course it won't be, because obviously whatever it is is going to be, at worst, something on the level of seriousness of, for example, some minor gum thing. I'm fretting about nothing as per, and she's just on a run of bad luck, despite the fact that they look perfectly fine to me. Well, of course they would. Do.

A few chirrups on the monitor that turn two circles green, but then silence and more silence and no green in the circles whatsoever, so that's him probably falling asleep. I study the monitor for a little bit longer, then I pick up the remote control and flick through the channels. Two teenagers arguing in a rather dowdy kitchen. Cartoon blue telephone ringing and grinning. Young man in T-shirt and jeans pushing a wheelbarrow along a garden path. Three men in suits debating in a commentary box about, I'd imagine, football. Newsreader. So, nothing.

I switch off, discard the remote and root around the jumble on the coffeetable, discovering, in all honesty by complete accident, one of Ali's catalogues, and I don't have the will-power, I just can't stop myself, with the result that I really should be drooling like a maniac as I flick past page after page of beautiful, beautiful women, pink of cheek, bright of eye, pert of nose, shiny and tumbling of hair, smiling of mouth, and, it would appear, keen on sailing. Also on trips to the countryside with their angelic children. Quite happy too, now that I've arrived here at last, to be seen in their swimsuits and knickers and bras and nighties. I unfocus, trying to see Ali in them . . .

God, yes, Ali in that nightie, the short, black one . . . Because there was a time when she used to wear nighties like that. Well, she still does, I suppose, occasionally wear a nightie, though it's nowhere near as short as that one these days, but, more to the point, she has a way of wearing a nightie, when she does wear a nightie, that seems to turn the nightie into a winceyette jim-jam . . . Although it can't be easy for her either, can it? . . . And it's hardly surprising, after a *birth*, for goodness' sake . . .

Still . . . It can be a bit difficult. Well, of course it would be a bit difficult, at times, often, usually, so that even a catalogue of women in shirts and slacks can set off a nigh-on insupportable yearning . . . Although it's fine, really, of course it is . . . Certainly nothing like the sticky patch of 1999, which had the potential to be as per predicted by astrology, the four hoarse men of the apocalypse gathering around us as they had done before in 1996 when the end of the world really did seem nigh and the name in the chant of doom was Jimmy Morgan. Jimmy Morgan. Jimmy Morgan. Jimmy Morgan. Jimmy Morgan. And now I have to not think, not to think, about Jimmy Morgan, and anyway, yes, the main thing, the only thing, really, is that we survived Jimmy Morgan and his apocalypse, and as for the sticky patch of 99, well, that suddenly got better, didn't it? and things turned back to how they used to be, if not how they used to be when we first started to go out together, because you can't expect realistically the initial oomph to keep going, though having said that it does sometimes seem to me that the oomph for me is just the same as it ever was, or at any rate the sort of yearning that the oomph seems to have transwhatsited into, then at least to how they were before the sticky patch, at least at times . . . Transsomething . . . Yes, things most certainly did get better and dramatically too, kicking off with that out-of-the-blue rosy period when we conceived Bongle – transmuted? – a never-to-be-underestimated rosy period, which can easily be recaptured, with the merest tweak to the, what's the right word? Dynamic. However bad it can feel at times when everything is in danger of appearing to be a bad omen, a portent of disaster, even a late arrival back from a dental appointment. Because that's all it would take. Really. The merest tweak. Because, deep down, I know, Ali's still the same wide-eyed girl that she was back in Aylesbury, when she could make me feel so man-of-the-worldish at being able to show her some of the world, even tiny bits of it, beyond the little council semi she'd grown up in on the edge of town . . . Of course it's much healthier now that things are more . . . equal.

Ten to.

. . . No, no, no. She must have been held up on the Tube or something . . .

But there follows a moment of weakness and a surge of

tremorous panic, a hammering of the heart and a gasping for air and a dizzying of the head . . .

Stop it, I tell myself. Pull your socks up. Get a grip . . .

I breathe in and I breathe out. I breathe in and I breathe out. I breathe in and I breathe out. And then there's a bit more breathing before I manage to get up and go over to the stereo cabinet and put, yes, yes, the radio on . . . Phil Collins, the one about the hill, quite near the beginning, I think. Okay, okay. Or maybe it's Genesis. Or someone else. Anyway, excellent.

Good.

Okay.

So I go back to the sofa and, breathing in and breathing out, sit where I was before, only this time stretching my legs out above the jumble on the coffee-table, and there has to be no touching of any part of the jumble until the song ends, and if I haven't touched any bit of it, then I'll know for certain that it's going to be okay, that it's going to be all right, as I do know, deep down, because it has to, it will, of course, be. All right.

. . . The song ends. I lower my heels.

7.32 p.m., Wednesday 16 October

EWAN

Guy there on TV. Kenyan farmer. Documentary about cheetahs . . . Aye, so this Kenyan farmer guy, he goes up to a
cheetah that's been stalking his herd. He's armed with a stick.
So who's higher up the food chain, the cheetah or the human?
Without the stick, I'd say the cheetah. With the stick, a tense
stand-off, then the cheetah backs down . . . Aye, cheetahs.
Programme before that was about . . . science. Parallel universes, string theory. How string theory could even explain the
Big Bang, if that was caused by some collision between two of
the other dimensions. Sounds fair enough to me. And I don't
have a problem with parallel universes. In fact, think about it,
parallel universes seem an excellent idea. That there's another
universe where, for example, I discovered skunk much earlier.
Had never married Carol. Hadn't been so straight and hard-
working.

Jesus, all that striving . . . Mind you, it's not my fault. I was
a lower-middle-class provincial Proddie Scot. What was I
going to be? Laidback? Happy-go-lucky? A free spirit? No,

173

I was a striver. All those years. That's what I did. Strive. I got up in the morning and I strove.

So what a complete waste of time *that* was.

. . . And there was me at 30 just knowing that I knew it all. Still in the middle of the striving, and still reassuring myself that, yes, of course I was in love with Carol. Ignoring the twinges of doubt. Oh, yes, I knew it all at 30. And at 31, kneeling in front of Carol and beseeching her to marry me. Aye, right, *very* sensible. Please marry me, you dim, shallow bore with symmetrical features.

. . .To mistake the set of her eyes for intelligence. To be so slain by cheekbones and a slimline nose. To be so taken in by a pair of perfectly arched eyebrows . . .

How long did it take me to realise that I didn't actually, as it were, *like* Carol? Three years. That's how long it took me to see past her beauty. Three years. It would have taken a woman ten minutes. But no. Three years. Some of them implausibly happy, with me walking around, pleased as Punch that I was sharing not only oxygen space with this beautiful specimen but a bed . . . The sheer thrill of walking around Soho with Carol. Early Nineties . . . Well, some women are sensible like that. Because let's not forget that huge faction of axewomen who can't see anything beyond their own neuroses. Not that Carol was one of those. Oh, no. Carol couldn't see anything beyond her own wonderfulness. Carol's fully reciprocated love affair with herself. That just being one of the things about Carol. But, Christ, how certain was I, at the ripe old age of 31, that this had to be it, the thing that everyone banged on about.

Love, love, love. All you need is love. Pa pa pa pa pa. All

you need is love, love. Love is only need . . . Don't talk to me about love. What's love got to do with it?

Fucking *love*. One of the big four lies humans tell themselves. We are special. There is a God. Death is not the end. But the greatest of these is love. Because it is, of course, if you think about it calmly and clearly for a minute or two, total sanctimonious *garbage*. Up there with Santa and Heaven. All those virgins waiting in eternity for the youth wearing a waistcoat of bombs. The resurrected Jesus. I love you.

. . . Now where did that start from? . . . Nope . . .

Well, it's been a busy old day, so I think I deserve another smoke. After all that hard relaxing I've put in. All that lying on the beanbag, basking in the warmth of the afternoon sun.

In October, mind you. Nothing like the epic heat of this year's ridiculous, African summer, of course. But, still, the kind of bone-warming warmth I don't remember ever having felt in, and I'm quoting Grassy here, Chillyjockoland. Back in fashionable Falkirk, city of café-strewn boulevards and evening *passaggiati*, you'd be lucky to have one afternoon a year like that and there would always be *some*thing. A hint of cool in the breeze from the Forth. A couple of worrying clouds. Snow . . . In fact, I do have a very clear memory of trying to find something edible in a school dinner one day in June, and looking out the window to see a flurry of snow. It was snowing. In June . . . First summer in London, 86 it would be, I spent marvelling at the continuing heatwave. Second summer, second once-in-a-generation heatwave in a row. Summer of 88, another heatwave, and it finally clicked. This was just what summers were like down here. Couldn't believe it . . . Just one of the reasons for living in London and not the land of deep-fried sweeties . . .

A whole evening of nothing ahead . . . So. What shall I do now? Oh, I know. I'll skin up, as I believe the young people say, another spliff, ditto.

I reach around and gather in the ingredients . . .

Some time later, and I'm now at the stage of looking around for a box of matches . . . Ah. Here's one, trying to sneak in under the beanbag. A white slimline restaurant's box. I pick it up and squint at the logo. Sanderson. Ah. The pre-dinner drink, couple of months back, with the girl I met at the GE Club. Designer . . . Karen. Of course. Karen . . . Typical Schraeger joint but in a building that was civic-Fifties. The banal geometry of the courtyard. I felt like I was back at high school or in a parallel universe – hey. Weird – where I worked for the Sheffield Water Board . . . First date, so nothing doing. A third-date one-nighter, as it turned out. With her having some sort of a boyfriend and me not being bothered one way or the other . . . Mind you, that one night was a roaring success. That thing she did. Impressive. So everyone a winner there, then. Apart from the sort of boyfriend, I suppose. Though why would he ever know? Unless she told him because they were into that sort of thing. Now that's a thought . . .

I strike a match, the doorbell rings and I nearly fall off the beanbag.

I pick up and shake the match which has been merrily blazing away on the floor, heave myself upright and stagger off to let Grassy in.

'Well, hello there,' says Russell. So, not Grassy, then.

'How did you get in?' I ask. One hand on the door, the other on the door frame. Trying my best to look like an unimpressed bouncer.

'The ageing hippie,' he says. 'He was on the front step, discussing matters of state with a mousy party. And he very kindly let me in.'

'That's Grassy. As you may have guessed. The mousy one sounds like the Public Sector Spinster in the basement. Anyway, more to the point, why are you here?'

Russell plonks down his briefcase and a carrier bag and crosses his arms. A crappy impersonation of, perhaps, a cartoon battleaxe greeting her sozzled husband. He needs a rolling pin for a start. 'Well,' he says, 'that's just charm . . .'

'Wait a minute,' I say, light dawning. 'You've just had sex. You've come round to boast about some sad, sordid coupling.'

'Well, as chance would have it, I—'

'At work, it must have been. Yes, maybe with her that likes the chair. Coatwoman.'

'Well,' says Russ, arms still folded but looking up and off, as though thoughtfully, 'as it happens, I . . .'

'Jesus, Russ. This is sick, you know. Why not cut out the middle man and just admit that you want to shag me?'

'Right. Because that's what I really want to do. Deep down. How perceptive.'

'Mick tae ma Keith.'

'I'll do no such thing. Look, are you going to let me in or not?'

'Only on condition that there's not even a mention of Coatwoman.'

Russ puts in some vigorous nodding. 'Okay, right, well, that shouldn't be so difficult.'

'You are *so* predictable,' I tell him.

Russ sighs, gives me a push and barges past. The carrier bag clunking against my shin as he does so. He marches straight to the kitchen nook.

'What's this?' I ask. '*Seinfeld*?'

'Supplies, you twit,' Russell calls over his shoulder while he sorts out my fridge. Then for some reason, he takes out his precious weekly wrap and starts chopping out two thick lines on the kitchenette's counter. The one that's meant to come with bar stools. Like your breakfast is a cocktail. 'More supplies,' he explains, because I'm wearing a puzzled frown, and at a normal pitch because I've padded back to the beanbag.

Russell snorts one of the lines. Then he darts back to the fridge, fetches out a can of McEwan's, cracks it open and takes a big swig.

'Russ,' I say, from the beanbag. 'What the fuck?'

'Shoa,' says Russell, putting on a daftie's look and wagging his head like one of those wee dogs you used to see in the backs of cars. 'Alwaysh shmoaking the weed, ya? Deshtroing all the memmry shellsh.'

'What's that?'

'Dutch.'

'That was *Dutch*?'

'Moasht shirtinly.'

'Ooshah.'

'You really don't remember, do you?'

'Remember what?'

'Here's a clue.' Russell throws his arms wide. And starts to sing. 'We. Hate. Jimmy Hill,' he bawls, vaguely to the tune of that old British Airways ad. 'He's a poof. He's a poof. We. Hate. Jimmy Hill. He's a poof. He's . . . Argh!' Russell looks in horror at his watch. 'The telly!' he shouts, with his hands slapped to his cheeks. 'The telly! What's with the telly!'

'What do you mean, what's with—'

'It's. Not. On,' he growls in his horror-film-preview voice. 'Put. It. On.' Spotting the remote on the floor, he makes a lunge at it, then shoots it at the TV.

'Gary Neville,' says John Motson. 'Up to Beckham . . . Back to Neville.'

I peer at the little box in the right-hand corner of the screen. '3:48,' says the top set of figures. 0–0 the lower. And now it does occur to me that Russell did say he'd come round to watch the football. On Wednesday, though.

Well.

This must be Wednesday.

We arranged to watch the England game . . .

The full force of this fact hits me. I heave myself up off the beanbag again, which shows the seriousness of the situation here, and head for (1) the fridge and (2) a can of beer. The line I'm going to be cool about, because it's all too easy to be very uncoolly avaricious when it comes to lines. But one of the many things I have been taught during the invaluable learning experience of my new life is that cigarettes are a must with alcohol. I light a Marlboro and offer the pack to Russell. Who looks at me as though I've just lit a fart.

'What in the name of the living Jesus are you doing?'

'Go on,' I say, squinting as a thread of smoke nears my eyes. 'Take one. They shorten your life.'

Russell shakes his head. Tut-tutting rather than refusing. 'O tempora, o mores, oh dearie me,' he says as he lowers himself onto the beanbag. He gestures to the empty floor. 'Take a seat,' he says.

'Who's it they're playing?' I say, propping myself up against a wall.

'Fucking Jonathan fucking Woodgate. *Look* at him. Can't remember. One of those new wee places you've never heard of. Ranked a hundred and something. So this could be good. Unless the bastards win by a shedload, it'll be a national disaster. Hey. Could be *great*.'

'. . . I don't know, Russ,' I say, although I do. Because I have had a moment of clarity. I can do the opposite here as well. Not have the line. Not watch England beating whoever it is. Macedonia. And I'm feeling done in after another hard day. So I'm going to leave him to it. Turn down the volume, shove in the earplugs, have a wee kip. Have the line afterwards. Yes. Sleeping, not watching. Bed, not floor. 'We're too old for this, Russ,' I tell him. 'Look, I'm off for a—'

'Are you in*sane*?'

I come to the end of a yawn. 'No, Russ, it's just daft. After all, we've both lived down here all these years.'

'London isn't England. Like New York isn't America. Who is it always says that? Oh, that's right, I remember. You. Come on. Come *on*,' he says again, but to the TV this time. 'Clear it, you divot . . . Okay, safe . . . I mean, think of the alternative. Think of if they win. Twevah. Ah we good enough to win the Wuld Cup? Yes, Gawy. We ah. And do you know faw why? I will tell you faw why. Because we. Ah. Ingglish.' Russell does his Homer shudder. 'The slightest chance. They beat fucking Liechtenstein and it's Twevah, can we win the Wuld Cup? . . . Okay . . . Yes, corner. Right . . .'

'Nah, Russ. Put the sound down, I'm going next door for—'

'Oh, you beauty! Oh, you *beauty*!'

'Yes!' I shout, when I realise Macedonia have scored. 'Ya beauty! Hey, hey, ya English *bas*tard,' I shout at a disconsolate David Seaman. Or rather, at a tiny moving picture of a disconsolate David Seaman.

'Come *on*,' Russell growls. 'Whoever the fuck you are. Get fucking *intae* them.'

'Right, then,' I tell him. 'Let's get tore in.' After all these years, a tiny part of me still feeling a right wee daredevil as I dip my head down over the thick thread.

I sweep up the last of the line with the pad of my right index finger, rub it over my gums, then open another refreshing can of McEwan's.

Feeling very, very happy. High, indeed. High on alcohol, cocaine, the panel lamenting a more-than-catastrophic draw and grass. And the cigarettes.

Russell is standing in the middle of the room, his feet planted on the laminate floor like it's newly liberated land, his arms thrown wide. 'We. Hate. Jimmy Hill,' he sings. So I throw my arms up as well, skooshing a small fountain of beer at the ceiling.

'He's a poof,' we sing. 'He's a poof.'

'Is this the last of it?'

'Yip.'

'We've finished it?'

'Yip.'

'Jesus Christ, Russ, no wonder I'm just buzzing here. Buzz, buzz, buzz. Just buzzing away. Buzz, buzz, buzz.'

'Enough wid da buzzin. So. I've got to tell you about earlier. Coatwoman, right? So this time Coatwoman turned up at the surgery with—'

'No way, no way, no way. I'm not having it, Russ.'

'That's not what she said, believe you me, when she was—'

'Honestly, Russ. I really, really don't want to hear about it. Really.'

Russell shakes his head, more in sorrow than in anger. 'You are so hung up.'

Maybe I should do the opposite thing here, too—encourage Russell to tell me all about it . . . No. This is one of those south-of-the-river rules that should not be broken. 'Garbage, Russ. Just because I don't want to listen to your self-aggrandising carnal blethers does *not* make me hung-up.'

Russell shrugs. 'Your loss. Makes for a great story. So. How about dem Bears, huh?'

'Those aren't pill*ows*.'

'Classic. Here. I've just remembered. Fucking Jonathan fucking Woodgate.'

'Aye, true, good point and very well made but let's not forget fucking David fucking Beckham.'

'Fucking Gary fucking Neville.'

'Fucking Rio fucking Ferdinand.'

'Fucking Jimmy fucking Hill.'

'This could go on for some time, couldn't it?'

'Oh yes.'

9 (I)

RICHARD

For some reason that escapes me for the moment I can't stare, although I obviously want to do nothing but sit here on the edge of the bed and stare and keep staring until my eyeballs itch, at Ali, who is, and I'm really not joking or anything, fastening her *stockings*, smoothing them up her thighs and now stepping into her new dress, the one from Selfridges that cost, as per invoice, two limbs.

Now she smooths down her new dress and has another tug at the stockings, a tug that's of a piece with the certain absence of any ceremony or alluringness about this operation, which she's conducting with businesslike efficiency, clipping and adjusting and tightening, like a hit man fitting a silencer. Which is probably just as well – the lack-of-alluring-ceremony aspect, I mean – because I'm in enough of a state as it is, trying to act normal while coping with the pang of longing that feels like a hollow in my stomach and has come from a glimpse of Ali's thighs framed by the black lace of her new panties and the tight black of her stocking tops. The new dress smoothed, Ali gives me a baleful look, at least that's the kind of look I think baleful is meant to mean, and sighs.

'Anything the matter, darling?' I ask, because I'm quick to pick up on the signs these days because it is, let's be honest, a source of some worry, Ali being so out of sorts, so that I fret over the doubts and fears that have been gathering, to tell the truth, as the frequency and duration of the out-of-sortsness have risen a bit of late. Was it, I ask myself, a good idea to move here? Were a small garden and an extra bedroom and an extra storey worth losing the old flat for? Was it such a good idea for Ali to give up work completely, even if it's only for a year or so, not on economic grounds, though actually there are some of those, which help explain why we're living in Tottenham and not Muswell Hill or Crouch End? But those are questions I ask myself only after I've completely failed to give any convincing answers in the main section of the exam: what am I doing wrong or not doing right or not doing at all or doing but in the wrong way?

'Oh, just your ceaseless chatter. Your endless prittle-prattle. I hope you're not going to be like this all day.'

'Like what?' I say because I'm genuinely bemused and can't stop myself.

'All hopeless-looking. Doing your strong, silent act . . . Well, silent act.'

It feels like I've forgotten her birthday. But it's no wonder that she's a bit on edge. Because it is a big deal. 'God, I'm sorry, Ali, I didn't, I mean I really didn't realise . . . I was just . . . I'm sorry. Really.' I reach out and rest my fingers on her sheeny calf, but something tells me to modify the rest to a pat and then to remove the hand at the earliest possible.

She has another sigh. 'Just don't do your usual, okay?'

'No, of course not,' I say, with a firm headshake. 'Er, what usual would that be?'

'Your usual. Going all clingy on me like it's your first day at school and I'm your Mum. Looming. Hanging about. Remember, it's a wedding we're going to . . . A party . . . a wedding party.'

'Got you,' I say with forced cheer because Ali's suddenly got her skates on here and careered off on to the thin, flaky ice that is the issue of us being about to go to the Orangerie in Holland Park for Peter and Jocasta's wedding party, but, and here's the thing, not the wedding as such, because that happened a week ago at a top-secret venue (no press, no nobody apart from two roped-in locals and a reputedly sozzled vicar, and, most important of all and never to be referred to again, ever, no Ali) subsequently disclosed to have been a beach on the north-west coast of Scotland. 'Looming forbidden. No hanging about. Do not cling. Danger. Hazchem. May contain nuts.'

'What?'

'Anyway, I'll be i/c Jakie,' I say in a bit of a hurry. 'If you want to go off and mingle.'

'Okay . . . okay, maybe I'll do that. Mingle . . .' Ali shifts sideways to inspect her profile in the mirror. 'Christ,' she says, after she's put on her shoes, her pointy, black, high-heeled shoes, let me add, and had a check of her watch. 'Is that the time? When did you book the car for?'

'Twelve-fifteen. So we've still got lots of time.'

'Oh, God . . . Jakie all set?'

'Shipshape and Bristol fashion.' And indeed he is, all dressed up in the outfit purchased (by self, on a successful mission to the Marks in Oxford Street during a lunch hour and a half) especially for this occasion – smart new khaki chinos and a little blue shirt with a dancing teddy on the pocket and a button-down collar. Bongle the top executive on his day off, kitted out for his eighteen holes or a jaunt to the country in his Porsche, although I suppose for the impersonation to be complete he'd have to lose the teddy.

'Where *is* Jakie?' asks Ali, picking at molecules of fluff on her dress. 'I thought you had him.'

'No, I . . .' Thought he was in the en-suite with you, is the bit of the sentence I don't say, because I can't, not with the abrupt dryness of the mouth and the suddenly pitching stomach. 'I'll just . . .' I say by way of explanation as I head off, at a merely smartish pace, on the grounds that sprinting to his bedroom and then bounding down the stairs five at a time, which is of course what I'm desperate to do and desperately straining not to do, would only ensure disaster.

'Where's the Bongle boy?' I say in a cracked sing-song as I reach the sitting room and give it a frantic scan. 'Must be in the kitchen, then,' I tell the empty room, as though saying it will make it real, although, come to think of it, I'm none too sure that the kitchen is the best place for him to be.

He's not in the kitchen either.

Not in the hallway. Front door shut.

Back to the kitchen.

'Bongley? Jakey?'

Definitely not in the kitchen.

Definitely not in the hallway.

'Bongley? Jakey? Bonglebongle?'

And he's not in the sitting room.

So this is how it happens. So this bit now, me standing here in the sitting room, is the bit just before, when it's still, however appalling with the hammering of my heart, normal, with a carefree Ali upstairs and me yet to witness it, us yet to turn into those poor people you see on the news, at the obligatory press conference, flanked by police, in front of a hoarding with the logo of whichever constabulary is on the case, the mother breaking down in mid-appeal, the father staring with hollow eyes at the middle distance.

'Namanamanama.'

'Oh, *there* you are.' And there he is, in all his Bonglicious-ness, sitting beyond the end of the sofa, chewing an oversized plastic ladybird and watching the muted telly. With a bit of a creak, I sit down beside him and give his chubbular knees a squeeze. 'What's this, then? Is it *Balamory*? Is it *Balamory* on the telly?'

He's too entranced by the chewing and the viewing to reply but the answer is, yes. It is *Balamory* on the telly.

'Is that Josie Jump jumping?' I say. 'Look at Josie. Josie's jumping, isn't she?'

My arm around Bongle, snuggling up close, my nose in his yellow hair, we watch as Josie Jump skips down the road to see PC Plum. Past the pretty cottages she goes, jumping and skipping.

I close my eyes as they fill with tears, which streak my face and fall onto the right shoulder of Bongle's new shirt, so I jerk my head back and I take a deep breath through my nose and hold the air inside me for a long moment . . . And then I breathe out and slump.

11.51 a.m., Saturday 26 October

EWAN

This is me padding back to the beanbag. No socks. The icy floor. The hot cup of tea in my hands. The beanbag sinking around me. The sip of tea. The re-igniting of the joint. The shaft of morning sun. The slant of it. The cloud of smoke turning 2-D and blue in the geometrical slice of sunlight.

I pat my hands around in a blind search for the TV guide and hit a loose sheet of paper. Ah. It's with a rueful humph that I pick it up and scan it. Yes. I remember most of this. Top left, a series of sums estimating income. Top right, a doodle of intersecting circles. In the middle, a pen-and-ink of my raised right foot. And bottom right, my thoughts of the day, the ones which were so good I just had to write them down. There are, I see, two that made it into print. 'NB,' one tells me. 'Breakfast tapas.' Which successfully reminds me of last night's business brainwave – a café which offered platters of free food (wee biscuity nibbles, doll's cakes, miniature muffins, as I recall) and merely charged for the exorbitant coffee and the extortionate juice. Up there with the one about selling kettles to the

188

French. The other aperçu is twice underlined and surrounded by asterisks. 'Living things live only because they *can* live,' it says. 'There is no design.'

I crumple the paper up and throw it in the general direction of the bin. Let the maid clear it up. Five cigarettes left in the packet, so that'll mean a trip to the shops later. Get milk as well. Tea. Pasta. Bottle of wine. Rizlas. The trip to the shops meaning that there's one task for the day. And for the rest of the weekend, come to think of it. And, come to think of it a wee bittie more, for the four days until the midweek trek down to SE57 with Grassy . . . I'll spend the afternoon watching the results come in on Sky. Just like those childhood Saturdays when I'd be condemned by the inevitable downpour to playing patience on the carpet and gazing up at a horse race or motocross in the mud. Except that I'll make sure to enjoy it this time around.

I'm getting into a proper reverie about the old *Grandstand* teleprinter when the phone rings. My first instinct is still to answer it but then I remind myself to let the machine do the work.

'Hello. I'm not here at the moment.' Beep.

'Macintyre, you wanker, answer. Answer. Come on, get off the beanbag and answer the phone. Answer it. Come on. I know you're there. Where else would you be? Answer. Answer. Answer the phone. I know you're there. And I'm going to keep on talking until you answer or the machine runs out of tape. Come on. It's important. Really important. Genuinely important that you answer the phone. Answer the phone. Answer the phone. Answer. Answer. Answer the phone. Answer the phone. Answer it. Answer. Answer. Answer. Answer the phone.'

'Who is this?'

'See, I knew you were in. Where else would you be?'

'So what's this genuinely important news, Russell?'

'Oh, yeah, there's a party tonight. Coming?'

'No.'

'I knew you'd say that. Come on. Saturday night. Party. Glamorous party. Exciting party. And I haven't seen you for ages.'

'I saw you last week.'

'Like I say. So. Come on.'

'No. Absolutely not.'

'Come on.'

'You don't get it, do you? I'm not going.'

'Come *on*.'

'No.'

'We'll meet first. Spot of supper.'

'We won't.'

'Andrew Edmunds? I'll book.'

'Can I remind you that I am, in fact, a man?'

'Somewhere cool and good. Meet at seven-ish, go to party ten-ish, have brilliant time.'

'No. No. No. Okay? Now, I don't want to put the phone down on you, Russ, but I am going to go now because I've got a lot of genuinely important stuff to be getting on with.'

'But the—'

'Bye, Russ. I'll talk to you soon.'

'But—'

'Bye.'

9 (II)

10.14 p.m., Saturday 26 October

RICHARD

A quarter, or maybe it should be just quarter, past ten, so this is, truly, a disaster sleepytime-wise. Of course, the Bongley man has been awake at this time before, but always in his bed and almost always crying for the sleep that is being denied him by his crying. And I suppose there must have been quite a few times when he'd have been up and about at this hour in those frantic first few weeks, when all three of us were all over the place so that I'd arrive at work with scratchy eyes and brain full of gunge, sick with exhaustion and enblissed as I'd never felt enblissed before, and of course there have been a couple of times when, a cherub strolling through the Gorbals at night, he's been mugged by a virus, and his sleep's gone all over the shop, and a couple of times of those when vomiting was involved, although I've no immediate recollection of just when this vomiting of which I so blithely speak happened, but I have to suppose that they would nonetheless have somehow entailed him being up and awake as late as or later than this. Not that you'd think he was any the worse for it, to look at him, new blue shoes stamping on the floor as his legs and indeed his arms jump up and down, the Herr Professor having been too preoccupied by his equations and his theories to have figured out which limbs, precisely, are responsible for the jumping.

Seventeen minutes past ten, which means that we've been here for eight hours and, say, ten minutes, since we did arrive just that tiny bit late, the man from the minicab firm having a child seat in the back, yes, granted, but also a rather cavalier attitude to the A-B principle, and eventually coming to a halt, after yet another turn when I hoped and prayed that this would be the cunningly revealed short cut which would justify every bizarre twist in what seemed to be not so much a route as a foray in a general direction, in what turned out to be a cul-de-sac, and pulling out an awfully crumpled *A–Z*. At which point Ali took over. Although I think we both felt that I was somehow to blame. Call it eight hours. A third of a day. One-third of one of the eleven thousand, more or less, of those days left, illnesses, terrorist atrocities, and accidents permitting . . .

But they'll have to leave soon, surely, because I happen to know that the not quite newly-weds will be spending the night in an undisclosed, or at least undisclosed to me, country-house hotel in Oxfordshire, preparatory to their flight tomorrow afternoon, in first class, it should go without saying, to whatever the airport is where one alights for three weeks in the Seychelles and a hotel of a magnificence I didn't even, until I looked over Ali's shoulder at the glossy brochure, suspect existed, where the marbled space-age swimming pools, note the plural, were miraculously full to the brim and the rooms weren't rooms but separate villas, built in panels of something like teak and with sloping reed-thatched roofs – huts, I suppose you'd call them, if you'd call Blenheim Palace a detached house . . . yes, so Peter and Jowotsit will have to leave soon, and that's the important thing because I'm guessing that that'll be our cue to head home and get the Bonglemeister off to bedfordshire. Guesswork confirmed, I think, by Ali's increasing antsiness – checkings of the watch, fiddlings with the napkin, twiddlings of glassware and cutlery – as the evening wears on and the bride and groom are still here and showing no signs of imminence of departure, and Bongle's still up and running, with a long cab ride back to boot.

But although it's inconvenient and a bit worrying and, actually, to be candid, horrible, lingering on in this room, even though it brims with happiness and success, yes, full to the brim of, as the song says, happy smiley people, healthy and wealthy and, for all I know, wise, but certainly wealthy because this is, let's none of us forget, one of Peter's parties, and therefore full of adults and, on this occasion, children who are all intimidatingly much better off than me, it makes sense. Naturally, Ali wants us to stay on until such time as the bride and groom head off into the night, quite possibly in a car decorated with a Just Married poster, balloons, and maybe some clanking cans in tow. She wants, quite properly, when you think about it, to support her big brother on his big day, waving a rattle, wearing a scarf in his colours and shouting hurrahs from the touchline. And, no doubt, to show him that she's not holding any sort of a grudge about the absence of any invitation to the actual troth-plighting. So of course she's been a bit on the edgy side, what with one thing and another.

'Can you look after Jakie for a bit?' she asks, quite out of the blue. 'There's someone I should say hello to.'

Quite difficult not to feel just a touch miffed at this, even though I have obviously but secretly preferred it this way than any other, because I have been doing most of the Bongle police duty, Ali having been drawn into conversations on a pretty regular basis, and the person doing the animal noises and reading *Kipper and the Blue Balloon* for a not inconsiderable number of times having been, not, as I say, that I've minded but still, self. 'Of course,' I say, and I take hold of the Bongler and sit him astride my right thigh. 'To market, to market,' I sing, with accompanying bounceage. 'To buy a fine pig. Home again, home again, jiggety jig.'

I go through the standard repertoire. Several rounds of to-market-to-marketing, followed by a few *Grand Old Duke of Yorks*, then a couple of demonstrations as to how the farmer, lady and whathaveyou ride, and, subsequent to that, a song of my own spontaneous invention.

> 'He's a bongly bongly boy.
> A bingly bingly,
> Shmongly, shmingly,
> Bingly bongly boy.'

With, if I say so myself, rather a catchy tune, but it seems that the Herr Professor's ever-active mind requires new subjects to tackle and master, because he squirms off my lap and down into the land of head-high chairs and knees.

I follow suit, sitting down with him on the floor, armed with a colouring book and some crayons, it being one of the Bongle's hobbies and interests to take a crayon and swipe at the paper. The floor's rather cold and there's no way I can't be fretting about the lateness of the hour and the demands this is making on the Bonglemeister's stamina, but to tell the truth it's so much nicer down here on the floor, between the chairs, behind the white tablecloth, than up there in the world of the healthy-wealthy, happy-smiley people.

I was about to add that this is all as per par for the course, given that this is one of Peter's parties, but that would be, I've just realised, a little bit misleading, because the guest list isn't quite as scary as Peter's usual, there being a few fewer TV and City types swanning around than one might fear would be the case, and a sizeable supplement of Jowotsit's fairly unscary family from Dorset (in contrast to the groom, whose family consists of Ali, their Aunt Betty and a single, anonymous cousin, everyone else somewhere else or, including their parents, dead, Mr and Mrs Standman having died within one disastrous year, soon after I first met them, before their mid-sixties, not necessarily from doomed genes or from having met me but because they'd both enlisted for the poor bloody infantry in the war against death, the first to go over the top, the condemned battalion of working-class smokers), plus a sprinkling of voluble young people, presumably Jowotsit's pals. Yet notwithstanding the below-average scariness of the guests, this is not only a Peter party, of sorts, but also a wedding, and weddings have a way, in my experience, of blaring out the great news that here are two people who've found the solution and sorted everything out, in marked contrast to certain parties at the party who, to be honest about it, really haven't found the solution and have failed to sort everything out, which is, push comes to shove, why they're not officially married, and maybe why they're not some other things as well . . . Especially this wedding because Peter so obviously has sorted everything out, in a Peterianly comprehensive and resounding way. Yes, of course there's been a regular supply of who'd-have-thought-its in the general chit-chat up there, but of course Peter was going to get married, and of course to a dolly-bird and of course a bit later in the day than most, because of course he was going to enjoy a protracted glamorous bachelorhood full of champagne and dolly-birds.

Bongle scores the paper with a crayon that he holds like a dagger, leaving a brief dash of purple, and, perhaps given the lateness of the hour and the fretting I can plead mitigating circs or reduced whatsit, but, whatever the reason or excuse, I allow myself an unworthy thought, to wit, that there's something so relentless about, I don't know, the display of it all up there that there's also something about it which is, and I don't like using the word and I don't want to appear snobbish but I really can't think of any other way of putting it, just a bit . . . vulgar.

Bongle turns a page of his book with force and flourish and attacks it with the purple crayon ditto.

'A circle!' I say, assessing a curving slash. 'Look, you made a circle! Aren't you clever?' I reach over to give him a cuddle. 'Aren't you clever? Aren't you a clever boy?'

'No!' he shouts with enormous glee, I think in mock protest at the cuddle rather than at the accusation of cleverness, but whatever the Herr Professor's reasons and motivations, that's him off on all fours, and now being chased by the Cuddle Monster, who's relentless in pursuit, even when Bongle decides to go for hyperdrive, pulling himself upright and tottering off at top speed for a mighty journey, fortunately round the perimeter of the room and nowhere near the dance floor, and the Cuddle Monster is in close attendance and every-thing's going swimmingly, Bongle chuckling, Cuddle Monster apparently in control of the whole situation, when, all of a sudden and for no apparent reason, Bongle trips and falls, in a way that's both slow and unpreventable, headlong, towards a pillar, his arms straight at his sides, his body stretched out for an instant, which I actually, to my utter shame, register as being just like a man in a white Lycra jumpsuit and a sleek, space-age-visored helmet shooting off the end of a ski jump. And then there's the next instant when his soft, new brow slams into the brick.

Not daring to examine the damage, I pick him up and hold him tight. He shudders then starts to howl into my shoulder. So he's conscious at least. 'Oh, little one,' I whisper, trying, without complete success, not to cry myself. 'Oh, little one, my little one, my little boy, my poor, poor, little boy, my darling, my little darling, my sweetheart, my darling . . .'

I carry him back to the bit of our table where we've made our family encampment. Ali's back, thank goodness, so I hand Bongle over and give her the newsflash about the pillar. She clasps him to her. After a while, when the howling is abating, she strokes his hair back from his forehead to reveal not an obscene bursting of flesh and blood but a small pink blotch, unspecifiably different in quality to the general pink blotchi-ness of the entire facecular region that comes with a defcon-three trauma.

'I just couldn't stop him,' I explain, hurriedly, as though guilty, which of course I am. 'He was fine and then he just tripped and right into this terrible pillar. God, it was . . .'

'It's okay,' she says, with a smile, a gentle smile, one of her gentle, heartbreaking smiles which, I realise with a lurch of sorrow, I haven't seen for a while. A long while. She cups Bongle's Teletubby bottom with one hand, strokes his feathery yellow hair with the other. 'He's fine.' Ali strokes his hair and his face, her long slender fingers stroking his face. 'Are you all right?'

'Me? Fine, I'm fine.'

'Good.'

Only towards the long process of getting Bongle to the stage where he can be distracted, in this instance by the melodramatic appearance from the changing bag of the squeaky frog, does it dawn on me what's been going on. Tummy trouble. Or, of course, period.

'You're back on the champagne, I see,' I say, risking the tease because it doesn't seem like a risk at all.

'I was bored.' She takes a tiny sip then puts her half-full glass down. 'We should go.' Ali puts Bongle back down on to his feet. He jumps up and down and laughs. Because he is SuperBongle, possessed of miraculous, mighty powers of recovery. 'What do you think?'

'What do . . .? Well, yes, I suppose we should go.'

'Let's order a black cab. So he can stay in the buggy.'

'Wrap him up nice and warm with the blanket over him.'

'And with any luck he'd fall asleep on the journey.'

'Give him a bottle of warm milk when we get home if he wakes up.'

'And if he doesn't, we'll just carry him straight to bed.'

'Yes.'

I reach for Ali's hand. Bongle buries his head in her legs. I stroke his hair.

And there we are. Together. As it should be. The three of us. Like the three bears.

10.14 p.m., Saturday 26 October

EWAN

'I was given to understand,' I say, smiling politely, 'that what I was being taken to was a glamorous and groovy party.'

'Not groovy, my friend. I'd never say groovy. Glamorous, okay, cool, very possibly, but not groovy.'

'No, I don't suppose groovy is the right word for this. Pointless. Rubbish. Shite. Those are more the kind of words that spring to mind. I mean, for Christ's sakes, Russ, take a look. What the hell are we doing here? It's like a . . . I don't know, a *wedding* or something.'

'Spot on, my fine young fellow. It *is* a wedding.'

'Oh, super. Weddings, they're just great. Such fun. So who do you know that's invited you to this happy event?'

'Well, I wasn't invited. Not as such. Not in the sense that I got a stiffie. Or at least' – Russ pauses to prolong my cringe – 'not *that* kind.'

'I see. We've come all the way to an oversized greenhouse in Holland Park to gatecrash a wedding reception. That makes sense . . . Russ, do you actually know anyone here or is doing the barn dance at strangers' nuptials just one of the things you do of a weekend in your lonely, tragic life?'

'My sweet young friend. So trusting. Yet so naive. As it happens, I *do* know the groom, yes. Pete. Mate of mine. Over there.'

'Where?'

'There.'

'Wait a minute. That guy over there?'

'Yeah, him.'

'Pete, you said?'

'Oh, this is very good progress, Mr Macintrye. You're doing awfully well.'

'I know him.'

'No, *I* know him. And you know me. That's why you've been not invited.'

'Yes, but . . . Pete? . . . Have I met him at your place or something?'

'. . . Don't think so.'

'Somewhere, then . . . Hold on. The girl he's with.'

'Bride, I think is the technical term.'

'The boat. The party with the boat. The house near the river full of wankers. That's it. The amazing girl.'

'You mean at Pete's place? Did I ever take you there?'

'No, I've got the gift of second sight and use it to only trivial effect. Yes. Of course you took me to that party. Six, seven months ago. The boat, remember? That's where I got off with Eunice. Or didn't get off with but first met.'

'Really? At Pete's?'

'Yeah. Definitely.'

'Oh, yeah, that's right, I did take you. The boat trip . . . Who's Eunice?'

'Eunice. I've told you about Eunice. Dirty Divorced Woman.'

'Dirty Divorced Woman is called *Eunice?*'

'Aye. Eunice.'

'Eunice. Bloody hell, no wonder you've kept that quiet. *Eunice.* Whoaboy.'

'I've just realised.'

'What?'

'Why we're here. Why you've dragged me halfway across London. I mean literally. Halfway across London. That's why.'

'What's why?'

'You're meeting up with that woman. Coatwoman.'

'Yes, I suppose she might be here, now you come to mention it, but only if the invites were extended to hangers-on like the groom's sister.'

'Christ, and maybe Eunice'll be here as well. Russell, you're a genius.'

'Quite so. Hey – Dirty Divorced Woman and Coatwoman in the same room. Just think of the possibilities.'

'Aye, that's exactly what I've always wanted, Russ. A foursome with you. Anyway, I can't see her yet. Eunice, I mean. Maybe not invited. So where's Coatwoman?'

'Dunno. Haven't seen . . . oh, there she is.'

'Where? You have to point or something.'

'Yeah, very discreet. Pointing. There, at the long table. Blonde hair, black dress.'

'God, so that's her?'

'That's her.'

'Her who turned up at the surgery wearing just a coat and a smile?'

'That's the one.'

'The one you took up the Orinoco?'

'The very same.'

'Good Lord . . . Aye, but where's the hubby? He's bound to be here somewhere.'

'Guy opposite her, maybe. I couldn't tell you. Unless he's wearing a name tag or he's got two little horns coming out of his head. Having said that, I couldn't tell you his name either.'

'Well, aren't you just daft as a fucking brush?'

'How so, my fine young fellow?'

'Well, what the hell are you doing here, when she'll be with the man with the wee horns? Hoping for a secret quickie behind the cake, are you?'

'I didn't know he was going to be here, okay?'

'Oh, brilliant.'

'Says the man who once earned a whopping five Highers, two of them at B and a plucky C in Chemistry, in magnificent contrast to my own poor, meagre total of six straight As.'

'Aye, no bad fur a darkie.'

'. . . I'm sorry?'

'Joke. Obviously.'

'Right.'

I have that sinking feeling. 'Aw, Jesus, Russ,' I say, 'don't go all PC on me.'

Russell takes his time, then he sighs. 'You're off your face, aren't you?'

'Not at all,' I tell him.

'The wine, the beers. And let's not forget the fearful amount of weed that's turning your brain into mush.' Russell shakes his head. 'Fackin ell,' he says, so it's obviously abating, whatever pissy little outrage it was, and high time too. 'Why don't you go roll yourself a big fat one and take a little walk? I'll meet you back here in a wee while, okay?'

'Eh? You mean you really *are* going for a quickie behind the cake?'

'We'll see.'

'Jesus. Okay, Russ, off you go.'

'Wish me luck.'

'Half an hour, *max*.'

'Oakily doakily.' Russell doing his Ned Flanders, confirming that he's back to normal. He goes off, taking a detour round the dance floor, which is surprisingly full of waltzing couples, some of them, much more surprisingly, under pensionable age. I put on a vague smile and try to look as though I've got a perfect right to take this glass of champagne from the platter proffered by a tiny Filipina in a white jacket.

So I wander round for a bit, vaguely looking about for Eunice. Maybe I really should roll myself another joint and go for a little alfresco stroll . . . I'm toying with this notion when a moon-faced infant staggers by, trips, nuts a pillar and falls on its face, like it's been shot by a marksman. A glancing biff knocks my arm, spilling most of my drink. Courtesy of the bloke who's marching towards the shot child. Arriving just in time for the howling to start.

Well, what the fuck, the drink's free. I make a detour towards the nearest Filipina. I'm still on the lookout for Eunice, although something tells me she's not here. Possibly something to do with the fact that I've scanned the entire room by now and haven't seen her.

Which means that this really is pointless. Fucking Russell. His idea of an excellent Saturday night. Absolutely. Yes. For him. With me in tow to keep him company in case he doesn't score with Coatwoman. Or, knowing Russell's little predilection, in case he does. Christ. This has got to stop.

I'll finish this champagne, I decide, and then skedaddle out of here, leave Russ to it. Cab it back to Dalston and a nice, relaxing joint. It's a cheering thought so I walk around for a while, beginning to enjoy the fraud of being here and thanking the Lord that I'm not one of this lot.

'Nothing doing,' Russell says, leaning towards my ear.

I sway away. 'Oh, I'm sorry to hear that. What went wrong?'

Russell shakes his head. 'Wasn't on. So we had a chat. And the tiniest little snog. Like *that*'s what I need. A kiss. Like I'm *twelve*.'

'A chat, eh? A chat? Well, well. This must be getting serious. You'll be getting engaged next.'

'Oh, settle down.'

'Exactly,' I say. 'Are you?'

'Am I what?'

'Going to settle down with Coatwoman?'

'Ewan, Ewan, my sweet, sweet, naive, young friend. No chance. And no danger. No, I'm just the buck nigger she has the affair with. I die in the first reel.'

'Christ,' I say, forcing the scorn because this is good news. An encoupled Russ, that really would be no good to me. 'The Mandingo Man. Never allowed in the Big House with the white folks. Dearie me. With your Armani suits and your practice in Devonshire Place.'

'No, it's a fact. She's not after moving in with me. Just away from him. Nothing to do with me. She's just one poor bored housewife.'

'You're completely blameless. How convenient.'

'And true. No, she's been dithering about getting the hell out for ages.'

'Christ. Either you want to leave and you do or you don't and you don't.'

'Oh, how wise, how true. What about you, then?'

'What about me?'

'You're the one who banged on and on, and for *years*, about how you wanted out of your marriage. But it was Carol who decided it, wasn't it? You just sat on your big bahoochie doing nothing about it but moan.'

'Aye, but there was the loft and everything. I wasn't going to make myself destitute and homeless, was I?'

Russell does his smoothie's raise of his right eyebrow. Annoyingly. 'Evidently not. So you had your loft, she has her kid. And she has other stuff to sort out. House, money, that. And she was about to scarper a couple of years back but then she got pregnant, thus relocating the goalposts a tad.'

'I don't see how.'

'Do you know why that is? I'll tell you. It's because you are, fundamentally, dim.'

'Oh, that's right. Of course.'

Russell sips his champagne. 'And the kid turned out to be a right Prince Harry.'

I do my own smoothie-eyebrow move. 'She sounds like a very, ah, friendly sort of a girl,' I point out.

'Or maybe she just got unlucky.'

'Ooh ooh ooh. Jealousee.'

'No, I'm not bothered one way or the other. And like I say, that's the way she wants it as well.'

I picture Russ in the middle of the Sahara, shooing people south. 'Good,' I say. 'You've got it all sorted, then.'

'Yip. I be cool. Now let's get the hell out of here. Unless you want to hang around.'

'Oh, that's right, Russ. That's what I want to do. Because I'm having such a good time.'

'Sorry, old friend, but needs must. What's the time? Right. I know a great place to go.'

'A sewing bee? Church?'

'Trust me, I'm a dentist. Come on, drink up.'

I do just that. We head off, Russell not breaking his stride as he picks up a glass from a Filipina's tray, downs it in one and hands it to the Filipina operating the door. My own exit is a bit less decisive. I weave past knots of people, feeling distinctly heavy-legged and incompetent. It occurs to me that I might be slightly more stoned than I thought.

As though to confirm this, I reach the cold, fresh outdoors and miss a step, my right foot jarring like a bad surprise.

'We're best going up to Holland Park Avenue,' says Russ, ignoring me, not out of politeness.

'Why not over there?'

'You dare question the King of Cabs?'

'No. No, I don't. Forgive me.'

'Again.'

We trudge – or rather, Russell marches and I follow, trudging – up to Holland Park Avenue, where, of course, a cab is approaching, yellow light like the wee barrel of brandy dangling from the neck of a St Bernard's.

'Where are we going?' I think to ask after a mile or two.

'This very cool place I know with a late licence. Christ, this country. If we were in Edinburgh, we'd be sorted until breakfast. And *for* breakfast. And after that as well. Right the way through the whole—'

'I am getting the drift, you know.' I look out and see the Albert Bridge. 'For fucksake. We're crossing the river. No way, Russ.'

'Jesus, your London,' says Russ, rather more volubly than I'd have expected. 'Three pages of the *A–Z*. You move a block east of Islington and you think you're the last of the great explorers.'

'No. All I'm saying is that this is now SOR. Nothing good can happen here.'

'And you know what you're talking about because you own a piece of it, don't you?'

'Exactly,' I say, ignoring the sarcasm. 'So which bit of England's Glasgow are we going to get mugged in tonight?'

'South London isn't England's Glasgow. *Birmingham* is England's Glasgow. Also Liverpool, Manchester, Leeds, Sheffield, Leicester, Coventry, the entire Midlands in fact, plus most of Lancashire and Yorkshire, that whole bit of England the English don't like to think about too much, that small patch the width of the country and the length of the M6, a huge tract of the country completely covered in tarmac and concrete and—'

'You've just had a line, haven't you, Russ?'

'One moderate, medicinal one, yes.'

'So that was your supposed chat with Coatwoman. You wanted to have sex crammed together in the shunkie, and when that didn't work and she'd gone back to the hubby, you thought, oh, well, might as well make use of the shunkie.'

'. . . No.'

'Christ, and you go on about me and *my* drug problem.'

The taxi rattles on, and on, and on. I look out at an interminable series of grim shops and terrible council flats with brick balconies for the local snipers. I let Russell do the talking. And after a while I begin to wonder if there was a part of my life when I wasn't slumped in this taxi, rattling through south London . . .

Eventually, the long trek ends. We pull up outside a nailbar and what a broken and filthy sign claims is the 'Lewisham 21st Century Auto Coin Laundrette'.

'Lewisham?' I say after I've clambered out of the cab. With only a small mishap near the spare seat. 'Lewisham?'

'This way.'

Russell walks off towards the nailbar, where he waits for me to catch up, what with me having a little trouble walking and all. Then he nips down what I soon find out is an unlit, narrow and crumbly flight of stairs that lead to a door. It opens, as though by magic, and releases a thudding racket, low and loud. A large, I'm guessing Jamaican, bloke nods us in. I follow Russell down a rank hallway partly painted, perhaps by a child, in bright orange, towards a steel door. I can feel my feet vibrating. Also my sternum.

Russell pushes the door open.

My first thought is that this has got to be dangerous. Surely the human frame was not built to withstand such a violent impact of noise? Jesus Christ, it's not just my ears, it's my internal organs that are in trouble here.

I take two deep breaths and follow Russell into the loudness. And, now that I've gathered my wits to peer into the smoky murk, a jam-packed room. Half the size of the loft's roof terrace, if that, but there must be thirty or forty people in here. Most of them men. All of them black.

I beckon Russell towards me. 'JESUS CHRIST,' I yell into his ear. 'I ACCEPT THAT YOU COULD FORGET THIS BECAUSE I'M INCREDIBLY COOL BUT I AM ACTU-ALLY WHITE.'

Russell smiles and shakes his head.

'I FEEL A BIT CONSPICUOUS,' I explain.

'EXCELLENT IDEA,' he shouts. 'I'LL HAVE A GUIN-NESS.'

I give up and head towards a counter which seems to be the bar.

Some considerable time later, after a lot of sidling, then a good deal of elaborate dumbshow with the man at the counter, I sidle back to Russell, carrying two cans of Guinness with plastic glasses for hats. Russell looks, I realise, pleasingly ill at ease in his suit. Only now do I think to wonder just why he's here. And brought me here. Well, what the hell. What I think is this. Life, you see, is a journey. This is just the bit where I get stuck behind a tractor.

There's a small commotion in the far corner. Caused, it turns out, by a guy lurching towards a stage. A stage that's so tiny there's barely room for the two enormous speakers and one microphone stand. The guy stumbles. He's stick-thin, shaven-skulled, uselessly tall. And, I'd bet, a major abuser of a major substance. He staggers to the stand and grasps it as a drowning man would grasp an offered branch. Then he leans down and rests his lips on the mike.

'Mowgli in da jungle,' he chants in a deep, hoarse monotone that's half a whisper, half a shout. 'Smoakin marijuana.' He takes his mouth away from the mike, turns his head, nods. Coming back in time for the beat. 'Baloo in da jungle,' he chants. 'Smoakin marijuana . . .'

Russell leans towards me, his mouth almost touching my ear in that distinctly unpleasant way of his. 'HEY,' he shouts. 'HE'S SINGING YOUR SONG.'

'Akela in da jungle. Smoakin marijuana. Bagheera in da jungle. Smoakin marijuana. Lion King in da jungle. Smoakin marijuana . . . PocaHONtas in da jungle smoakin marijuana wit TIGga in da jungle smoakin marijuana . . .'

Shoom? Yip, went there. Trade? Yes, tick the box. Reykjavik? Tick. Ibiza, early doors? Yes, early Nineties, so tick. But I have no idea if this guy is the local nutter or bawling a chant like this is the thing to do here of a Saturday night. No clue from the crowd, who are all too busy smiting or looming or jostling or yelling into each other's ears to pay him much notice. Maybe this kind of thing has records in the charts and programmes about it on the telly, its own celebrities and magazines and radio stations, and I haven't registered any of it because I'm losing my grip . . . Oh, well.

'Winnie da POOH in da jungle smoakin marijuana an PIGlet in da jungle smoakin marijuana Bab da BUILda in da jungle smoakin marijuana Bill an BEN in da jungle smoakin marijuana . . . Andy PANdy in da jungle smoakin marijuana Looby LOO in da jungle smoakin marijuana . . .'

Despite the thumping racket, I find myself drifting off into one of my favourite new reveries – the one about how things might have been different if I'd somehow been a completely different sort of young person and got into drugs earlier on. Because say what you like about drugs, but they are terrific. Ecstasy – tried that last week. Got one from Grassy. Didn't do it with Grassy, obviously. No, on my own, in the flatlet. Marvellous, it was too . . . Why didn't I discover Ecstasy when it was MDMA? Why didn't I spend the Summer of Love jogging on the spot in fields by the M25 with blissed-out girls? Because I was too busy trying to get noticed at Paxton Gallagher Pieface, fizzing with ambition and self-delight.

'SPAT in da jungle SMOAKin marijuana Peeta RABbit in da jungle SMOAKin marijuana an tree BEARS in da jungle SMOAKin marijuana GoldiLACKS in da jungle SMOAKin marijuana wit NODdy in da jungle SMOAKin marijuana . . .'

Russell gives me a nudge. He jabs his index finger at the stage then taps it on his forehead and twirls it around. Then he lifts his head to acknowledge someone. I look over my shoulder. It's a woman in a spangly blue dress. A strikingly almost-beautiful black woman in a very short spangly cocktail dress. Maybe about thirty. Fit, good legs . . . She looks familiar . . .

'JESUS,' I yell. 'YOU TART. BUT WHY DID YOU HAVE TO DRAG ME ALL THE WAY DOWN HERE AS WELL?'

Russell frowns and puts his hands by his ears.

'I'll tell you why you dragged me down here with you. Exactly the same reason as you dragged me all the way over to

Holland bloody Park. You're showing off again, aren't you? It's because you've bucked the penis stereotype, isn't it?'

Russell smiles and shakes his head, places his fingertips to his ears.

The important thing now, I realise, is not to dwell on the sheer pointless waste of this Saturday night. And not even the hint of a line. And him sneaking one. Even by Russell's standards, this has been a remarkable performance. I'm going to have to get my own back for this one. 'Well, good luck, Russ,' I say. 'She looks great.' I have seen her before . . . The waitress. She's the waitress from the goat-curry emporium. Well, at least that confirms that he really isn't getting serious about Coatwoman. 'But if you don't mind.' I poke myself in the chest then jerk my thumb thataway. I give an annoyingly smug-looking Russell – not concerned, far less guilty, just smug – a flappy mock wave goodbye then start to sidle through the throng back to the orange hallway. And the crumbly stairs. And the sudden ringing silence and the cold night air.

I look around this empty, dull street. Litter lifting in the cold breeze. A bus stop. A bus-stop queue of people I have never laid eyes on before and will never see again.

I light a cigarette before I set off. You're never alone with a Marlboro Lite.

Part Three

10

9.58 a.m., Monday 24 March

RICHARD

I'm late. I'm late. For a very important date. Well, not exactly, because I'm not late, I think, and certainly hope, and the last very important date I had, or date of any sort, regardless of the importance issue, was with Ali, of course, and we'd be spooling back the years to find the most recent date we had. Not that we don't go out, although actually we don't go out at the moment very much, or, I suppose, at all, what with us being parents and so on and so forth, but we used to go out, used to do nothing *but* go out, especially in the old days, before we started to live together, because seeing someone in the evening for the cinema or something can't really count as a date, if you and the someone are going to go home together after the cinema, can it? Or not?

Hmm.

Spool back the years, back to the era of the bedsit in Battersea and Ali commuting down from Aylesbury for the weekend, before, of course, that era went pear-shaped in the ghastliest possible way, though not to be thinking about that . . . Where . . .? Yes, spool back to that era when we'd always have dates, out at one of the big Americany cinemas, in Leicester Square maybe, because we used to like going into town, into London as I used to think of it, since Battersea really didn't seem to belong to London or at any rate London as I knew it from family-treat trips, of a Friday or Saturday night, then back to the small and crumbling pad in Orbel Street, rechristened by us as Horrible Street, and with some justification too – one of the many examples of the kind of bantering patter that Ali and I used to have, and still have, of course, though perhaps with less opportunity, probably because of our lives expanding to take in the emotional enormousness of the family unit increasing in size and number by fifty per cent, or maybe that should be thirty-three and a third, because that was one of the real bases for the relationship really, that kind of bantering together being one of those things that do so much to turn two people who fancy each other into a proper couple. Plus Ali was so good at it, so funny, and still is or can be, that it'd get me in my innards, the surge of love for her giving me a real, physical biff, so that it was a wonder I couldn't see any evidence of it, as I later could observe her tight, round, basketball belly biffed from within and, on one memorable occasion, clearly see, when she pulled up her stretched-taut T-shirt, tiny little bumps that looked very much like bumps made by a teensy little fist. Yes, that I do remember. Well, sort of. As clear as any memory can be.

Anyway. I'm late. I'm late. For a very important date. Because it's the rhythm that's the important thing. Anything to keep the legs going until the next hold-up or this uphill bit ends, whichever comes first.

. . . What will the boy they call the Bongle boy be doing at this very moment? Up to his usual japes and scrapes, I'll be bound, romping around the place and jumping up and d—

Goodness.

. . . I mean, really.

. . . Blimming hell.

Because that's all it takes. A chap opening the driver's door without looking, or even with looking but not seeing, because of a blind spot or an intervening object, me, and my front wheel slamming into the door and me being catapulted into the sky. Luckily for me, my legendarily quick reflexes, together with a state of awareness rigorously maintained on high alert, meant that I had enough time to react and remember that I had enough space to swerve out of harm's way, but twenty yards further along, past Kingsland or the Kingsland Road's next traffic light, where I'd have been picking up the pace downhill, and who knows what might have happened? Not that I can afford to dwell on any of that because I have to keep concentrating.

The lights are at red, so I begin to sneak up the inside of the traffic, pushing off the pavement where a lorry is blocking off all but the tiny alley of the gutter, then, towards the front of the queue now, walking the bike forward, an ungainly business that has me shuffling in a stiff-legged fashion, like an ageing robot, squeezing alongside a behemothic artic. And now, with my legs propped astride the spar, just off the saddle, waiting at the front of the queue for the lights to change, I see in my head a clear, focused snapshot of the chap getting out of his car, an old Volvo, the chap old and thin, dressed for a day at the beach, with a red bandanna, a frayed T-shirt, flip-flops, oblivious to my swerve. Oblivious because, it only now occurs to me, he was quite obviously drunk. Or something.

An incident that can only confirm the apparent lunacy of this cycling, but it has to be said that, on the other hand, there are times when it's fine and some of those times when it's not only fine but wonderful, times of soaring exhilaration and triumph. Zooming along past all the cars stopped at a red light. Zooming along past all the cars stopped at a green light. And it's cheap. And the rustbucket's in the garage with the big end gone and a massive bill I can't pay looming, I get nervous on the Tube, and the buses are acceptable if you have four hours to spare. Most important last, it's all part of the new regime, you see – the new regime of the fitter, leaner, and, yes, better me, a me who has not only taken the fitness whatsit by the whatsits but also rolled up his sleeves, put his bottom into gear and generally got going to face the going that's got tough, because push comes to shove, that's what's happened to the going, it's got tough, or if not tough as such then at least a bit on the sticky side, as sticky as they've ever been at *Bricks and Brickmen*, stickier even, what with *Construction Now* and the redesigned redesign designed to keep *B&B* as the nation's pre-eminent domestic-construction-related title, and the annual-appraisal season upon us, so that it befalls to self to put in the hours because there are times in life when you just have to buckle down and this is one of those.

Ali's been a brick, of course, though having said that, matters domestic haven't been quite as serene and joyful as in an ideal world they might have been, Ali being a bit down in the dumps at the moment and with a tendency to employ the Reply Curt and the Observation Sardonic, completely understandably, of course, her being stuck at home all day with the Bongle boy for company, although to be honest being stuck at home all day with the Bongle boy seems to me to be a rather wonderful prospect, but then I don't have to do it day after day, although doing it day after day, larking about with the Bongle boy rather than being stuck in a boring old office, does also seem a rather wonderful prospect, but then I . . . oh, well.

So, yes, I'm two weeks into this new regime. That's to say, this is the start of the regime's third week. Two whole weeks I've already done of cycling into work. Not whole weeks, of course, but every workday. Apart from one day last week, Tuesday I think, or maybe it was Wednesday, when there was the monsoon and I steeled myself to take the Tube. And Friday, the day of the worrying poo and the even more worrying listlessness at breakfast, which did turn out in the end to have been probably caused by an earlyish start, likewise the poo which only smelled malevolent, the day of the eventual mad dash to work *in a taxi*, yes, a taxi, and a taxi which headed straight for the gridlock at King's Cross and sat there perfectly contentedly for several months. But every day apart from that.

Not that I've had a health scare or anything, although it did really take me aback at first just how taxing it was to get up a hill, because the last time I went up a hill on a bike I was wearing Dunlop Greenflashes and taking Wendover Hill (542 ft) in one heroic go, reaching the summit a little out of puff and a bit achy about the legs but still able to dismount, ramble about and admire the scenery, whereas now I wouldn't be halfway up before I'd be struggling to press 9 three times on my mobile. Something I hadn't quite appreciated until I started this malarkey. So the whole bicycle experience is completely different – actively painful in an entirely unexpected and partly disturbing way, and when not painful, as has just been so efficiently demonstrated, terrifying in an expected but a disturbing way with knobs on. Also, you didn't wear helmets. And you didn't have these mountainbikey bikes, you had proper bikes, racers, with drop handlebars.

A good twenty often hair-raising minutes of apparently normal pedalling which still seems to have constituted a stern cardiovascular workout later, I make it to the office, at 10.17 (seventeen minutes past the notional beginning of the working day but early for *Bricks and Brickmen*, where things can be properly said to have got going usually round about eleven, Bob permitting), dismounting with a flourish, swinging the right leg round and over the saddle with my left foot still on the pedal – a manouevre which makes me wonder for a moment why I'm about to go into a grown-up office and not a chum's house or a Scout hut or a tennis club. But I persevere, removing my ghastlily purploid helmet and my snappy cycle clips with the speed of a guilty man, then taking off my anorak and stuffing it into my holdall, to reveal – ta-ra – the besuited executive all set for a hard day's top-level grind.

'Mor*ning*,' says Callum in reception in a noticeably meaningful manner for no reason whatsoever.

'*Good* morning,' says a friendly girl in the lift, a rather beautiful girl in the tradition of the Timotei advert, with conspicuously brushed blonde hair hanging down her back, and, rather continuing the Timotei-ish theme, wearing an apple-green dress that's too short and too flimsy by half, revealing not only the kneecapulae reversums, but the lengths of slim thighs some distance above them, and I have to remind myself that I'm not at the tennis club but in a lift at work and looking at the reflection in the mirrors that are the lift's walls of an incomprehensibly middle-aged man, avuncular at best, so I just nod and smile and turn away, ostensibly to inspect the row of numbers that denote which floor we've reached, in this case 2, beside the door.

Then it's 3 and the lift pings and I can make my escape, striding down the corridor, or perhaps beetling might be a better word, because this is the only way for any heterosexual man, or, I suppose, though of course I couldn't say this for certain, lesbian woman, to handle a corridor as full of girls as this, girls who have a terrible habit hereabouts in the land of *Life & Style* and *Mode* of being distressingly pretty, their long legs scissoring, their heels clicking, their little skirts swinging. He, or she, keeps his head down and makes a run for it.

'Good *morn*ing,' says a girl I vaguely recognise, maybe from *Life & Style*. I stretch my lips in another smile and look determinedly at her eyes because she's wearing a T-shirt that stops well north of her navel. One stunning miniskirt and a visible thong later, I make it to the very end of the corridor and the relative safety of the *Bricks and Brickmen* nook. All I have to hope for now, I think as I push open the door, is that Shirley's wearing something loose and baggy.

'Antarctica,' says Bob. 'Before the ice. Channel 5 last night. See it?'

'No,' I say, walking on with the air of an uninterruptable man with a mission. 'No, Bob, I was . . .'

'Proves my point,' says Bob, who's sprinted out from his

workstation to accompany me en route to the editorial cubicle. 'What we think of as a continent covered by an ice sheet yay thick was once a fertile, even tropical place, so it stands to reason, doesn't it, that it could easily have—'

'Morning, Richard,' says Shirley. She's wearing a stripy Sloaney-looking blouse, two buttons undone, a black skirt, down to just below her knees, black hosiery, pumps. Not one of her worst outfits but still one that will have to be coped with. Or, I tell myself, else. 'Have you got a moment?'

'Quite easily have—'

'Of course.'

'Supported an advanced—'

'Excuse me a minute, please, Bob.'

'Society which—'

'Yes, I just have to talk to Shirley here, you see. Be with you in a moment, Bob.'

Bob narrows his eyes and shoots me with his index finger. 'Later,' he warns. I push the cubicle door shut.

'So, Shirley,' I say. 'What can I do you for?'

'Well, mainly I just thought you might need a break from the Pyramids.'

'Oh, right, well, yes, absolutely, and thank you.' I plonk the holdall down on the floor, take off my jacket, drape the jacket round the back of my chair, switch my computer on, sit down and swivel a quarter-turn. Then steel myself to ask her, '. . . How's things?'

Shirley shakes her head with the air of someone who has long since resigned herself to disappointment. 'You don't want to know,' she assures me.

'Ah. The MM was away in the country again.' Please.

'No, well, yes, but he came back early, left the wife and two veg in the sticks, so I did see him last night.'

'Ah . . . See *to* him, more like.' Trying to enter into the spirit, you see, but the price to be paid for that little joshette is now having to try very hard not to think about Shirley naked and magnificent and seeing to someone.

'Well, no, not exactly. I mean, he came round to my place and I was all primed and ready, I can tell you. And wearing the whole kit and kaboodle, because, I think I might have told you before, the MM's a great fan of the suspender belt and the stocking and the what-have-you.'

Oh, good Lord, have mercy.

'So there I was, all the gear on, all trussed up and no place to go, underneath a black dress, I don't think you'll have seen it, it's not a work thing. Quite tight-fitting.'

No, no, no.

'Specially round the bum.'

No, no, no, no, no.

'And I might as well have been wearing my biggest Sloggis and a pair of jeans. I mean, no action whatsoever. Not even a hint of you-know. And there was me ready to drop to my knees in front of him soon as he walked in the door.'

Doodee doodee doodee doodee doo . . .

'But he just marched in, saying he couldn't stay long, dumped himself on the sofa, had a drink and switched on the TV. So there was me, crossing and uncrossing my legs like I was doing a sitting-down version of the can-can.'

Alalalalala. Not li-ih-ih-ih-ih-istening . . .

'And you know what he did? He fell asleep. Right there on my sofa. Sparko. I wouldn't have minded so much but it's been weeks since we've had sex. Literally. Weeks. Like *three weeks.* Can you imagine?'

Tumty deedle tumty doodle . . .

'So I went into the bedroom, climbed out of the fancy dress, put on a kimono and pottered around in the kitchen until he woke up a full hour later. Looked at his watch, said, "Is that the time?" like I'd be holding him there against his will or something, and shot off. I mean, that's NBG, isn't it? I mean, what's the point in having an affair with a married man if there isn't going to be any sex?'

'. . . Well, I . . .'

'Anyway.' Shirley straightens her back, in doing so thrusting out her unavoidably substantial chestal region. 'Oh, God, now that I remember, there was a bit of work stuff I had to tell you.'

'Oh?'

'The MD's secretary. Whatsherface. Selina?'

'Samantha?'

'Serena?'

'Susanna?'

'Selina, I think.'

'Sharona?'

'Anyway, her. Semolina. She was on the phone for you.'

'For me?'

'For you.'

'What for?'

'I don't know.'

'Hm. When was this, did you say?'

'Dunno. I was just in. Tennish?'

'Bloody hell, it's all go, isn't it?'

'No rest for the wicked,' says Shirley, doing a joky little squirm that does me no good.

'Bad news,' says the arriving Bob. 'Ads aren't looking too clever.'

'What's the matter with them?'

'They just lost the back page.'

'The back *page*?' I squeal. 'How? Who? How?'

'Kingdom Cement. They just withdrew it. Saying something about a budget restriction but Valerie in ads is convinced they're going to go with *Construction Now* instead.'

'Bloody hell.'

'Well, you know what Valerie in ads is like. One finger always on the emergency button. But she was already two pages short so it's no wonder she's in a panic.'

'Hm, with press day on Thursday,' I point out. And then I have an idea. 'Tell you what. Why don't I call in some of my contacts? In the industry,' I explain. 'On the PR side,' I continue to explain because Bob and Shirley still look puzzled.

Mere moments later, I, the boss with the most, the man in control, have phoned Valerie, calmed her down, phoned Marcus, shot the breeze, and given him the inside info on a back page ad space going cheap, told him to pass it on to whomsoever it might concern.

I was quite impressive there, though I say it myself.

9.58 a.m., Monday 24 March

EWAN

'Oh an look, man, look at iss one. An iss one. Oh, man, an iss one. Swimming pool, a lot. An iss one, look, man, check out a fucking *stables*, man. *Stables*, man, you know what I'm saying? *Stables*, where . . .'

'Grassy, what the fuck?'

'Juss ave a look, man. Check it out. Iss one. Ix bedrooms an, like, *acreage*, man.'

I'm standing in my doorway, holding on to the door. I've got my glasses on but I still can't see. It's my eyes that are smudgy. And because I'm wearing only a dressing gown, there's a disconcerting airiness around my calves. 'Yeah,' I say with a surprisingly sore croak. 'Yeah, very promising, Grassy. But could it not have waited a bit?'

'Why?'

'Because it's the crack of ten. I went to bed at four. As you may know, because that's when I kicked you out.'

'Yeah, but shit, man, it's a brochures, they arrived in a post.'

228

'Anyway, how come you're so lively? In fact, how come you're so conscious?'

Grassy shrugs. 'You want me to go, I'll go. Fat's what you want. Seriously. Few want.'

'Grassy, no offence, but I want. I'll come down and see you in a wee while. After I've had my bath. Say twelve. All right?'

'Hey, scool,' says Grassy with an ostentatiously forgiving air. 'I'll take these but I'll leave you iss one, yeah? Bring it down with you because I will be jonesing for another look at it, you know what I'm saying? *Jonesing*, man.' He hands over a thick, glossy brochure and pats it. 'Enjoy,' he says. Reminding me strongly of a bloke at school called . . . Brian Hawley, I think it was, who used to do that with his *Mayfairs* and *Whitehouses*. Like he had shagged every girl, quaffed each to the lees, slaked himself sober. Grassy gives me a reassuring nod and shambles off.

I bum the door shut. I look at the brochure but can only register that the cover is mostly blue. And that I won't be going back to sleep. No. That's me condemned to gritty-eyed insomnia. Thanks for that, Grassy. Cheers, mate.

I shuffle into the kitchen to make a coffee. With the Gaggia, one of the recent additions to the household. Not that there are many. Hardly any. The sofa. The sofa cushions. New blinds. A table. Chairs. Nothing in the bedroom apart from the bedside table and lamps. And the ornately gilded, wall-sized mirror, for obvious reaons.

Well, it was just daft having nothing. And even the nothing included a bed, a kettle, the beanbag, the TV, et cetera, et cetera. And I might as well spend some money on something.

I pour out a large espresso into a cup . . . Okay, another

piece of new equipment . . . And take a sharp, quick sip of steam. I stand there like a dummy, staring blankly at the blank walls, until I can risk a proper go at the coffee. Then I remember that I smoke. Soon I'm in a position to give my head a shake and have a look at the brochure. Either that or morning TV. So – brochure.

I flick through, past pages and pages of yellowed mansions and vast, ivy-covered farmhouses. All beneath purple skies. And all for risibly low prices. Small chateau in the Loire valley? Three hundred thousand Euros, call it two hundred sterling. For the cost of this box in Dalston I could buy the Normandy farmhouse on page 48 and have change for the *gîte* on page 52.

We're going to go halves. A hundred grand each. Courtesy, in Grassy's case, of the bequest from a recently expired aunt who had the good sense to have few friends or relatives and to have been the outright owner of her semi in up-and-coming Ashford.

We're going to buy a house in France. A house with land. Growing alfresco as well as indoors.

At least that's what Grassy thinks we're going to do. Buy a house in France with Grassy? Aye, that'll be right. Become a skunk farmer? I don't think so. But I'm letting him down gently and slowly. Keeping him sweet for as long as I can. Two more crops out of Mottingham, and I'll call it a day. Dare over. Box ticked.

But it has to be said – Mottingham is going very well. There was an interminable month at the beginning when I had to do some actual work on the place. But only a month because the repairs were straightforward. As was the decorating. And I have worked wonders. So that the place now looks . . . Well, no, it still looks like shit, but no worse than the rest of the street or any other part of south London. Better, in fact, than most. But still shit. Highly sellable, though, minus the hydroponics. And the property market's still going mental.

Plus there's Grassy's indoor gardening. Which seems to be going great guns. Fandabadozie, in fact. As evidenced by the large bin-bag of grass that I have stashed in a kitchen cupboard. One of two bags in this house crammed to the gunwales with grass, because Grassy's got another concealed he will not say where in his flat. And that's just the first crop. The second imminent. I'm telling you, take a peek inside the bag I've got and you'll be hit by (1) the pungent and unmistakable reek of marijuana and (2) the resemblance to a Customs seizure on the news: a whole bin liner of weed, enough grass to make a teetering yet extremely relaxed compost heap.

Which does sometimes give me the heebie-jeebies. Occasional outbreaks of pure, chilling fear that I'll wake up one day to find a helicopter overhead and an elite squad of drugs cops abseiling down into the bedroom. But, really think about it, what are the chances? Anyway. Prison, that might not be so bad. They've got TV in prison. Drugs, also. And, knowing my luck, my cellmate would be Kate Moss . . . Well, you make your own luck in this life, don't you?

No, heebie-jeebies apart, I have to say that I can't quite believe how well things are going. Heebie-jeebies apart, I haven't felt like this since . . . arguably, since the days after I took that train home after finishing with uni. Certainly, not since I got Tim and Robin on board to set up the company.

Full of daydreams about just how successful we might become. (Eventual answer – fairly. Eventual supplementary question – so what?). But this present business venture is very different, requiring, as it does, no, as it were, work.

I reach over to the table for the zip-sealed bag of grass, the Rizlas, the broken cigarette, and the rolling machine. . . .

The first of the day. Perhaps with a glass of refreshing orange juice? From the new juicer? Mm. What a good idea. First I have to get up off the sofa. So I'll be doing that in a minute.

Yes . . .

. . . That rolling machine. It's made for king-size Rizlas. So somewhere a perfectly legitimate company has a perfectly normal factory where they make machines designed to roll only marijuana cigarettes . . .

I tie my dressing gown tighter, then lie back on the sofa. Puffing away. Just puffing away. Ashtray on the floor. Curtains shut but light's sort of ambiently coming in. If I opened the curtains, it'd be really bright. Facing south. Even just one of the curtains.

Julia. The thought just comes to me. Julia. Picked her up at a party. We snogged on a sofa. Last time I did that at a party, it was with Fiona Henderson at Deke McCulloch's house, third year at school. Face like a plate, plumpish arms, pink skin, freckly back. Julia, that is. Not Fiona. God, Fiona Henderson. When did I last think about Fiona Henderson?

She's Jules to her mates, or so she claims. Julia to me. Christ, it might be Jools. Or – whoah – Joolz.

Joolz. Ooshah. Ooshah booshah. No. Surely not. Julia. Two nights I've spent with *Julia* since the night of the sofa.

The first, what, three weeks ago at that party Russell dragged me to in Belsize Park. Then again last week.

She has a husband, thank God. And they've been very enjoyable, all three nights. That thing she has about not moving, that works for me. Though it was weird at first, when I wondered if there might have been some misunderstanding. But then it dawned. So I was a bit more forceful than the usual. Which seemed to work. Second date she was pleading with me not to, powerless as she was, astride me.

Still. That seemed to work, too . . .

Yes, she's married to a posh psychotherapist. They have a house in Highgate. She's 38. He's 61. She has her needs. And I'm happy to help out.

What I'll do, I'll have a glass of orange juice. Real orange juice from the new juicer. And another espresso. Glass of water, maybe. A cigarette. Yes. In a minute . . .

I I

7.28 p.m., Thursday 3 April

RICHARD

Ali's downstairs, watching *Lofty Ambitions*, or it might be
House Rescue . . . or *House Hunt* . . . or that gardens one . . .
Well, whichever it is, I've got much the better of this deal,
seeing as I'm upstairs and busy giving the King of all the
Bongles his bath. And it is a busy old process, with the playing
with the ducks and the cups and the magic stick and the smiley
shark and the squishy tortoise and the pink dolphin who
squeaks when he goes into the water, to say nothing of the
washing (easing a warm, wet ball of cotton wool over his new
pink skin and his Aryanly yellow hair, gently twiggling it into
the little whorls of his ears and trying to do likewise with the
other orifician regions whenever the opportunity presents
itself, say during a reach for the squeaky pink dolphin bobbing
under the taps, followed by a small bout of splashing and the
newish game where he flicks water at me, eyes huge with glee,
and me staring at him, mouth ajar, small Earthling brain quite
unable to comprehend a vision of such overwhelming, unbearable gorgeousness) and then the persuading out of the bath and
onto my lap and then the drying and the jiggling, the prolonged
jiggling because there have to be at least three *Grand Old Duke*

of Yorks mingled with at least two *Jack and Jills* followed by the scampering out of the bathroom and into our, i.e. mummy and daddy's, bedroom (or rather one of us trotting teeteringly, as though he has an invisible companion in a three-legged race, around the bathroom and the bedroom while the other one of us tries not to think about the times when such times as this have gone horribly wrong and one of us has tripped up over his own feet or simply fallen over, or crashed into a pillar at an uncle's wedding party, or, on one occasion, outside the giraffe house at the Zoo, bent down to hold one foot in one hand and the other foot in the other hand and then, in very slow motion yet also somehow unstoppably, toppling, not very far of course and thank goodness for that, onto the ground, forehead-first) and thence – or would it be hence? – to his bedroom, where or whence there's still stage two to deal with and the whole business of actually getting him ready for bed.

Stage two goes swimmingly, as it happens, so I'm soon tugging a top over Bongle's more-or-less dry hair, shoving arms into sleeves and generally mauling and hauling and then, after all this tossage and turnage, while he's becalmed on the mat on his bedroom floor, all the chasing and struggling done, ready for bed now, looking up at me and looking particularly angelic in these PJs (the blue ones, with the red trim, the ones with Bob the Builder, Pilchard and Scoop on the front), but there can be no dawdling so I have to concentrate and seize this chance to cram him into his latest sleeping-bag boy-in-a-bag whodyoumaflip, which is already getting too small and really should be replaced, right now, if only Mothercare or, let's be honest, Asda could immediately have a branch next door which stayed open late.

So now it's song time. 'What shall we sing tonight?' I whisper. 'What song will we sing tonight? Mm? What song will we sing, do you think? How about *Twinkle, twinkle*? Shall we sing *Twinkle, twinkle*?' Having selected *Twinkle, twinkle* completely not by chance, this being my favourite because El Bonglero often has a real stab at it, and however short and uncertain the attempt, it's a guaranteed show-stopper, the little fluting voice, and the tune all over the shop.

But he scrunches up his face. 'No,' he says.

'*Aiken Drum*?'

'Aikay Dum.'

So *Aiken Drum* it is. That's to say, our own customised version of *Aiken Drum*. I start, singing almost but not quite under my breath:

'There was a man lived in the moon, lived in the moon, lived in the moon.
There was a man lived in the moon and his name was Aiken Drum.
And he played upon a ladle, a ladle, a ladle.
And he played upon a ladle and his name was Aiken Drum.
And his best chum was called . . .'

I pause for the squirm of excitement at this bit – and there it is.

'Bongle, called Bongle, called Bongle.
His best chum was called Bongle and his name was Aiken Drum.
And they both went to the sea. The sea. The sea.
And they both went to the sea. To see what they could see.
And they said hello to the doggie.'

'Woof woof.'

'The doggie.'

'Woof woof.'

'The doggie.'

'Woof woof.'

'They said hello to the doggie.'

'Woof woof.'

'The day they went to the sea. And they said hello to the wolf.'

'Ha woo.'

'The wolf.'

'Ha woo.'

'The wolf.'

'Ha woo.'

'They said hello to the wolf.'

'Ha woo.'

'The day they went to the sea. And they said hello to the . . .' (because I want to hear his backwards miaow) 'pussy cat.'

'Ow-eem.'

'The pussy cat.'

'Ow-eem.'

'The pussy cat.'

'Ow-eem.'

(Allegro ma non troppo. If that's the one for slower and quieter.) 'They said hello to the pussy cat.'

'Ow-eem.'

'The day . . . they went . . . to . . . the . . . sea . . . Ready for bed now? Ready for bed? Let's go to bed now, shall we? Here we go to bed now. Here we go to bed.'

I gather him in my arms and hoist him up, with appreciably more effort than used to be the case, in the distant past of, say, a week ago, so that he's looking over my left shoulder. Whence or hence to bedfordshire, carrying him up and over the cot's bars and down, tucking him in and giving him a kiss and instructing him to sleep tight and not let the bugs bite and clicking the monitor on and dimming the light and tucking him in a bit more for good luck and giving him a final kiss, on my fingertips this time and then my fingertips touching his forehead, his wondrously soft, smooth forehead, and whispering a last goodnight and tiptoeing back down the stairs, via our, i.e. Ali's and my, bedroom and the en-suite to do a quick tidy-up, to the sitting-room lounge where Ali's flat out on the sofa, completely done in after a day of Bongling – and who can blame her with the pace that the Bonglemeister sets? – watching a pert gay man put on a yellow helmet, turn to give the camera, with pursed lips and ooh-er-matron raised eyebrows, a scandalised look and start climbing a ladder.

'Can I get you anything?' I ask, picturing a glass of water or a pot of tea and certainly not anything remotely alcoholic because today has been, as yesterday was, only yesterday was much, much, much more painfully even more so, a day of coping with a hangover, a hangover of ginormous stonkocity, so that yesterday was a day of being overhung the like of which has not been seen since the New Year when I was sick out of Sophie Godfrey's dad's Mini Metro's window. God knows how I made it into work yesterday. Well, so do I actually – by waking on the sofa at ten minutes past five and lying dismally awake thereafter, ashen of mouth, gritty of eye and dangerously queasy of breadbasket, until Bongle eventually stirred, at the ironically late time of ten past eight and the day officially began. That's how.

'No, I'm fine,' says Ali. The pert gay man wiggles his way up the ladder.

'Sure?'

'Yeah . . . Actually . . .' Another camera, presumably on the roof, shows the pert gay man poking his head over the ladder and the gutter and now inspecting the tiles, which look very much of a piece with the brickwork, which in turn looks very much like it belongs to a semi in suburban London, mid-1930s, I'd bet, or maybe it's a camera held by a cameraman standing on the top rung of another ladder, though that would surely be rather precarious. Suddenly, the pert gay man's face, peeking out between the gutter and the unsuccessful fancy dress of the yellow helmet, one of those luridly bright-yellow construction-site helmets conventionally accompanied by a nauseously greeny-yellowy-coloured safety bib as also favoured by lollypopladies, crumples. He seems to have burst into tears, so I suppose it's bad news on the roof front. Or maybe it should be lollypoppeople.

'Mm?'

'What?'

'No, no,' I say with a touch of a stammer and feeling very much on the back foot because that was the Query Curt, 'you were saying something.'

'Oh. Yes. I was about to say, before I was so rudely interrupted, that I might pop out for a bit.'

I stand there, blinking, rather stupidly, I suppose, but, mitigating circs, I am a bit taken aback. Puzzled also. 'Er . . . sorry?'

'I might pop out for a bit.'

'Pop out? . . . Now?'

Ali looks up at the clock on the mantelpiece. I follow suit. Both hands point to VIII. 'Yes, I suppose I should get going,' she says.

'. . . Don't you want to watch the end of your programme?' I ask, possibly rather foolishly.

We both look back at the TV and speeded-up footage of a team of workmen repairing a roof in the jerky, marionette-y way of speeded-up footage.

'No,' says Ali . . . 'It's Marion. She just called up.'

'Did she?'

'While you were doing bathtime.'

'Oh. Right.'

'She just called on the off chance. She's in a pub with a friend of hers who's just about to leave.'

'Right.'

'Really just to keep her company.'

'. . . She's a bit, well, needy, isn't she, Marion? You only saw her last week.'

Ali shrugs. 'She is a bit needy, I suppose.'

I nod my head then shake it. 'What pub?'

'The Wells.'

'The Wells? . . . That place in Hampstead?'

'Yeah, well, I'll take the car.'

'Gosh . . . Better not drink, then,' I say, wagging a finger to show that this is mock-stern.

'Okay,' says Ali. She stands up, zaps the TV with the remote and sighs. 'I'd better be going,' she says. 'Jakie go off okay?'

We both look over to the monitor. There's one green light showing and dimly at that, exactly consistent with the breathing of a tiny little Bongle boy who's fallen fast asleep. 'Yeah, Jakie's fine,' I say with a smile back to show that everything's fine, which it is, really, mainly, mostly.

'Don't wait up if Marion gets going,' she says, moving to the door.

'Okay. Bye, then,' I say, smiling. 'Have a good time.'

Ali replies with a wave, a light little stiff-fingered wave, rather like, it occurs to me, the gesture we do for a snapping crocodile, in, for example, the second verse of 'Row, row, row your boat,' where, instead of 'Merrily, merrily, merrily, merrily, life is but a dream', the words go, 'And if you see a crocodile, don't forget to scream', and then you scream, in a gorgeous little high-pitched squeal if you happen to be a Bongle, a final line which confirms, now that I come to think of it, the whole song's underlying horribleness, with its chirpy reminder that life is a fleeting, airy thing of no substance, soon gone and forgotten, and then its blithe conjuring-up of this image of Bongle naked but for his nappy tottering along the muddy bank of a swampy river, coming face to face with a crocodile, and, in the happy confidence that this'll solve the problem and have him safe back in mummy and daddy's arms in no time, letting out a gorgeous little high-pitched squeal, while the crocodile's jaws yawn.

'Bye,' I say again, perhaps a bit feebly, certainly too feebly for Ali to have heard. She disappears down the hallway and soon the front door clicks shut.

. . . I don't know about this Marion. Someone who all of a sudden comes back into your life and starts persuading you out at all times of the night, it's okay, perhaps, if you're single and keen on going out and so on and so forth, but it's not quite as appropriate somehow to ask all that of someone like Ali, who, on the other hand, *has* been cooped up in here all day, and the rain pouring down, so, fair's fair, it's only natural that Ali'd want to pop out for an hour or two should the chance arise.

So that's her off on an impromptuous evening out and me left wondering what on earth to do next . . .

A glass of water, that's what. I wander through to the kitchen, deciding to make it Evian from the fridge for a treat. It's one of those things nobody warned me about being middle-aged and that happened to me as soon as middle age threatened – your body will sprout grey hair and you'll have to start trimming your ears, you won't know who anyone is on *Top of the Pops* and the life expectancy of a hangover will double. The two-day hangover. It'll be bifocals next. The onset of arthritis. Trouble peeing. Prostate trouble. Prostate c-word . . .

Weakened and enfeebledly vulnerable, I can't resist the assault that follows, which, having begun with the thought of cancer, continues with the thought that even if I don't get cancer I'll definitely, one hundred per cent certainly, get death . . . and now here it is, the full-blown attack, looming over me like a pterodactyl, and what it says, isn't 'Cancer!' or 'Death!' but 'Jimmy Morgan.' 'Jimmy Morgan. Jimmy Morgan. Jimmy Morgan. Jimmy Morgan.' Though of course the impact of Jimmy Morgan's name isn't quite as great as it once was – well, yes, it isn't, not really – when to start with I was baffled more than anything, a disbelieving incomprehension, and not only at the stark, undeniable fact that what had allegedly happened with Jimmy Morgan had actually happened with Jimmy Morgan, but also at what was happening to me, and not only the terribleness of my obsession but the physical me, the way I was being eaten up by the very thought of Ali and Jimmy Morgan, really as if a pterodactyl were ripping at my innards, so that, yes, I was struggling at one point even to take on board the fact that this kind of jealousy seemed to be very like an actual physical ailment, which just shows how un-prepared was I for anything remotely like that. At that early stage, Jimmy Morgan was a dark, swarthy, hairy-backed, meaty-handed, sausage-fingered brute of my poisoned imagi-nation, though he was soon to be burnt into my memory, with a vividity so few things are, as the smooth operator in the stripy shirt and blood-red cords of the grimmest of grim realities, and here he is still, Jimmy Morgan, in his stripy shirt and red trousers, always keen to turn up at moments of enfeeblement such as these, and other times . . .

Stop it. Stop it. Stop it now. There's no need for that kind of nonsense, which is why it doesn't happen nearly as much these days, and no wonder, because we've moved on, yes, we *have* moved on, and a good long way as well, the arrival of Bongle having propelled us into overdrive, I mean hyper-drive, so that we're literally light years away from whatever happened to have happened long, long ago, in 1996. Or in 99 . . . But back to 96, and, looking at it objectively, one would have to say it was not only understandable but nigh-on inevitable. Me in Battersea, Ali in Aylesbury, young, pop-ular, beautiful, lovely, and Jimmy Morgan in Aylesbury hovering, sniffing prey.

And in any case, who am I to be casting stones? When I'm suffering from not only the second day of a stonking two-day hangover but also from the second day of skulking mortification and guilt and shame.

Oh, God . . .

I lean against the fridge door.

Breathing in and breathing out.

Breathing in. It's going to be okay. And breathing out. It's going to be all right. Breathing in. It's going to be okay. And breathing out . . .

Soon I have recovered enough to shuffle to the kitchen door and then, slowly, back to the sitting-room lounge, where I put the TV back on, lie on the sofa and look at the pert gay man, who has returned to terra firma. Still wearing the helmet, chatting to a bodybuilder who must have taken up roofing repairs as a hobby and sipping at an enormous carton of it would most probably be coffee.

And breathing. With long, slow, calm breaths.

I jab at the remote. A silver car whooshing through water. Car ad. The silver car in an eerily exaggerated evening light swishing into the driveway of a rectangular modern house, of the kind I assume you get quite a lot of on the coast of California. Football – a team in red tops playing a team in white tops. Two working-class women in their sturdy fifties looking meaningfully at each other, worried – a soap, most likely. Laughing model flicking her russet bob. Ad. Diagram of molecules racing down a tunnel. For shampoo or maybe hair colouring. The rectangular house in the eerie dusk. The handsome driver getting out of the silver car, being greeted by his beautiful wife with an adoring kiss. Football – one of the red team lying on the ground, holding his leg in a silent howl of agony.

Exactly what I wanted to do, more or less, apart from the silent bit, and not holding my leg, when I used to obsess about Jimmy Morgan – Jimmy Morgan, Jimmy Morgan, Jimmy Morgan – in the bad old days of the apocalypse: howl with the agony of it, just give up, sit down on the ground and howl, the only feasible response to the pictures in my head, the pictures of Ali and . . . him. The pictures that, shamefully, shamefully, continued long after that terrible, terrible business was over and done with and Ali and I were getting back to normal, or as near normal as the circs allowed, the pictures keeping the torment fuelled, which only goes to show that the torment was – and, however less it, of course, is, is – in actual fact all very sortoutable because the ghastliness was all of my own making – my obsessing, my torment, my problem, my fault.

And now I do some more deep breathing to quell another wave of panic and self-loathing . . . And it works, the deep breathing, unlike yesterday when the hangover was at its peak and I wasn't up to doing any quelling and the entire day was filled by waves of panic and self-loathing, and no wonder. No, today, I'm feeling much better, yes, only off-colour and weak and headachy and parts mouthian still coated with membraneous fur and in need of a good sandblasting, but all symptoms of rude good health compared to yesterday, even after I managed a nap, or rather napette – ten winks, I thought, at most – with the phone off the hook and my head on my desk, or more accurately, my keyboard, so that I roused myself to find that the article on the screen had acquired in the meantime two additional pages of rs and 5s, and to see Selina or

Serena or maybe, it occurred to me yesterday because my mind had gone a complete blank, something completely different like Marjorie or Gwendolen or Jane, before I came to my senses and decided that it was Selina, or Serena, one of those at any rate, and only then taking in the fact that, whatever she was called, there she was, the MD's beautiful and scary PA standing in all her scary beauty at my cubicle's doorway, having knocked at the open door and ostentatiously maintaining what I subsequently realised she probably thought was professional composure but came across as cold disdain as she reminded me that I had an appointment with Simon, i.e. the MD, at three. I remember staring at her for some time, then persuading my attention to turn, quick as an oil tanker, to my watch, and then staring at the watch, which alleged that the time was now quarter past three, for a considerable period, working out all the while that I hadn't bothered putting it in my diary after Selina or Serena phoned to propose a meeting with Simon the MD tomorrow, i.e. today, i.e. yesterday, at three, yes, not putting it in the diary on the sensible grounds that nobody in his or her right mind would forget an appointment with Simon the MD for the following day, and promptly forgetting about it.

Cartoon blue telephone beaming up at a young housewife, handset dancing merrily. The pert gay man, still with the yellow helmet on, pushing a wheelbarrow towards a ramp. People jumping onto sofas, a girl reclining on a sofa, people dancing around sofas in a big building full of sofas – sofa ad. Football – the severely wounded player back on his feet, limping slightly, then breaking into a run to kick the ball.

'I'm sorry,' I said in a croaky whisper, panic making me brilliant, and acting the part beautifully because I wasn't really acting at all, 'I'm not feeling terribly well. A stomach bug, I think.'

'You're ill,' said Serena or Selina or whatever she is called. 'Look at you. Shall I call for a doctor?'

'No . . . No, I'm sure it's just a bug.'

'Have you been sick?'

'Twice,' I said, sincerely.

'Diarrhoea?'

'. . . Er, a bit.'

'Was it discoloured?'

'Er . . .'

Selina or Serena nodded once at this, in a, for no reason that I could see, decisive way. 'I'm phoning for a cab,' she said, not actually phoning for a cab but striding towards me or rather towards the telephone on my desk. 'I do think you ought to go home and get to bed. I'll tell Simon and we'll reschedule.'

For the next day, that's to say today, at my insistence, keen as I was when I left a message on Selina or Serena's voicemail first thing this morning to show that I'm the kind of chap who's not going to let the small matter of a virulent stomach bug, with its accompanying bouts of sickness and attacks of probably discoloured diarrhoea, prevent him from getting in to the office, pressing the nose to the old grindstone and putting in a solid shift of editing and man-managing and attending rescheduled high-level meetings with the top brass. Rather successfully too, certainly insofar as the high-level meeting was concerned, because that went pretty well, all in all, benefiting as it did from the sympathy vote on the illness front as well as, I'm pretty sure, from appreciation of self's heroic recovery and dedication to the company cause, in piquant contrast to the reaction of Ali yesterday when I arrived home early and in style, wrapped up in a tartan blanket in the back of a black cab, and I had to remind myself that I wasn't really ill, proper ill, but hung-over and that, unlike Serena or Selina, Ali was well aware of this. Not that I needed too much reminding as Ali made more than a few comments at the point of my early re-entry into the house and thereafter about this being binge drinking and that not being good enough, and quite right too, although it's not as if I'm being sent home early in cabs every week, or every month or indeed ever before, yet, nonetheless, the fact remains that it's pretty rich of me to feel miffed, even slightly, about Ali popping out for one civilised drink.

Bald man in a long coat running in a dockyard at night. He's chasing another man. Whatshisname from that series on yonks ago, a comedy, sort of a sitcom I think it was, Whatshisname being a lad about town as I recall with a girlfriend and her parents, but here he is now, jumping over a stray girder. A player in red fetching the ball then holding it above his head, trying in vain to throw it back into play. A group of young people wearing jeans and fleeces inspecting a dilapidated hallway and staircase, the pert gay man, minus helmet, wiggling up to them.

Yes, the meeting went pretty well, although it turned out to be slightly different from the usual, when it's been a case of me covertly reintroducing myself to Simon the MD and both of us pretending to be acquaintances of some standing who are completely at their ease, politely catching up on each other's news. This time it turned out to be not just Simon but Beverley the head of Personnel to boot, and a chap I'd never clapped eyes on before whose name, occupation and purpose in being there escaped me. Not the usual meaningless, embarrassed exchange either, with Simon actually asking proper questions, about the Thames Gateway stories mainly, to the extent that I had to reveal my source (Marcus, of course) and could only pity the poor sods who edit the proper, grown-up magazines, if this was the kind of high-wattage light they were shining on one of the company's not-quite-so-high-profile titles. I asked Angela, the editor of *The Haberdasher* on the fifth floor who has upsetting breasts, about it, inadvertently putting the wind up her because she hadn't had any, ah, wind of any upcoming appraisal, so she immediately began to worry that Beverley in Personnel must have overlooked her, and therefore most likely must have forgotten about her very existence, and remindable only at the cost of reminding management to close *The Haberdasher* down. Angela's a bit of a worrier.

Puppy playing under a washing line. Ad. Probably for, yes, it is, washing powder. Bald man slamming Whatshisname up against a wall. Woman's manicured hand reaching for a phone. Call the Friends Bar. 0898 something. Calls cost 80p a minute.

So when Shirley popped her head round the door this afternoon to ask how it had gone, I was able to reply with a dismissive wave and confident pursage of the lips, because although there had been an unsettlingness about the meeting, overall it hadn't been so unsettling as to prevent me from doing a pretty convincing, and sincere, job of being reassuring. So it was all fine to start off, even when Shirley took that as her cue to tell me her news. 'The MM came round last night,' she said. 'Had a couple of drinks, then upped and left. Just got into the car and went home. So obviously,' she said, 'I'm anxious.'

'Oh, that's all right, Shirley,' I said, well settled by now into my role as Mr Reassurance. 'If it was only a couple of drinks and he'd had dinner or something, he'd probably be below the—'

'No, I was worried because we didn't you-know. Again.'

'Oh. Right.'

'That is, after all, supposedly the point of the MM coming round. The you-know.' And that was round about the point that Shirley shifted forward in her seat, or rather her legs did and her skirt didn't, a discrepancy which allowed another inch of her legs to hove into furtive, fraught view. Far too low a denier for comfort – ten at the most – and I yearned for the thick woolly tights of Shirley's winter wardrobe, especially when accompanied by the jaunty multicoloured stripy ankle-muffling mini-leggings.

'Of course.'

'Except there's been a lot less of that recently. Much less of the you-know and much more of the distracted.'

'Right.'

'I'm just hoping it's work because he was like this once before. And what worries me is that he's got into a panic again and will say something like he did before about this not going on and him having to stop seeing me.'

'Is it because his wife suspects?' The only good thing to be said about Shirley's hosiery is that it meant I didn't take too much notice of her bosom. Yes, there was that.

'I don't think his wife suspects a thing. I think it's pure guilt.'

'Well, you would feel terribly guilty, wouldn't you?' I pointed out.

'Would you?' Shirley put her head at a little tilt at this point to show that she was making a joke of it, the mischief of it being, you see, that she'd shifted the question to direct it at me.

So I smiled. I think. 'Of course,' I said. 'Of course you'd feel guilty.'

'Aaaah, but would that stop you?' Shirley wiggled her eyebrows and, continuing the patter, made a little thing of uncrossing and crossing her legs, a harmlessly teasy, flirty thing and no more, of course, I do realise that, but the skirt was already creeping up her thighs and I'd like to add the mitigating circs of the hangover as well as the hosiery, given the clear and present danger that those could have been stockinged legs that were being uncrossed and crossed, with a tiny suggestion of a rustle as the underneath of one leg smoothed across the top of the other, but whatever the reasons and excuses, the basic fact is that I found myself entranced by those distressingly fine, hosieried legs, so that I just . . . well, I just sat there, gaping at the curve of the neat feet into the black shoes with sort-of-stiletto heels, the tendon at the ankles, the slenderness and length of the calves.

Bald man in a coat running after a car and soon giving up. Player in white running to a jubilant crowd, telling them to shush, for some reason, his finger at his mouth. American police car bouncing down the rampy hill of a street in, presumably, San Francisco.

So there was a pause which was growing into a silence by the time I managed to say something. 'Well,' I said, feeling very much as I did when I was pushed on stage at the St James's nativity play, a dishcloth on my head, remembering that the purpose in being out on a stage in front of an audience of ten thousand people was to say, in a loud voice, 'Lo, a star' only when I heard an adult voice whisper, with some menace, 'Lo, a star', as I then said, 'That would be telling, wouldn't it?' Which left me wondering why on earth I'd said that instead of something else completely different and what on earth Shirley's question had been in the first place because in truth I was all over the shop at that point, and the point is that *Shirley noticed*, even if it was only for a second or two, although of course she covered the whole situation with her usual adeptitude, saying, in quite a normal voice, 'Well, now, wouldn't it just?' and then saying, 'Well, I suppose I'd better,' and then nodding towards her desk and then moving off and out and away.

The moment she'd gone, I let my rictus smile fade and screwed up my eyes. I do another wince now. What the *hell*? What the *hell* did I think I was playing at? All these years I've worked with Shirley and I've behaved myself. The peck at a company party last year that turned out to be a peck on the lips, that was about it. A transgression but pretend-it's-minor-and-forgotten-able. But in the space of four or perhaps five seconds – one thousand, two thousand, three thousand, four thousand, five thousand, yes, five seconds, at the most, most probably four, in truth – I blew it. For those four or five entire seconds, my guard fell and my mask slipped and that was all it took to let Shirley see that her boss, colleague and friend was a slavering sex addict. Not to mention the obvious fact that, every bit as much as at the party last year, I had just, in a very real sense, betrayed Ali.

Hold on, though, don't panic, Mister Mainwaring, because isn't there a chance, looking at this in the cold light of eight hours later, that what happened constitutes not a Big One from which Shirley and I will never recover but another easily-passed-over moment? Shirley will put it down as just one of those stupid little things, won't she? Maybe it happens – well, it probably does, bound to, in fact – all the time to such an attractive, sexy woman as Shirley. On a daily basis. Men just losing it in front of her very eyes, if only for a second or two, but usually it'll be worse, awful sometimes – strange, ghastly men suddenly asking where they've met her before, wolf-whistling drunks, the pair of eyes that won't stop staring at her on the Tube, as I've seen men stare and leer at women, wondering how on earth they can do it, the men that is . . . Although knowing full well why, because there are times, so many, many times, when the lust level rises higher and higher, to such a height that the defences and barricades and barriers can't hold it back any longer and the lust surges over, I mean, I am a man, flesh and blood, with my urges, and it has been so long since . . . since anything, really, nothing at all of any sort, to be honest, since the rosy period when we conceived Bongle. But that's no excuse so I knew while I sat at my desk and stared unseeingly at the toasters, as I know it again now sitting here in the sitting-room lounge and staring at a woman on TV standing in front of a plate-glass window in a fashionable riverside penthouse at night, that what had happened with Shirley was a thing of shame.

And, now as then, because I was and evidently still am, too fragile to prevent it doing so, the Shirley shame passed and passes to the onrushing Big Shame, the shame of the reason-for-the-two-day-hangover shame. And whatever the longevity or seriousness of the Shirley shame, they will be as nothing compared to those of the Big Shame, which is one of those ones that will stick around for a long, long time in the front of the brain, before edging back, gradually, as the years pass, to a recess, at the back of the head but always accessible, alongside calling Miss Taylor 'Mummy' and asking Sophie Godfrey to *Saturday Night Fever*. Yes, this shame was a Big One, up there with the Bournemouth Incident – i.e. big enough to make me start and gasp years and years from now. And nothing for it now but to slump back in the sofa, just as yesterday I slumped in my chair in my cubicle, and put my head in my hands and howl under my breath. 'Oh, no. Oh, no. Oh, no . . . Oh, no. Oh, no . . .'

I twanged the girl's thong. The girl with the red thong in the club. The beautiful Asian girl with the blue-black hair at the exit of the club, and the lovely smile. And the red thong. Which I lifted to place a five-pound note on the surprisingly brown, surprisingly cold skin of her upperest thigh. And which I replaced with a, oh, dear, oh, dear, hearty twang. Before, oh, God, here it comes, I . . . patted her bottom.

Sitting here now, on the family sofa in the family sitting-room lounge, in the family house, the ghastliness of this hits me anew. I patted her bottom. I patted a stranger's more-rather-than-less bare bottom. Oh, God . . .

Mind you, it was a wonderful bottom. Quite brown, I mean brown the colour of . . . chocolate, milk chocolate, and remarkably round and firm, really . . .

Oh, for God's sakes, what kind of hellishness is this? Stop it. Stop that right now. For God's sakes . . .

Bloody hell.

Bloody hell, bloody hell, bloody hell . . .

Bald man looking perplexed. Cartoon blue telephone. Police car chasing another car down another rampy hill presumably still in San Francisco. Player in white top sitting on the grass, looking up at the referee.

I slump further into the sofa.

Why did I have to get so drunk? A perfectly fine evening out with Marcus and I just got plastered. It was okay to start with, well of course it was, at some pub in the City, full of men in suits who were noticeably bigger, stronger and younger than me. And, needless to say, much, much richer. So a couple of pints of some flat, bitter bitter there, but somehow I hardly noticed the taste as I kept up with Marcus, a tribute to the conviviality of the evening, with Marcus on excellent form. And then it was on to a restaurant. Near St Paul's. I think. A very brightly lit place, with a sparkling stainless-steel kitchen on open view, and done up with curiously purple, where you'd really expect white or cream or even red or blue, upholstery. Linen so starched that it belonged in a black and white film, in a scene set for example in a steam train's dining compartment. Also, comically large plates, where the food looked like islands of whatdoyoumacallthems, pagodas. So we must have drunk a couple of bottles there, and Marcus might have drunk a bit more than me but only a bit, *cogito ergo sum* I was pretty squiffy by the time the double espressos hoved into view and Marcus passed me, secretly, under the table, his fingers tapping my knee and then seeking mine, as though he was playing footsie except with his hand, and I truly didn't know what to think, until I realised that he was trying to get me to hold on to something, a small rectangular paper packet, as it turned out. As I recall, I just sat there, clasping it in my suddenly wet fist, feeling like a criminal. Because, I suppose, I was. A criminal.

'Loos are that way,' said Marcus and he winked. 'It's good stuff.'

'Right,' I said, at a slight loss as to what to do next, except to register that it might be generally advisable policy to be on the move. So I edged out of my seat and away from the table and found myself heading for the loos, via an extraordinary corridor of tiny lime-green mosaic tiles and deep-blue-sea blue lighting, where I now found myself heading for one of the pair of cubicles which clearly came in the job lot for the kitchen. I locked the strangely metal door behind me, feeling like a fugitive from justice. I'd stay here for a moment, I told myself, calm down, collect my thoughts, then go back up and thank Marcus with a wink, pretending to have taken the stuff. That was my first thought. And then, whether it was the drink or just plain and simple complete absence of moral fibre, my second thought was to wonder this – why not give it a go?

And then I dared myself to do it. Go on, I thought . . . Why not?

Because I didn't have a clue what to do was one, minorly practical reason but that didn't stop me. No, I did my best to improvise, relying on nothing more than cloudy memories from telly or films where people have taken cocaine, for that is what I held in my fist, I was pretty sure, a whatever it is of cocaine. Wrap? Wrapping? Wrap? Wrap. So I pulled the lid down on to the seat whereon, with me by now kneeling on the floor, I placed the little packet and, having taken the precaution of taking a deep breath, carefully undid what transpired to be a surprisingly intricate, origamian packaging. I unfolded it with some trembly fiddling and opened it out to see a rectangle of powder, three or four big pinches' worth, some of it in tiny grains, some of those sparkling, some of it in tiny pebbles, most of it apparently of a granulosity, say, halfway between sugar and flour. I licked my finger, dabbed it in and licked the grain I'd gathered. It didn't taste of anything and nothing whatsoever happened. Then, just as I'd got to the stage where I thought I might well not know what to do next, the vision came to me of Thingummyjig, the actress, in a film, taking cocaine, using a credit card to scrape out a thick thread . . . then leaning over the thread with a rolled-up banknote up her nose. Of course.

So that's what I did. Elizabeth Hurley. Still kneeling by the toilet, I took out my credit card and started to scrape at the grains, even more carefully after a couple of pebbles leapt up and down somewhere on the floor. But how much to scrape off? Half of it? Was this meant to be half each? Probably not, I thought, or at least not in one go, so I settled on half of a half. I tried to leave the rocks behind on the grounds that they just looked a bit daunting, and concentrated on the less intimidating sparkly grains, amassing them in a tiny pile on the toilet seat, all the time telling myself, like one of those yoga things, 'Don't sneeze. Don't sneeze.' Mantras. Although I had been alone in the gents' all this time and although there were no noises to indicate anyone's imminent arrival, I paused and waited, guiltily, for some considerable and considerably nervous time before I told myself to go through with it and then, taking a deep breath, went through with it, leaning over the miniature heap with a rolled-up fiver stuck up my right nostril, taking quite a few quite alarmingly noisy goes at it until I had inhaled all of the thick white thread right up my right nostril.

And then . . . Well, and then I put my credit card and five-pound note back in my wallet, and I refolded the paper, with possibly rather less origami than it had once had, and I stood up, and I dusted myself down and I sniffed a bit to combat the sudden itchiness in my nose.

Manicured hand reaching for phone. 0898 something. Player in red top, in close-up, shouting. American detective looking out of a skyscraper window with an aerial view of, one presumes, San Francisco.

I don't know what I'd been expecting exactly but I had been expecting *some*thing. Bright colours, weirdness . . . But nothing was happening. On the contrary, things seemed to be unhappening. My head had cleared. I felt quite sober again.

Perversely disappointed by the complete absence of goblins and the complete lack of things going woozy or wibbly, I made the best of it, and rather successfully too, being in, though I say it myself, rather good form when I got back to the table, and very happy to take Marcus up on his proposal that we repair for a post-prandial tincture. Marcus being very keen at this point, as I was also, to talk, and Marcus being very enthusiastic in his reassurances that of course this was all on him, this being what expenses were for, and quite properly too in this case, because wasn't this a legitimate celebration, the celebration of the latest *Bricks and Brickmen* scoop about certain construction companies and a certain government contract re: new housing development in an area not unadjacent to the Thames Gateway? A scoop that, Marcus confided, with a disconcertingly naughty-looking look, had done the share price no harm either. So all the more cause to celebrate further, with that family holiday in Portugal long overdue – and, more immediately, a move on to this place he knew of. That'd be great, I said. Great idea, fantastic, brilliant, terrific.

A taxi ride later, east, I think, to Whitechapel or perhaps it was Bethnal Green, but unarguably one of those here-be-dragons parts unknown, and we were in a darkened, empty street, where later I would stumble and fall so ignominiously, outside somewhere called something like Rumours, or perhaps it was Whispers, having jauntily, merrily, appallingly twanged a girl's thong, with an awning and a doorman, the cuboid doorman, who made it clear that he was allowing us in only because he wouldn't lower himself to bar us.

Not that the place looked like any kind of place that would bar anyone for anything. It was a large, square room, unashamedly bunkeresque in appearance, with one ginormous blank television screen occupying much of one wall. The room was inhabited by scatterings of men – men in suits, studenty types, a quartet of crop-haired and wardrobe-sized older blokes who could equally have been carpenters or call-centre operatives or notorious gangsters – all watching a naked black girl with a strange, complicated hairstyle, one patch of it stretched across her forehead in a way that the normally tousled mop of a *Just William*y sort of a boy would once have had slicked down for a Sunday visit to a ghastly aunt's, dance around a pole on a small podium in the corner, turn her back to her audience, bend down, grasp her ankles and reach up and round to slide a finger with an incredibly long, possibly dangerous fingernail over her para . . . peri . . . pera . . . perimeneum? . . . There, anyway, between, and shocking rather than even remotely sexy it was too, so at that point I was honestly just busy being taken aback and feeling somehow to blame for not being her GP or not knowing her well enough. Heavens, I don't know *Ali* that well enough.

Then, every bit as surprisingly, a moment or two after Marcus had returned from the bar, a nearly naked girl, no more than twenty, appeared right in front of us, smiling up at us, revealing unusually small teeth and broad gums, wearing a bikini, teensy spangly triangles covering her n-words and no more, and holding out if not actually jiggling a pint glass half full of coins and notes, the breasts themselves not only bulky but wonderfully sticky-outy – perhaps my first pair, it now occurs to me, of surgically enhanced boobs. Peremeun?

That pint glass came round quite often, and it was carried by, I came to realise, all the six or seven girls who, when not up on the podium slinging themselves round the pole and showing their peremeuns, would spend their free time wandering round the bunker, wearing clothes but only just, asking for donations in the pint mug, chatting, in the case of the quartet of huge, middle-aged, i.e. my age, yeomen as though they were old friends, though I can't see how that could be, or perhaps they were regulars, and, and here's the point, I'm afraid, asking if anyone would, well, like a private dance. The same procedure here, apparently, as at the other places, a girl every now and then going off, leading the lucky winner or winners to another room, past the thick, red rope slung at knee height between two aluminiumish poles . . .

The American detective walking along the gravelled driveway of a large, clapboard, American house. The American detective ringing the front doorbell. The American detective waiting at the front door.

Twenty pounds each we had to hand over, me becoming rather insistent on paying my share, as I recall, the grounds being that this was above and beyond the call of anything claimable on expenses.

Oh, God.

Oh, God, oh, God, oh, God . . .

Well, one thing's for certain and it's this: I'm not doing that again . . .

I mean, what was I *thinking* of? When I should have been thinking of all the things I have, which is all I want, so that all I want is to keep things going. Not ruin them or behave like a moron.

Oh, God . . .

I've got to pull my socks up. Player in red jumping to head the ball and missing it. Yes, pull them right up, while also applying the nose to the old grindstone at work, as well as taking all precautions to be a proper husband and father and not a drug-crazed sex maniac, and, yes, generally knuckling down.

Player in white passing the ball to a team-mate. The team-mate passing the ball to the goalkeeper. The goalkeeper kicking the ball into the crowd.

I'm going to get my act together. I'm going to sort things out.

Yes.

. . . It's going to be okay. It's going to be all right.

7.28 p.m., Thursday 3 April

EWAN

'Well,' I say, now that I've recovered. 'That was a first for me.'

  'Really?'

  'Really.'

  '. . . So how was it?'

  '. . . Good. Great. How about you?'

  'I liked it.'

  'Good . . . So . . . have you done that a lot?'

  'Not a lot, no.'

  'But a fair few times.'

  'It's not a usual thing, like, it's Tuesday night, nothing on the telly, so might as well. Anyway, how come you're so interested? You're not getting jealous, are you?'

  I smile at my luck in stumbling across a woman who's perfectly sincere in this tease. Because she really doesn't care. How great is that? 'No, Eunice, I'm not getting jealous.'

  'How is that possible? Oh, well. On with the show.'

  'Where you going?'

  'Shower.'

'I don't know how you're even upright.'

'Because I go to the gym every day and I'm meeting my friend Amanda for dinner in an hour.'

'Are you? You didn't mention that.'

'No, but I kind of lost track of time and I didn't think that we'd go on for quite so long.'

'Fair point.'

'Well, I could stand here chatting all day, but that shower won't run itself. Join me if you want.'

'I can't move.'

'Suit yourself.'

Why I don't know and how I don't know but a minute or two later I slide off the bed and shuffle over to the heap of clothes on one of Eunice's Biedermeier chairs.

And start to get dressed. Rather creakily. Wobbling a bit putting on the trousers.

I'm shambling about looking for my shoes when Eunice comes back in. She's wearing a turbanned towel and the regulation White Company dressing gown. She unwraps the turban, drops it, unties the dressing gown and shrugs it off. She steps over the towel with pleasing grace and comes towards me. She throws her arms around my shoulders, pressing her breasts against my chest. She reaches up and lands a kiss, a kiss that soon turns luscious and then lascivious. At the very time when I've been working under the assumption that I won't need to have sex ever again, a hot stab of lust jabs at my stomach. By jingo.

The kiss draws to a close.

'Bye-bye, then,' says Eunice.

'Is that my cue to leave?'

'Well spotted.'

. . . So it is with a moist groin that I walk through Maida Vale. Maida Vale at night. The empty streets of Maida Vale at night. The emptiness bit explaining how I manage, with a superb sense of daring, to smoke a joint.

I'm walking past stuccoed, pillared houses.

I feel like a young rake. A buck.

I stop, take a deep breath and flex my shoulders. Stretch out . . .

I could face down a wolf. I'm a strong, fit, six-feet-tall human male in my prime and I could take on a fucking wolf.

. . . I could run all the way home.

I could sprint to the end of this street.

I could climb that high fence.

I'm not going to because I'm also far too fucking *cool*.

But I could.

. . . Seriously, a wolf.

A cheetah, for fucksake. A cheetah and me, one on one? I win. And no need for a stick.

Because I am an alpha male. An alpha male. There's an alpha male walking down this street, people. A fucking alpha *MALE* here.

. . . Except there's still hardly anyone about. A couple of burdened-looking women at a bus stop way up the road. Two old blokes this side of the street but at least a hundred yards away. And now, across the street a young, spiky-haired guy. He catches my eye, immediately lowers his.

I look around. I take in another deep breath, far as it will go. My chest swells, magnificently.

. . . I'm going to walk home. Through Camden, over to the

Highbury Corner roundabout, down St Paul's Road, Balls Pond Road, Dalston. Piece of piss.

My shiny black shoes slap the pavement. Shiny black Oxfords, no-nonsense. Just the thing for a good long walk.

I march up to Edgware Road. Across and along St John's Wood Road. Past the mansion blocks and apartment blocks, gleamingly new or kempt Edwardian. And now Lord's. The new media centre looking like it belongs in Eunice's special drawer.

I've reached a roundabout that's slinging out traffic. A hotel to the right. Far opposite, a wall of what might be Regent's Park. Four-lane racetrack up to the left. Facing me, the side of a rather appealing squat church and what looks like a wee park.

I cross the suddenly car-free racetrack.

I assess the railings. Then check out the street. Not a copper or parkie in sight. I jump onto the knee-high wall, get my holds, then push myself up and over the railings with ease. God, I'm good.

Possibly from instinct or some distant memory of hunting for Jerry soldiers, I dart into the shrubbery. Pushing through to a sort of path. Made of wood chippings, it looks like. So that's what park paths look like these days. This particular one, I discover, leads up to a kiddywinkle's playpark. I veer right and head for an open space. Fenced in by large trees and the size of a posh lawn but it feels like the veld.

I dig out another spliff I made earlier in the programme and smoke the sucker, assessing the neon sunset and the curvy special-drawer media centre, then the very Londony mansion blocks and then past the trees to the glass penthouses overlooking Lord's. Ivan lives round about here, I think. Something on the ground floor, I trust, with a view of the traffic.

Ivan. The transparently scheming Ivan. Jesus, he was crap. I take a final puff of the joint and start to wander back to civilisation. But, fair's fair, Ivan being crap did mean that I could make my plans and get out in the nick of time. I saw the tethers were coming loose and I jumped early . . . Christ, I could sing a song. I could sing a song, right here by the fence.

As it happens, I vault the fence with cool dignity. And find that I've landed next to, of course, a parked cab with its light on.

Heedless of the taxi's whirring meter, I spend the journey gazing out the window at roads that become less wealthy then poorer as we head east. Like the world if you start in California. Finally, we reach the border with Tajikistan. Smiling, I hand over a ridiculous £26 and stride up to the front door, then three steps at a time up to the flatlet.

Where I spend the next hour or two savouring a few glasses of Macallan and smoking a joint plus some cigarettes for good measure. Finishing off with a blurry inspection of the kitchen cupboard that's mostly occupied by the black bin liner bulging with the first crop of Mottingham Gold.

And so to bed. Ears humming with the earplugs I need to survive a yowling Dalston night, head falling towards the pillow, I manage to see, like a station sign glimpsed from a hurtling train, that it's 12.16 by the alarm clock. That used to be about the regulation bedtime and now it seems an absurdly early night, I think to myself, before I fall unconscious.

For five seconds.

Someone's shouting.

I sit bolt upright, staring at the dark.

More shouting, muffled but loud and violent.

What the fuck?

Some clattering and banging. More shouting.

What heavy objects can I arm myself with? Shoes? The heaviest things I can see are my black Oxfords. Christ, why don't I keep a seven-iron in the wardrobe? Or a baseball bat? Why don't I have a baseball bat under the bed?

A door banging. Some yelling. Where's it coming from? I still can't make anything out. Except that there's several people doing the yelling and that they're males. Males who are very pissed off.

For no useful reason, I check the time. 4.49, says the alarm clock.

The alarm clock. The heaviest thing in the room. I'm going to have to go out there, in my dressing gown, armed with an alarm clock.

There's a crash, then a sort of splintering noise, but again, muffled. It sounds as though someone's downstairs, trying to batter down a door with a duvet.

The thought reminds me. I'm still in bed. I jump out and stand naked in the darkness, feet planted apart, poised and waiting for . . . what? The bedroom door to crash open and . . . a horde of hooligans to rush in? The SAS? A bunch of Yardies high on crack and an indiscriminate killing spree?

This waiting goes on for a moment longer.

And another moment.

And another.

Then I glimpse something to my right.

Jesus Christ. Someone's there. Someone's already in the room.

There's a stab of fear in my chest.

Then I turn to face him. I am buzzing with adrenalin. 'Come on, you fuck,' I whisper. 'Come *on*.'

I can make out a figure. He's hunched, ready to strike.

The mirror. It's me in the big boudoir mirror.

I look around, shiftily. There's still something of a racket going on from somewhere down below – banging and clattering, raised voices – but it seems even more oddly muffled than before.

Ah.

I take out the earplugs.

The racket clarifies into clattering and banging. Also some stomping. It sounds like a moonlight flit gone violently wrong. And whatever it is that's going on, it's going on in this house. A commotion in Grassy's flat, is my first thought, but the noise doesn't quite fit that. I tiptoe to the window and peek out between the curtains.

Nothing going on down in the back garden that I can see.

I shove on a shirt and trousers, then steel myself to open the bedroom door and venture out into the main room. Okay so far. I tiptoe over to the nearer window and look out.

At a police van. Right outside. Also two police cars, each parked at a slant across the street and with their doors open. And, logically enough, police. Four, five, six police. Kitted out in the baseball caps and jerkins of cop battle fatigues. They might even be armed. Right outside this house.

Christ.

This is a raid.

I let go of the curtains and jerk my head away from the window, like a peeping Tom who's been caught in mid-peep. There is a huge great big bin liner of marijuana in my kitchen. Cleverly concealed, where no cop in battle fatigues would ever think of looking, in a cupboard. And no need to worry about sniffer dogs because a plod with a heavy cold could smell that bag from the landing.

I shiver. One enormous shiver that starts in my skull and works its way down to my feet.

There's nothing I can do. Nothing.

They seem to be starting with Mrs Longname on the ground floor or the Public Sector Spinster in the basement. They'll work their way up the house, but how much time does that buy me? Five minutes? One minute? And what am I supposed to do in that time? Burn it all? Cram it down the bog and flush it away to safety? I could claim that it's for personal use but even Grassy would take several years to get through that lot. Or I play the respectable innocent and it turns out that the bin liner's been hidden there without my knowledge. Yeah. With my fingerprints all over it. And it being in my kitchen cupboard.

Then I have another thought which makes things much, much worse. Mottingham. Very soon after I get cuffed for that bin liner, I'm going to get screwed for Mottingham.

So, basically, if I hear a knock at the door, that's me fucked.

There's a knock at the door.

I pinch the bridge of my nose and shut my eyes. '*Shit*,' I whisper.

Then I tell myself to get a grip.

More knocking at the door.

Okay. Here I go.

I pad slowly through the flat to the hall. I remind myself
how to breathe then prepare to play the part of respectable
homeowner who's just been woken by a racket and definitely
does not have enough weed in his kitchen cupboard to supply
Glastonbury. I give my hair a tousle, make my eyes a bit
blearier and take another deep breath.

Then I open the door.

'Ucking hell, man, you know what I'm saying?'

'Grassy, what the . . .?'

'A fucking pigs, man, it's a . . .'

'I know.'

'Ucking *raid*, man . . .'

'I know.'

'Ucking pigs all over a . . .'

'Grassy, I know.'

'A fucking *basement*, man.'

'The basement.' An extraordinary thought occurs to me.
'You mean *only* the basement?'

'Yeah, a basement. Sylvia's. Below Mrs, Mrs, Mrs . . .'

'Mrs Longname?'

'Ucking Mrs Longname, man. Sylvia, man. Ucking Sylvia's.
They're doing Sylvia's place.'

'Christ. So they're . . .'

'No need for alarm, sirs.' We both look down to see a cop's
baseball cap hove into view. And now an upturned podgy face
underneath. 'A police operation. Everything's under control.
Sorry for any disturbance.'

'Anks, man,' Grassy calls down. 'Only we was worried, you
know what I'm saying? With a disturbance.'

'Well, the situation has been dealt with, sir. No need for alarm. Sorry for the disturbance.'

'Well, okay, but at was some shit, you know what I'm saying? Some real fucking . . . disturbance, man.'

'I'll let you get on, sir. Thank you for your cooperation.'

'No problem, officer . . . Ucking hell, man,' says Grassy, when the copper's gone back down the stairs. Only now do I fully register that Grassy is naked. His dick a tiny acorn in a patch of grey scrub. 'You know what I'm saying?'

'What do we do?' I mutter. My brain whirrs. 'They've done the wrong flat. And we can't feasibly get rid of the stuff in time. So we hang tight. We move the stuff soon as the cops leave. Hope they don't realise their mistake. Okay?'

Grassy shrugs. Then he scratches a shank. 'Ingers fucking crossed, man.' Grassy steps back, nodding his head. 'Scary shit, man,' he says, then he turns and scurries downstairs. I shut the door and lean against it.

I'm safe.

Probably. For the moment.

I have to get to work.

Two minutes later, I'm washed, dressed and making coffee. Also forcing myself to peek through the curtains to see what's going on, now that the racket's died down for the moment.

. . . Three cops outside in battle fatigues. Another one getting into the van. The van driving off. The three cops below starting to move off. Another cop, in regulation ello-ello *Dixon of Dock Green* kit. Just standing at the end of our path . . .

Good news, good news. Right. Now for the bin liner. Checking first to see that nobody has snuck in during the past five seconds to open the curtains without my noticing, I look in the cupboard.

There is a very distinct waft of marijuana. I fetch out the bin liner for the second time tonight. Sobered this time, I notice that fetching it requires a small but still surprising degree of effort. I plonk the bin liner down on the floor. With a discernible thump. I pick it up again. It *is* a bit heavier than I remember. I put the bin liner down again and frown at it for a while. Then I hunker down, unfurl the scrunched-up top and look inside at the poly bags of grass. Could they be a fine or a suspended sentence? No. With the Mottingham set-up, I'm looking at about a year inside here.

This really is daft. There really must be better ways of unstraightening myself. Dogging. On-line poker. But not this.

It's while I'm mulling over this thought that I find myself gazing at one of the bags. The way it's wrapped, it's different somehow. Or, no, the wrapping's the same but the shape of it's different.

I pull it out. I tear off the wrapping. I am holding not a bag of grass but a strange brick-shaped parcel tightly bandaged in gaffer tape. I reach over for a knife and cut through to arrive at another parcel. 'Enough with the parcels,' I mutter as I cut a slit halfway up one side. I pull the cut open.

That's not marijuana. Marijuana doesn't come, as far as I know, in the form of white powder.

I lick a finger and take a dab. I rub it on my gums.

. . . My gums have begun to tingle.

I get to my feet and start pacing the room, still holding in my left hand a hefty brick of cocaine. Worth I don't know how much but a good few years, that's for sure.

'Grassy,' I tell the empty room. 'Fucking *Grassy*.'

12

8.33 p.m., Friday 4 April

RICHARD

The one on the left has blonde hair which is just long enough to justify the ponytail. Her friend has a browny-black bob, and maybe it's the bob that gives her the air of a pre-talkies movie star. Only the air, not the actual physical appearance, which isn't at all evocative of the silent screen, because she and her friend on the left are both wearing sports kit, and of a distinctly contemporary kind – chunky white trainers, wristbands, sports bags slung over their shoulders, sports tops under sports hoody jackets, and, because there's no point not being honest about this, sports grey tracksuit bottoms, and I'm saying bottoms here rather than trousers because bottoms are exactly what I'm thinking about as I'm looking at those two sports girls' bottoms and the movement under the flannely-looking grey material, which isn't a wobble so much as a shimmery, shivery ripple, because, despite the fact that both bottoms fill the tracksuits, they, the bottoms that is, are possessed of such muscly firmness as to obviate wobblage, if that's what obviate means, and I'm in a position to appreciate the mesmerising firmness of the bottoms because there they are, right there, directly in front of me, at exactly the place where I can maintain an apparently innocent

274

eyeline, at the bar, where they, the sports girls, are trying to catch the barman's eye, and in doing so have begun to lean forward over the counter, thus thrusting out the bottoms, which would be bad enough but then there's a significant additional factor to take into consideration here and that's that they are both wearing, obviously and, I'm afraid, very, very upsettingly, thongs.

'You are a sad pervert,' I tell myself, though not, I think and certainly hope, out loud. 'Look away.' And then I do look away. Eventually.

Feeling cheap and nasty now, on top of everything else, I move my gaze down slowly to my hands, and find that they are crossed on my lap like a footballer in one of those human walls. For something to do, I push back my sleeve and check my watch. Eight-thirty-five.

That's crazy, because that means that it's somehow already nearly two hours that we've been here.

Two hours.

Although I suppose that would account for the recent outbreak of lasciviocity regarding the two tracksuit bottoms, which I'm still coping with, incidentally, still busy ordering myself not to take another peek, as well as for the floppy, water-balloony state of the stomach, the nearly two hours of drinking beer.

That means it's also two hours since I walked out of the building and thought: I will never again in my life lay eyes on Callum in reception. Well, not thinking it, really – telling it to myself but not believing it. Not really.

Which is just as well. Because here he is! Callum in reception. At the end of the table. Snuggled up next to the older woman from the *Life & Style* ad department whose name may nor may not be Vivienne.

On reflection, I don't suppose it's as much of a coincidence as all that. Given that the White Lion must be the pub nearest to the office, though maybe the Mitre might just shade it. Or even, if you cut round the back, that new trendy place . . . Hyphen? Circumflex? . . . Something foreignly punctuational. Anyway, he, Callum in reception that is, seems to be pally with possibly Vivienne from *Life & Style*, ergo, therefore, thus we can see that, it is perhaps more inadvertently than advertently that he, Callum in reception, has joined our merry throng.

But what merry throng can this be? Who precisely are the revellers? Why, bizarrely enough one might have thought, Callum in reception, might-be-Vivienne, Valerie in ads who's might-be-Vivienne's friend, Bob, Shirley, self. All gathered here in the White Lion. Why, then, this post-works drinks bash? Could there possibly be some sort of special occasion being marked here? Why, yes. Yes, there is, as a matter of fact. There is a very special reason why we're all gathered here, in the White Lion, at what must now be a quarter to nine. We're all here to celebrate . . . Yes! That's right! The end of my last day at work!

Everyone seems to be having a great time of it, too. Callum in reception snuggled up between Valerie and maybe-Vivienne, sharing a giggle. Bob drinking with astonishing purpose, having just returned with a tray of top-ups and crisps and, I suspect, being about to continue his monologue about the Pyramids and the ancient mariner civilisation of Antarctica. irley, to give her her due, has been much more appropriately low-key. Upset, even. So, for once, I think we're both feeling rather grateful for Bob's witterage.

Sure enough, as soon as he's distributed the drinks – a half for me, nothing for Shirley, nothing for the two ad girls, a vodka for Callum in reception and a supplementary pint and squintuple whisky for himself – and the crisps, Bob's off again, talking, either oblivious to the situation here, or perhaps indeed coping with the situation by pretending, in his own Bobbular way, that no situation exists, so quite probably with the best of intentions, and quite loudly now. '. . . carbon-dated to ten thousand years earlier,' I hear him say before I tune out again and find my gaze making its way, slowly but surely, back to the two girls at the bar, who are now turning away and out of sight and serve me right.

Bob seems to have ground to a halt. Or maybe this is him just having a drinks stop before he resumes the long slog of telling us everything he thinks and knows.

. . . The sack. The sack . . . Even with the considering-the-circumstances-I'm-sure-you'll-agree-more-than-generous three months' salary pay-off and the tactful official phrasing, it's still the sack . . .

I've never been given the sack before. Not counting the holiday job for Metcalfe's when I announced my resignation the split second after I reversed one of their vans into their other van. That I recognised immediately, even as a callow sixth-former, to be a resigning issue, the unwitting of course but nonetheless extremely effective crumpling of one van's radiator grille into the other van's rear. But this? For the life of me, I still can't see that anything I did was so terribly wrong. The drop in circulation was inevitable, and, if the Thames

Gateway stories hadn't quite held water, hadn't they also helped create a stir, possibly even slowed that inevitable drop in circulation, and shown *Construction Now* a thing or two? And what was so wrong about me, my, me, my selling a back-page advert? That there were dark mutterings also about timekeeping only goes to show how out of touch Simon is. Or, as Shirley adeptly pointed out, it also shows how Simon was just casting around for excuses rather than reasons. As if a new editor who always gets in at eight o'clock sharp every day and doesn't carry any controversial scoops will miraculously restore sales figures and immediately consign any new rival publications to the recycling pile of history. Although I didn't actually tell Simon any of that, or of anything else, really, being far too stunned to do anything other than take in the extraordinary reality that Simon actually had it in for me. Infamy, infamy . . . The truly perplexing and horribly public nature of this out-of-the-blue, iceberg-of-urine-falling-from-a-plane-slap-bang-down-onto-your-house calamity was just so overwhelming, the mere fact of this event was so difficult to cope with, that I think I just muttered something politely regretful at the end, left the room and operated thereafter in a complete daze.

'. . . one hundred and fifty thousand years of human evolution,' Bob's telling Shirley, even louder now, so that I have no choice but to tune back in. 'And we're expected to believe that civilisation started only ten thousand years ago? I don't *think* so.'

Shirley shrugs. 'Seems reasonable enough to me,' she says, and I take a swig of lager, grateful for the way that lager has of thumbing up the dials of general vagueness, and for Shirley and her adeptitude, because here she is, soldiering on, keeping the conversation going, for my sake, it has to be for my sake, ultimately, surely. Surely, Shirley. 'That's when you had population growth after the end of the last Ice Age. And farming. They had to discover farming first.'

Bob leans forward. 'So humans only discovered farming in 8,000 BC? No *way*. Plus,' he says, pointing an index finger at the ceiling, 'there's the fact that you have the same culture springing up in Peru, Egypt, Cambodia, the Indian coastline,' and such is Bob's fervour as he declaims his list that it's not at all difficult to picture Bob losing it, going crazy, tipping up the table, the glasses tumbling onto our laps, then Bob bursting into tears and running out of the pub, or Bob leaning further forward and, all inhibitions gone awol, grabbing Shirley by the hair and pulling her face towards his. No. Not that. But something. Something unhinged. '. . . Like different branches,' he's saying now, as yet not unhinged, keeping things under control, with increasing success, it seems, the crisis, or imminent crisis, over, such being his visibly growing thrill as he prepares to unleash his next point. 'Like a tree, like the branches of a tree, like they're all coming from the one trunk, a trunk further back in the past.'

What on earth is he talking about?

'Yes, but,' says Shirley, who seems to have a rather firmer grasp of things, 'what are the supposed similarities?'

Bob ticks off his fingers. 'Astronomy. Mathematics. The same legends.'

'Legends are legends, read them how you like. And people have always measured things. Especially stars.'

'Okay, then,' says Bob, obviously not conceding anything

but preparing Shirley for the knockout piece of evidence he's about to produce. 'Pyramids. They all built huge pyramids. It cannot be coincidence that you get. Quite independently. Exactly the same. Structures. All over. The planet.'

'Well, it's not coincidence, no. But it's not because they were taught how to do it by the descendants of the ancient civilisation of Atlantis.'

'No?'

'No.'

'Really,' says Bob, with a ghastly as-though-polite smile. 'How, then?'

'Because,' says Shirley, carefully, and perhaps it's something about the way that she's looking at her lager that makes me think of a policewoman taking off her policewoman's hat then taking a deep breath then knocking at a door, 'pyramids are what you build when you want to build something really high but you don't know much or anything about for example engineering and you don't have any heavy plant. Actually, if you don't know much or anything about engineering and you don't have any heavy plant and you want to build something really high, pyramids are all you can build. So of course they all built pyramids.'

Bob stares at Shirley. This goes on for longer than it should. Much longer. 'No, they're not,' says Bob eventually.

Shirley frowns and nods. 'No,' she says. 'Maybe you're right.'

'Yes,' says Bob. 'Yes . . . Right.'

The problem solved, Shirley asks Bob if he's going to Chelsea on Sunday so that's Bob off on another incomprehensible lecture which gives me lots of time to be visited by images of my editor's cubicle, my editor's desk, my editor's flying toasters, and then a snapshot of the view from Simon's office, the rooftops beyond the huge windows and me holding on to the back of the chair in front of me while Beverley looked serious and Simon talked in a distinctly I-am-being-sad-but-resolute sort of way. Simon behind his bed-sized real-mahogany desk, Beverley sitting purposefully in the comfy chair, leaving only the less comfy seat for self and neither of them even inviting me to sit down, not inviting me to the extent that my, me, my sitting down would have been an outlandishly inappropriate manoeuvre, like spitting on the carpet. So I stood, you see. I stood. Holding the back of the uncomfy chair. As if to show . . . something or other. Some small act of assertion. While Simon told me that he was sure I would agree when he said that this was for the best.

Bob hoicks up a shirtsleeve and inspects what I've noticed only now at this last gasp is a curiously sizeable watch. 'Right. I'd better run for the train.'

'Charing Cross, isn't it?' I ask.

'That's right. No time to lose. So.' Bob stands and pulls on his scruffy leather bomber jacket with a drawing of an eagle on the back and below the eagle the word EAGLES. It strikes me that I may never now know what that EAGLES means, if it's some American team or a motorbike thing or what. The same feeling I had with Callum in reception in the foyer, except of course I did see . . . Odd. Somehow or other, Callum in reception and Doodah have disappeared. Valerie also.

Bob drains his pint, knocks back the last few molecules of his whisky. 'Better scoot,' he says. 'See you Monday. Er, Shirley. And, Richard, I'll . . .'

Not see you on Monday and probably never again. I smile and nod. 'Thanks, Bob,' I say. 'Safe journey. Have a good weekend.' Now, was that a smooth or an absurd thing to say?

'And you,' says Bob, and he's off, scuttling away to Charing Cross and thence or whence to the flat in Eltham that I've never seen but confidently imagine to be rather small with pictures of the Pyramids sellotaped to unmodishly wallpapered walls. He lives on his own and he doesn't have any kids, I know that.

'So,' I say to Shirley now that it's just the two of us. 'So . . .' I smile at my knees.

'Just as well,' she says, 'that I didn't tell him about the Giza pyramids not being exactly aligned with Orion's belt.'

'Right.'

'Poor Bob,' says Shirley.

'Yeah, poor Bob,' I say.

'And poor you.'

'Well . . . it'll be all right. It'll work out okay.'

'Oh, Richard, of course it will . . . You'll be fine.'

'*Nil carbonara illegitimi*,' I say, smiling although somehow Shirley's sympathy only makes me rather wish I were Bongle's age and could burst into tears. 'Thanks for being so good about this,' I say, and then I cough, because there was a dangerous crack in my voice on the 'good', and the cough seems to work because it comes out fairly okay, a touch wobbly maybe but basically okay, when I then say, 'I really appreciate it, Shirley.'

'If it's any consolation,' she says, 'I know how you feel.'

'How come? What's the matter?'

'I've been given the push too. By the MM. He chucked me on Wednesday.'

'Oh, Shirley. Oh, no.'

'I couldn't bring myself to tell you before. Although, I know it's not the same, I mean it's only . . .'

'No, no, it's love. Mine is just a job.'

'Love. I don't know about that.'

'Didn't you love him?' I say, and it occurs to me that I'm now walking along exactly the conversational path I shouldn't be walking along. 'I mean, I'm sure you probably still do, but . . .'

'Yes. Yes, I did. And I suppose I still do. Not like it used to be. It's been on the wane, truth be told, certainly from him, the love stuff as well as the lust stuff, the past year or so. But I suppose. Oh, well,' Shirley says with a smile and she offers her glass for a chink. 'A toast,' she says. 'To the sackees.'

'The sackees,' I say and I remember to chink.

'If you think about it, though,' says Shirley, 'there are similarities. And the things people always say are the same. It's not the end of the world. There's plenty more where that came from.'

'Yes.'

'All true enough as well but completely of no use if you're the person on the receiving end.'

'Yes,' I say, although I'm not so sure that I'm not about to lose Shirley's drift, and the silence that follows leaves us both looking straight in front of us at nothing in particular.

'. . . So when did this happen?'

'Wednesday.'

'Wednesday. Right . . . So how are you about it?'

'Okay. I mean, it could be a lot worse. A *lot* worse. No, really, I'm pretty good, considering. After all, when you think about it, that's seven years that the MM's been on the go.'

'God. Seven years. Ten per cent.'

'. . . Ten per cent of what?'

'Your lifespan.'

Shirley looks at me. 'I suppose it is . . . So. What do you want to do?'

'Ah, do you mean for employment or for the next thing after this drink?'

'Next thing after this drink.'

'. . . God, I really don't know. What do you think?'

'Let's have *another* drink,' Shirley advises. 'What can I get you?'

'No, no,' I say, banging the table with my knees as I half-rise from my seat, thereby almost knocking over several glasses. Rather painfully also. 'It's my . . .' But Shirley's already up – 'Um, another half?' I suggest – and off and away to the counter. And now that she's there she too leans forward. Good grief . . .

So there's that to be said against staying much longer but on the whole it's actually not so bad at the moment, here in the White Lion with Shirley, two and a half pints of lager down, another half to come, Shirley being so nice and, let's be honest about this, looking so very sexy, although I've not to think about that, although it will be so bad later, of course, of that I have no doubt . . . Perhaps I'll become one of those men who leave the house at eight-thirty-five sharp, besuited and be-briefcased, off to spend a day at the park.

'Forty-two,' says Shirley, plonking down the half of lager for me and the glass of gin or vodka and tonic for her.

'Sorry, Shirley?' I say, and it occurs to me that much more lager and that'll be quite difficult to say.

'Forty-two,' she says. 'That's how old I am.'

'Really? I thought you were . . .'

'What?' she says, raising an eyebrow. 'Forty-five? Fifty? I don't look that old, do I?'

'No, no, no, the opposite,' I say. 'I always thought you were a couple of years younger than me. Thirty-seven, thirty-eight.'

Shirley laughs, her curiously hearty, mannish laugh. 'Ha, ha, ha. You'd better stop there. . . . No, it's forty-two. Weird . . . I still feel like I'm thirty-one.'

'Well, you look terrific for forty-two,' I say and I feel my heart hammer because this is dangerous, forbidden territory, for both of us I'm sure because she has to be as aware as I am of the whole situation, the whole unspoken issue of the terrificness of Shirley's looks.

'Thank you,' she says, as composed and competent as ever. 'I'll take that as a compliment.'

'Well, I . . .'

'And that's the thing that really hurts about the MM, the fact that I've wasted so many crucial years being the MM's bit on the side. When I could have had . . .'

'No, no,' I say, immediately anxious about how to cope with this heart-rending development, 'you still have time. And there's IVF and all sorts.'

'. . . A proper relationship, I was going to say.'

'Right.'

'Anyway, the good thing is that that really is it with the MM this time.' Shirley raises her glass. 'The sackees again,' she says.

We chink again.

'The sackees again,' I say and I drain my lager. 'My shout,'

I declare, banging the glass on the table and then heading off to the bar.

. . . A short while later it seems to be closing time.

'How about we go on somewhere?' says Shirley, as the Polish or Russian or Czechoslovakian or something barmaid with the amazing haughty cheekbones clears our glasses and empties the ashtray full of crisp packets into a bin liner, before propping the door open to usher in a wintry wind, presumably as a hint.

'That'd be yes,' I say, incompetently, granted, but with no hint of a slur. Where on earth can we go, though? The only places I know which are open after closing time are ones Marcus has taken me to and I really doubt that Shirley would feel at all comfortable in any of those.

'How about we go on and have one for the road at my club?' says Shirley, and she takes my arm, a purely chummy linking but one that causes first a jolt and then a strict talking-to in my head about this being a purely chummy thing and the advisability of not revealing myself to be a sad maniac and pervert.

'Club?' I say, possibly belatedly registering the question. 'What club? Do you mean we're going to go clubbing?'

'Not that sort of club. A club club.'

'Right,' I say. Although I still haven't a clue what to expect until our taxi draws up outside a Georgian town house somewhere in the middle of Soho. We totter down a flight of wrought-iron stairs to a basement door, where a black girl greets Shirley with a broad smile. I follow Shirley through to a sort of bar area, full of reprobatishly bohemiany types, not too intimidatingly young though, and in fact by the hatch that seems to be the bar there are a couple of sixty-something soaks whose clothes are sheeny with overuse. Not the kind of place I'd have thought Shirley would have had much to do with but that's exactly what she seems to have as we head for the hatch, her in front and exchanging hellos and hi-theres with an impressive proportion of this basement's population, self in her wake like the bodyguard to a star.

It transpires that Shirley does come here a lot, with the MM, because the MM's been a member for ages, although he won't be here tonight because he's gone to Shanghai for a week and Shanghai is welcome to him. We've settled in a dark corner of a dark panelled room upstairs by this time, and I must say I do feel rather fine, especially considering. Residually hungry, and, I'll grant, a tad squiffy, but who wouldn't be getting a tad squiffy in the circs? But mainly rather fine. All credit to Shirley as well as to the brewers and purveyors of strong Continental lager for that state of affairs, because here she is beside me on a cushioned banquette underneath some prints by the eighteenth-century chap, or it could be seventeenth, and still with her spirits up and doing by far the lion's share of the chat, and most entertainingly too ... Hogarth. And Shirley looking so, well, so very, very sexy. The unassuming but still rather sexy black skirt, just tight enough. The gently ribbed black jersey, now that she's folded her jacket beside her, showing the always impressive curve of her breasts. Her auburn hair. The slant of her eyes. Her eyes. Her somehow very, very sexy long nose. Her mouth. The thin upper lip, the full lower lip.

Suddenly and God knows how, we're kissing. Kissing.

Right here on the cushioned banquette. I am kissing Shirley. Shirley is kissing me. We are kissing.

We clamber up the wrought-iron stairs and out into the immediately dodgy street with the expressed intention of getting a taxi, I'm presuming for Shirley's flat, although now it does strike me that I could have got this all hopelessly wrong. Then it strikes me that I don't care about that nearly as much as I should. In any case, just how are we going to get a taxi at this time of night? And with this many people on the streets? Who are all these people and what are they all doing at . . . two in the morning, wandering around and milling about?

'Cab?' says one of the crowd of millers by the first corner. 'Cab? Cab?'

'Ah . . .' I reply.

'We're going to Wandsworth,' says Shirley and my heart thuds. 'How much?'

'Wandsworth, eighteen pounds.'

'Deal. Where is it?'

'Here. Here. Here. Here.'

I'm getting into the back seat of a green Mazda 323, quite possibly to be held at ransom and/or sexually assaulted by the day-patient sitting motionless in the driver's seat. Before I know it, we're hurtling down Shaftesbury Avenue and, more remarkably still, Shirley and I are kissing again. Hers is an urgent, pressing-and-pushing kissage technique, but I feel, nonetheless, almost overcome, head a-whirl and even more so when, as an accompaniment to the kissing, I dare myself after a while to move my hand under her black skirt and, slowly, up, up Shirley's long, firm thigh, until, until, until the tips of my fingers register not continuing tight but abruptly smoother elastic or Lycra and very soon after that not elastic or Lycra but cool, smooth skin.

So, precisely at the time when, a tiny part of my brain still realises, I really should be sobering up and acknowledging what a despicable fool I'm being, sitting here in the back seat of a Mazda 323 with Shirley, right hand around her shoulder, fingertips of the left hand registering cool, smooth skin, I don't. And the Mazda 323 hurtles on, heedless, unstoppable, south, down Vauxhall Bridge Road, and over Vauxhall Bridge. And now I have my whole hand on her bare thigh. And Shirley's tongue is wriggling even more vigorously in my mouth. And now she's sliding her hand forward until it rests along the top of me, the angle rather obvious. And we keep on hurtling.

Eventually, Shirley pulls away and a few moments afterwards the hurtling stops. 'Eighteen pounds, he said,' says Shirley, handing over a note. 'Keep the change. This is me,' she says to me with a hint of a sh in the esses.

'Oh,' I say. 'Right.'

Unrepentant and in the open street, Shirley puts her arm through mine and leads me towards a somehow rather straitened-looking, early-Victorian, flat-roofed house.

Shirley opens the door. 'I'm at the top, I'm afraid,' she says, starting up some stairs, so I follow three steps behind, staring straight at her behind, and it occurs to me as I do so that, however preposterous the notion still seems to me even as I climb these stairs to Shirley's flat, it really is odds-on that I could soon be looking at this behind unprotected by its black skirt. My eyes, I'm now aware, have gone goggly, in addition to which, I also realise, I've been forgetting to breathe. My nose and ears should be sending out little puffs of steam.

Just when there's the danger that what's going on here will soon seem an absurd human folly, like football or line-dancing, I hear a sentence inside my head: 'I've picked her up at the fairground,' and I couldn't tell you why I heard that sentence inside my head or any sentence at all, only that the same thing happened to me a couple of times, years ago, pre-Ali, when I was going out with Susan Hartley so I must have been in my early twenties, twenty-three maybe, and I occasionally used to find myself telling myself that sentence as Susan Hartley and I had, to be candid, not terribly good sex – 'I've picked her up at the fairground' – instantly transforming, in my head, the business of having sex with quiet, obliging and, to be candid, unexciting Susan Hartley into an all-out shagging with the kind of dirty, sexy piece of work who'd hang around fairgrounds, wearing a lot of lipstick, smoking. As did it then, so does the sentence work now. I've picked her up at the fairground, runs my internal commentary. I've picked her up at the fairground and she's asked me to fuck her so I'm fucking her at the fairground. I'm fucking her at the fairground. I'm fucking her at the fairground . . .

When it's over, I try to keep my arms locked straight but the strain's too much so I lower myself down beside Shirley and lie there, spent and gasping, ashtray-mouthed, eyes shut.

'Well,' says Shirley, who's obviously about to be as adept with this situation as with a difficult headline or a wonky computer. 'Goodness,' she says. 'So,' she says, I think raising herself up with her right elbow propped and turning towards me, 'what was it with the fairground?'

My eyes spring open. I stare up into the blackness.

'The fairground?' I say, above the racket of my heart biffing my ribcage.

'I thought you said something about a fairground.'

'A fairground?'

'That's what I thought you said.'

'No . . . I can't remember . . . But I don't think I could have been saying anything about a fairground. Maybe it was "very good" or something.'

'Very good?'

'Or something. I can't remember. Heat of the moment and so on.'

'. . . Do you always talk to yourself like that?'

'No. No. Not at all. So I really can't explain it, this one, if that's what I did, I mean. No. Not one of my things, I'm afraid.'

'. . . Oh.'

'. . . Yes.'

'A pity we didn't have the light on.'

'. . . Yes.'

There follows what I'd like to think is a companionable silence, a wordless communing of some nature, but, although of course I can't be certain, I rather suspect that the reason we're not saying anything is because this is, suddenly and overwhelmingly, beyond words and not in a good way. I can't tell for certain how Shirley is, of course, since it's so bloody dark – maybe she's all right but I can't imagine that she's filled with a loving glow – but personally speaking I just want to curl up and hug myself tight.

'Are you okay?' whispers Shirley.

'. . . Yeah,' I whisper back. 'Are you?'

'. . . I suppose,' says Shirley, still whispering.

'That was lovely,' I say.

'Yes,' says Shirley under her breath. 'Lovely.'

'. . . Well,' I whisper, 'the thing is, it's so late, I really ought to . . .'

The next bit could well have been, I realise, awkward, the bit where I have to get up and hunt down my clothes and get dressed and say goodbye and get out of here, had Shirley not been so adept.

So not nearly as long as it could easily have been afterwards, having assured her that I'll get a cab on the street with no difficulty, I find myself out on the street, with absolutely no clue which direction to walk in. Shivering a bit also. I head right, for no particular reason, remembering only after I've gone past three or four parked cars to turn and offer a wave in case Shirley is standing at the window to watch me go. I turn and search for her silhouette at one of the top-storey windows, but in all the contenders the curtains are closed.

Maybe we should have built up to it a bit more . . . If she'd only switched a light on . . . I reach the end of Shirley's street, turn, for no particular reason, left and see, miraculously, a hundred yards away and closing, a cab, a proper black cab, with its yellow light glowing like the barrel of brandy round a St Bernard's neck, although that wouldn't, of course, glow, but like it anyway despite that. I thrust my hand out and in my anxiety find that I've also shouted 'Taxi!' like people do in films but not in real life, especially not in a suburbany-looking street in south London at . . . good God, ten to four in the morning.

'Halesworth Street, please. In Tottenham. South Tottenham. Just up from Stamford Hill.'

The cabbie looks at me without any discernible expression for a while.

'Please?' I say.

The cabbie keeps looking with no discernible expression and then he gives his head a tiny jerk backwards, which I take to mean that I can get in. So I get in, slump down, close my eyes and let myself be warmed by the cab's heater, on full blast, thank goodness, and soon the warmth is enough to soothe, and I need soothing because this does not feel at all good even now, in a warm cab and at this first stage when it's all still a blur and too much to take in.

It's the heater that does it. Just as I've got comfy – propped up in the corner, trying not to think, gazing out instead at a row of semis whose gardens have all been converted into alfresco garages – and the back bit of the cab is warming up, I get a really strong whiff of perfume.

I sniff the air, like a predator. Yes, it's definitely perfume. So strong I can almost identify it.

I sit bolt upright as it dawns on me. It's my jacket. And not just my jacket. It's me. All of me. I smell like I've been standing under a shower of perfume.

I reek of adultery.

We're crossing the river, going back across Vauxhall Bridge, guarded now by new blocks of flats that aren't called flats but apartments or suites as in penthouse, by the time I manage to calm down enough to begin to think of a plan.

Ali will be asleep, so I'll have a very, very quiet wash in the bathroom by Bongle's – Bongle! No, I can't think about him now. No, and I wasn't thinking about him earlier when I was boffing my deputy, was I? Erstwhile deputy. Oh, God . . . No. No, I wasn't – room, maybe sponge down the clothes, or shove them surreptitiously into the washing-pile, including the jacket even if it's dry-clean only, or sponge them all first *then* shove them all surreptitiously into the washing-pile, or, better, straight into the machine and cover them with a towel or something, with the excuse ready that . . . that . . . the excuse that . . . the clothes smell of perfume because . . . because . . . because the . . . because the . . . I have no idea.

. . . I got drunk because I got sacked and . . . someone sprayed me with perfume . . . for a lark . . .

Maybe if I tell her about being sacked she won't be too concerned about the stink of perfume.

We're coming up to Buckingham Palace, so that means we're – what? – twenty minuts from home. Fifteen at this time of night. I have to get my act together. I have to think of a plan, a plan of action.

I take another deep breath and expel the air like it's smoke. I'm still brainwaveless but I think I've got a basic modus thingummy. Silence being the key.

. . . And the key refusing to go into the lock, so that long after the taxi has gone, I'm still standing at the front door, drunk, knackered, useless, perfidious, fiddling about to no bloody effect whatsoever. Until, at last, the key slides in.

I take off my shoes and tiptoe along the dark hallway, remembering to keep to the right of the coat-stand and the little table that—

'Hello.'

The light has come on. I stand there, frozen, on pause, like I'm an escaping convict and I've been caught in a searchlight.

Ali is coming down the stairs. In her dressing gown. She reaches the bottom step and comes towards me.

I attempt a smile. Her nostrils twitch.

'Coco Chanel,' she says. 'You're drunk,' she says.

'Yeah, sorry, don't know how, seem to have got a bit tiddly,' I say, arguably with the hint of a gabble. 'Thing is, Ali, the thing is, you see, the thing is, I got sacked today so we went to the pub and—'

'Sacked?' she says, peering at me.

'Yeah, well, with a bit of a pay-off, quite a handsome one really if you—'

'Sacked? You mean you've been fired?'

'Yeah, well . . .'

'You're saying that you've lost your job?'

'Yes, but I . . .' I come to a halt because I don't know what to say. Instead, I look at her shins and give them a feeble smile. Then I shrug my shoulders.

'We went to the pub,' says Ali.

'Sorry, darling?'

'That's what you said, isn't it? *We* went to the pub. We. You mean you and Hilary.'

'Shirley.'

'Forgive me. Shirley.'

'And Bob. And Valerie from advertising and a chap called Callum and a woman called, well, I don't know for certain what she's call—'

'But Shirley.'

'. . . Yes . . . Yes. Shirley was there. Of course.'

'And Shirley wears Coco Chanel.'

'. . . I don't know what she wears.'

'You're lying.'

'What?'

'You're lying. I can always tell. Whenever you lie, you do that thing with your eyes, then you look off and up somewhere behind me. And that's what you just did. You did that thing with your eyes, then you gazed over my shoulder. Now, why would you lie about Hilary's Coco Chanel?'

I tell myself to look Ali in the eyes. 'Did I?'

She does a little half-smile. 'You really are such a crap liar,' she says. The little half-smile fades away. 'What's that on your face?'

I whisk my right hand up to my cheek, the fingertips resting on my skin like it's an instrument I'm about to start playing. 'What's what on my face?'

'Looks like . . . lipstick. Above your mouth. See.' Ali brings a tissue out of the dressing-gown pocket, and, as my innards turn to water, dabs at the bit that because of the advert I know is called a fultrum. She inspects the dabbed tissue and smiles thinly. 'Lipstick,' she says. 'Lipstick.'

'I . . .' I say, knowing that the next thing I'm going to say is going to have to be brilliant and brilliantly performed. I look Ali in the eye again, steadfastly, confidently, resolutely. 'I,' I say. '. . . I . . .'

'How long has this been going on?'

'No, no, no, oh, God, darling, nothing like that, for God's sakes, no, oh, no, God, no, it was just tonight, just . . .'

Ali's mouth stretches in another thin smile.

8.33 p.m., Friday 4 April

EWAN

I stretch out my right foot and nudge the hot tap off. Job done, I settle back into the rewarmed water with a wee sigh of contentment. I'm going to add up my blessings. One, this bath. What better way to relax and wind down after a long, hard day of chilling out and smoking spliff than to take it easy for an hour or two in a lovely hot bath? Blessing number two, the full and certain knowledge that I'm not going to be interrupted. By, for the sake of example, Grassy. No. No chance of that, and I thank my lucky stars. Three, here I am, having a bath in my flat and not, as might have been the case, taking a quick, fearful shower in my cell block.

Oh, and four, the saucer in the corner with the half-smoked joint in it. Five, the neighbouring box of matches. I lie back and puff away, moving only to puff and to stretch out the occasional languid arm to flick the ash into the saucer.

Six, Mathilde. Here to learn English. Returned to her husband and family couple of days ago. So that couldn't have worked out better.

. . . My fingers have gone all wrinkly. I used to love that when I was a kid. Touching the white whorls on my fingertips . . . I should invest in a duck. A proper bath duck – a bright yellow plastic number with a bright red beak . . .

Where was I? Before the ducks? . . . No idea . . . Something about sex, maybe? Well, I'll make it about sex now in any case because sex is another blessing to count. Got it. I was counting my blessings. So blessing number whatever is sex. Particularly since my brainwave. When was it? A month or so back. Couple of months. No, wait a minute, it must be . . . No, that's right, two months or so. Say. Anyway . . . yes, brainwave. A couple of months back, lying on the sofa, watching German football, smoking a refreshing joint. Pot of tea on the go. And it just came to me. A revelation. Yet so blindingly obvious. Prostitutes.

In the olden days, I'd probably have used the Net. But no way am I getting a computer. So next day I strolled down to Liverpool Street, went into one of the richly decorated phone booths and took the least strange of the cards. Jodie, she's called. Or at least, that's what she calls herself. Late twenties, I'd guess. Great figure. Enormous brown nipples. 'Tie n tease', her card said. I asked her if she did straight sex and she said yes she did. So we did. Eighty quid for the hour. A flat off Columbia Road. Very neat. Very clean. Well, straight*ish* sex.

And the convenience. I just call her up when I'm in the mood. I can see it catching on. Last time, I asked her about her card so she showed me her wardrobe. Crammed with outfits. Shiny uniforms, leather gear, enormous high-heeled shoes. Some of it for TV stuff. But mainly it's light bondage she does. The blokes being the ones who're tied up. Her prancing round them, tickling them and giving them a pinch now and again. I don't quite see the point, but you never know, I might give it a go some time. Why not? . . .

Here's a thought. Reincarnation. How come folk always used to be somebody important? A Pharaoh or Napoleon? Never an average person, a farmer's labourer or a kid that died at two . . . And here's another thing about reincarnation. How come the population explosion? Answer me that. I mean, are there billions more souls around now than there used to be? Or are billions more souls currently being given life in human form? In which case, what forms were they being reincarnated in before? And why the sudden wholesale transfer from fish or fowl or whatever to human? According to the Discovery Channel, we're all descended from basically the one tribe, of about two thousand people. So where were all the souls then? Or before that? But then, every religion has questions like those, questions that religious types spend lifetimes mulling over. Not because they're nigh-on-unanswerable in their metaphysical complexity. No. No, you know why? Because they are very simple. And so are the answers. How come, if God's so great, He allows suffering and dead babies? What do folk actually do in Heaven? Where is it? Are pets allowed in? What happens to them if they're not? How do Santa's reindeer fly? How does Santa get down every chimney in the world in one night? How does he get the presents to you if you don't have a chimney?

Chimney . . . Chim ney. Peculiar word . . . I stub out the joint on the saucer. Maybe I'll have a go with the Clinique Body Scrub. In a minute, maybe. Quite a good idea, though, because I'll soon be seeing Eunice. Seeing quite a lot of Eunice,

I imagine. Ah, that's what I was thinking about. Sex. And the sex with Eunice just gets better and better, believe me. We seem to have settled into this once-a-week routine. Which suits me dandy. And tonight's the night. She says she has a surprise.

So that should be good.

God, when I think of the years with Carol. Once a week, then once a month, then never a month . . . Carol. Get this. Carol's engaged. And not the guy she two-timed me with. Some other arsehole. She rang me up to tell me. 'I thought you'd like to know,' she said, in a very Carol manner – prim, prissy and full of herself at the same time. 'I'm engaged to be married.' Engaged to be married. Dearie me. Well, good luck to whoever he is, poor bastard. Even Russell's at it. He denies it, of course, but he seems to be getting rather keen. Russell encoupled – inconvenient but it would have its amusement value.

. . . All these cities getting bigger and bigger all over the world. Cairo. Rio. Unheard-of megaconurbations in China. But there's still only two truly international cities. One, New York. Two, London. So although I've been living down here all these years, I haven't been living in England all that time. No. London's a city-state. Just like New York.

. . . New York, London . . . cities getting bigger everywhere . . . Nope.

. . . Maybe I should get the bathroom redone after all. A chrome ladder instead of this crappy wee radiator. Retile the walls. Plain white, probably. Get rid of that lino, see what the floorboards are like underneath, or replace it with . . . slate tiles? Nice, but a bit cold on the feet. Well, who cares? I won't be the one with the freezing feet. In any case, no, yet again, to all of the above. I might pass a paintbrush over the place but that'll be it. Ravi from Butcher & Stockley's coming round tomorrow and what he sees then is what he'll soon be selling for a, fingers crossed, ludicrous amount. Upwards of a hundred and ninety-five, Ravi said. Mad.

So, sell this place, buy somewhere just a bit more expensive somewhere better. Warsaw. Glasgow. Joking, of course. Camden, maybe . . . Kentish Town? No, Camden. Then I collect the exorbitant sum I'll get from the Mottingham hovel, buy a place somewhere the property market's going to go even more mental. . . . Canterbury, I reckon. Rent the sucker out. Plus spend a hundred grand or so on a house in France. One of the ones in Grassy's brochure, even. Rent that out. Go there myself a bit, off-season. Maybe Eunice could pop down for a week or a weekend. Then, seeing how that's all working out, maybe even spend the rest of the cash on other places. Another couple maybe, some crappy town in the Thames Gateway. Rent them out too, and, hey presto, there's a very handy income. While the property value wheechs upwards. And if I needed some ready money, simply sell one.

Yes, it's a blue sky up there. A couple of fluffy wee clouds. Which don't have silver linings, because they're made of silver. They sparkle and shimmer. But mostly it's blue. A dark, summery blue. A dark, purply, French-property-brochure blue. The one anxiety I used to have — the faint and silly worry that the police would get wind of the bin liner and raid the flat — has gone. Been there, done that, got away with it.

And the bin liner has gone. As has Grassy, on an extended vacation. Being able to use all his limbs because I let him off.

On condition that he remove the coke and himself immediately and until further notice. Because here's how much coke there was in Grassy's flat – none. Grassy having concealed his entire stash in my bin liner. I think I know his source, though he denies it hotly. Like he also denies that he wasn't going to tell me about the coke bricks before selling them on, having incurred zero risk to himself. Brilliant . . . Aye, as for the grass in the bin liner, the Mottingham Gold, minus a bushel or two for personal use, I sold to a local dealer for a knock-down grand. And who was this local dealer? Some twatted hippie? A shuffling kid in a hood? No. The dealer I sold it to was . . . Go on. Have a guess . . . No. Way off. The dealer I dealt with was Mrs Longname. The criminal mastermind at the centre of a vast network of potfiends and teaheads at her church. Which, being Anglican, is attended only by the old and the ill. Plus, I have no doubt, the occasional woofter. But mainly sick biddies. Many of whom swear by their teatime reefers to stop the shaking and ease the pain . . .

How did I get on to that? . . . Right. So it can still be said that one hundred per cent of the homes and occupants of this house have been intimately involved in the production and/or delivery of narcotics. Because it also turns out that the Swat Squad raid on the Public Sector Spinster's place wasn't a mistake. Turns out that the Public Sector Spinster did not toil in a library or teach the young. Nor was she a spinster. Turns out that the Public Sector Spinster was a biggish-time coke dealer. With, it was rumoured by Mrs Longname, three passports, a pile in Marbella and an estranged husband in the Scrubs. And, I'm presuming, the previous possessor of Grassy's white bricks.

. . . What else? Hard to recall, really. My memory doesn't seem to work as it once did. So that's another blessing of marijuana.

. . . That's right, I was counting my blessings. On wrinkly fingertips. White whorls. I used to love that when I was a kid . . .

. . . What's today? Friday. So it's tomorrow that I'm seeing Russell. He's been making threatening noises about some party. Aye. That'll be right. Wild horses, my friend. Wild horses . . .

This is me reaching over for my watch. Time to get going . . .

I'm dryish and saronging the towel when the buzzer goes. Prompt as ever.

I ignore the phone and press the button, open the door and pad out to the landing. Soon, where in a previous life a cop once looked up, Eunice appears. She's wearing a peach-coloured A-line dress. Her skin looks like caramel. Caramel or milky coffee.

'I've brought you a little present,' she says, holding up a vivid-pink carrier bag. From, now that I can see the logo, Agent Provocateur. Well, well.

She comes up to me with a smile. A knowing smile.

We kiss. Politely, a peck on each cheek.

She holds the bag open. 'What do you think?' she asks. 'You like?'

I look down. 'Wow.'

13

8.38 p.m., Saturday 12 April

RICHARD

I'm trying to look the part of someone waiting purposefully on a corner as a chap saunters by, a young chap with a way of wearing his baggy jeans as though for the benefit of any passing fashion photographer. He's carrying a brown paper bag of groceries just like the ones in American films, except there wasn't a baguette sticking out the top as there usually is with brown paper bags of groceries in American films, but he was carrying the bag in front of him, cradling it with both hands, just like they do in the movies. What must it be like to saunter through life like that, and what kind of job must he have at twenty-whatever-he-is to be sauntering home down this street? It might not look much like it – in fact, it might actually look like a Wimpey condominium in the middle of a wasteland of rubble – but the plain fact of the matter is that they don't give you residency hereabouts unless you're on a million a week.

I check my watch again, not least because checking my watch makes me look like someone who's meeting somebody or has to go somewhere or has something of some nature on his agenda. Nearly ten minutes I've been at this particular spot so it's probably time to head back, take another walk past and resume my other post at the other end of the street.

So I go back, slowing for the walk-past, which reveals only one more arriving invitee – male, mid-thirties, smooth – crossing the road towards, although of course I'm only presuming this, because I'm not going to be obvious about it and turn round and stare, the same house I've just been walking slowly past.

Soon, now that it's obviously in full swing and evening's turning into night, I am going to have to smuggle myself in. I still don't know the exact details of that self-smugglage but I'm going to have to get in somehow. Go in round the back, probably, because, I've checked, there is a climbable wall. Yes, that would probably . . . Unless Ali arrives now, of course. Then I'll be able to intercept her, possibly even go into the party with her, Ali and me, together, if the conditions seem favourable . . . Though best not to expect that, I think. But, no, she must be in there already, bound to have arrived as early as she could . . .

Looking on the bright side, though, forgetting all the obstacles, I should be grateful to be here at all, really, when you think about it, it being sheer good fortune that the phone should be answered that time and by Joanne, that Joanne should be happy to chat, about herself, Joanne being Joanne, but in doing so that she should let slip the news that she'd also be babysitting on Saturday, i.e. now, what with Ali planning on going to what sounded and sounds a very Peterish party to celebrate his split-up from Jowhatsit. And not to think, if humanly possible, about Bongle all on his own, at the mercy of Joanne. Or about Bongle at all, far less about, for example,

Bongle's PJs, which ones he might be wearing tonight, the Bob the Builder ones or the newish Winnie and Tigger ones, but I really do have to stop right there, because even the reminder not to think about him has made my insides lurch like they were on the high seas.

Anyway, whatever happens, it's got two hours to happen in before I have to scoot to get the last train or bus back. Unless, and this is a thought I've had with increasing frequency, I miss the last train or bus and sleep . . . rough, I suppose. Paddington, maybe, a bench there. Or a park. Or just keep going throughout the night, find a late-night coffee shop and ply myself with espressos. Espressi? Espressos. Almost preferable, in fact quite possibly actually preferable, to rushing for the last train and eventually slinking in long past midnight, tiptoeing up the stairs, past the all-being-well-fast-asleep ageing Ps, to my old bedroom, my bedroom whose walls have long been neutral white, but might as well still be decorated by Blu-Tacked posters of Ian Botham and Debbie Harry in a short yellow dress. Not Ian Botham in a short yellow dress, obviously. Just Debbie Harry.

. . . It's as well I'm not tied to an office and office hours, although that doesn't apply so much to today, today being Saturday, but any other time, during the week, I can be on standby, ready to drop nothing and hop on a London train at a moment's notice.

And it's all a temporary measure, that's what I have to remember. No matter that it feels at the moment as hopeless and irreversible as this mortal coil's off-shuffling. But in fact this is just the bit before the bit where it gets better again, that's all. And if I can see Ali tonight, that might well speed things along. Who knows? The effect could be so immediate that I could be sleeping tonight in our bed. Although now I have to give myself a stern talking-to along the lines that I really can't afford to think along those lines either, however much, believe me, I want to. Think along them. Those lines. The lines about me sleeping tonight in our own bed. But that's . . .

'For God's sakes, pull yourself together.'

I breathe in. And I breathe out. Breathing in. And breathing out.

. . . Anyway, who's to blame for any upset, panic and hollowing misery that certain parties might be currently experiencing? Self. That's who. Self. So who am I to be getting all churned up and pathetic about what is, after all, Ali's entirely reasonable response, her *correct* response, in fact, to my terrible, terrible, terrible, terrible mistake? What self has to remember is that despite how this feels at the moment – which is, yes, probably about as bad as the stickiest parts of the sticky patch, worse than then even, to be honest, so somewhere between the sticky patch and the Jimmy Morgan apocalypse – what we are having to deal with is a one-off mistake which is very easily sortoutable, because this isn't as relationship-threatening, no, of course it isn't, the Jimmy Morgan thing having been an . . . affair, I suppose I'd have to call it, not a silly stupid, drunken, heinous – yes, heinous but nonetheless mainly just stupid – one-off, one-night-only, ghastly, ghastly, ghastly, ghastly mistake. Much more easily.

Yes.

So, first things first, and that's to get into the garden, monitor – no, better make that survey – the scene from there because there's no way Ali would be arriving now, surely, which means she has to be inside. Yes, it's definitely time for stage two . . .

It's going to be okay. It's going to be all right. It's going to be okay. It's going to be all right.

8.38 p.m. Saturday 12 April

EWAN

Having mustered a last, tiny line from Russell's precious wrap and licked the packet, I leave the shunkie with rather more vigour than I entered it and a numbly fizzing tongue. I edge past the queue and go downstairs. Russ nowhere to be seen, so this is me wandering around the place, pretty aimlessly but feeling fine.

Wandering around a party of dull strangers does have, however, a limited appeal, even in a chemically enhanced mood. Especially when there are only a few women and all of them are obviously encoupled. Also, no Eunice, busy mini-breaking with her pal Amanda in New York. No, this is a very male gathering. Give it an hour – much sooner if the shunkie continues to be so well used – and this lot'll be singing 'Swing low, sweet chariot.'

The thought spurs me on, through the noisy kitchen and out, down some stairs and into the garden. Which is as uninhabited as I'd hoped. I make my way in the sudden gloom over the regulation decking towards the regulation wrought-iron garden furniture. Where I get settled, or as settled as it's possible to get on a cold wrought-iron chair, and fetch out a joint from my wallet. 'And here's one I made earlier in the programme,' I say out loud, before setting it alight and taking the first few fragrant puffs.

'Er, hello.'

A man's voice. And its owner emerging from behind a dark patch of large new shrubs. Drunk? Nutter? Someone with a pissing-in-a-bush fetish? Not the aggressive type, at least. More shambolic. Unsure of himself. Hey, I'd be unsure of myself if I was dressed like that. A leezhur jacket from Marks and Sparks, pleated slacks fresh from the Corby Trouser Press. Very civil servant at the weekend.

I blow out a long thread of smoke. 'Hi,' I say pleasantly enough. 'You want?' I hold up the joint.

Shrub Man comes closer and takes a good look, then steps back. 'Er, no. Thank you.'

I nod. 'Be my guest,' I say, pointing at the chair nearest him, the one that's south to my north.

'Thank you.'

He drags the chair back. Scraping it against the concrete with a noise that's not quite up there with nails on the blackboard but not for the want of trying.

'Ewan,' I say. 'Ewan Macintyre.' I offer my hand over the table.

'Richard,' he says, taking my hand and shaking it with one vigorous yank. 'Richard Fossett.'

'Good to meet you, Richard,' I say. I take a look around. The decking. The wiggly path of what in daylight must be brightly spray-painted pebbles. The lots of plants in rectangular metal pots. An ironic gnome, fishing over a pool of stone chippings. 'Shite garden,' I say, companionably.

'Oh. Do you think so?' says Shrub Man, puzzled or worried. 'It's designed, you know. By a designer.'

'Oh, well then.'

'A garden designer, I suppose it would be.'

'I suppose it would,' I say. 'Well, give it two years and this'll look as cool as a blow-wave. Grass'll be back in. Talking of which, you sure you don't want some of this?'

'Really, thanks, but I won't, if you don't mind.'

'Cool. All the more for me. So. You a pal of his?'

'I'm more family, really. Well, sort of family. Peter's my, um, wife's brother. Except that . . . Well, long story.'

'I don't know the guy. I'm here by mistake. Ligging along with my mate and his . . .'

'I see.' Guy smiles and shakes his head. The smile belongs to someone in the line-up after a funeral. Not to worry. I'll finish this then head inside, leave him to it.

'So which part of Scotland are you from?'

'. . . Falkirk.'

'Ah.'

We sit in silence. Fine by me, though apparently not by him. 'Are you married?' he asks, all of a sudden.

'Nah. Well, I had a wife once. What was that all about, eh?'

'Ha,' he says. '. . . Do you have any children?'

He's a man for his blurted-out questions. And where did that one come from? 'No,' I tell him. 'Not that I know of.'

'Ah . . . I've got a little boy.'

'Right.' So that's where that came from. '. . . How old?'

'Eighteen months.' He purses his lips and puts in a good spell of determined, speedy nodding. 'Year and a half.'

'Right,' I say.

'Of course, things are a bit difficult at the moment,' he says, the world's number one at the blurted-out non sequitur. Now why didn't I stub the spliff out early and go back in when I had the chance? 'But only at the moment,' he reassures me. 'I mean, it's all very sortoutable.'

Okay, absolutely no cue for a farewell there, so I'll have to ride out the next sentence. Then I'll skedaddle. 'Good,' I say.

'I mean, this wasn't something that was planned or anything, no, no, that'd be different,' he says, with more than a hint of a gabble, squeezing his hands between his knees. 'But no, you see, this thing, it's just a temporary thing, a few weeks, that's all.'

This is mind-busting skunk I'm smoking here. And I've been smoking it all afternoon. Plus there's the coke Russell's spared me from his precious ration. All of which may help to explain why I find myself thinking about what he's just said. 'You're right,' I say. 'Knowing that it's been planned does help but the most important thing—'

'Yes, but the great thing about my little thing at the moment is that it's just a one-off, a silly, stupid thing. And completely my fault, of course.'

'Aye, well, that's just it, because the important thing with Carol and me is that she was in the wrong. Because . . . what's the point of these wee walls, do you think? Like they're keeping out trolls. Hey. Troll walls.'

'Ha.'

Troll walls, trolls . . . Nup. Gone. 'What was I saying?'

'Troll walls.'

'Yeah. No. Before that.'

'Um, something about your wife.'

'. . . Oh, aye, got it. No, Carol being in the wrong, that meant she couldn't play silly buggers when it came to the division of the spoils. Whereas . . . aye, where*as*, if she'd found out about one of my little indiscretions, she'd have shafted me. Of that I have absolutely no doubt.'

'Though mine is completely my fault, you see. Completely my fault. It's just a terrible, terrible, terrible mistake, that's all it is. Not one that means the end of it all. No, no, no.' He does a wee snuffle of a laugh at the daftness of such a concept. 'This isn't the end.'

'Hey,' I say, 'everything ends.'

'Well, that's—'

'Three things you've got to remember, my friend. One. We are accidents of chemistry in an empty, meaningless universe. Two. Shit happens. Three. We're all going to die.'

'Ha.'

'Oh, yes,' I tell him with an avuncular air. 'Everything ends. We end. The universe ends.'

'Well,' he says, as if he could argue the point, 'you say that but . . . some things last for ever.'

'Aye, but only when you're at the theatre.'

'Hm,' he says with one of his halfway brave smiles, not really getting it. 'No, yes, anyway, it'll be okay,' he says. 'It'll be all right.'

I nod. 'Sure it will,' I say. 'Fandabadozie.' I take a final puff, then stub out the roach on a shin-high wall. Oh, yeah. Troll walls. 'Getting a bit nippy,' I say. 'Think I'll head back in.'

I get to my feet. He stays perched on the edge of the wrought-iron chair. His hands clasped between his knees. He looks up as I turn to go. Our eyes meet.

So I nod my head and I say, 'Good luck.'

And he nods and he says, 'Thanks. And you.'

I go back inside and soon see Russ, in the hallway, shrugging on his coat. Alison living up to her nickname, putting hers on too.

'Hi,' she says brightly, being nice.

'Hi,' I say, being nice back.

'Listen, we're off,' says Russell.

'Eh?'

'Yeah, godda split. You want to share a taxi back to civilisation?'

'Aye, well, I'm not going to hang around here, am I? Here, give me your mobile, Russ.'

'Why?'

'So that I can use it to make a telephone call.'

'Oh, I see.'

'Come on, Russ. Saturday night, and I'm in the mood for love.'

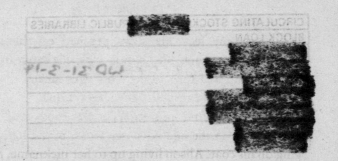